Edward Bulwer Lytton

Miscellaneous Prose Works by Edward Bulwer Lytton Vol. 1

Edward Bulwer Lytton

Miscellaneous Prose Works by Edward Bulwer Lytton Vol. 1

ISBN/EAN: 9783742811639

Manufactured in Europe, USA, Canada, Australia, Japa

Cover: Foto ©Andreas Hilbeck / pixelio.de

Manufactured and distributed by brebook publishing software
(www.brebook.com)

Edward Bulwer Lytton

Miscellaneous Prose Works by Edward Bulwer Lytton Vol. 1

NOTE TO THE READER.

In these volumes are for the first time collected into one whole, miscellaneous criticisms and essays written in different periods of life, from early youth to the commencement of old age. Naturally, therefore, they embrace an unusual variety of subjects, suggested by such acquaintance with books, and such experience of life, as so long a space of time may have afforded to one who has ranged over a somewhat wide surface of literature, and been brought into active contact with many diversities in the characters and pursuits of men. In such a collection there cannot fail to be many blemishes which no revision, however careful, will remove. Differences of age necessitate inequalities of treatment; essays written in early youth will be too light for some; those written in later life too dry for others. The first dealing chiefly with sentiment will be often too sentimental; the last dealing chiefly with reflection will be often too reflective: and in a whole, of which the several parts have been composed at such wide intervals of time, there can scarcely fail to be sometimes repetitions, sometimes contradictions, of speculation or opinion. For these and similar defects, if excuse be needed, I can venture to make none.

But perhaps in the main cause for the blemishes thus frankly owned may be found the best chance of that originality which consists in the exposition of any single mind, throughout a long course of years, in those native and acquired differences from the minds of others which mark its characteristics and constitute its idiosyncracy.

Whatever the worth of these volumes, they will be
thought, perhaps, a not unnecessary accompaniment to
the works of fiction by which I am more popularly
known as a writer, — comprising as they do a reper-
tory of the opinions and sentiments, the reveries and
the reflections, the studies of mankind and the critical
theories of art which, herein expressed subjectively to
the influences of my own mind, are objectively represented in the world of fable by images invented to
realize or to typify the truths of life.

One word as to the contents of the volumes: —

The first volume (of the London Edition, forming
vol. I. and II. of this Edition) consists of criticisms contributed to our principal Reviews, to which, since most
of them treat of human character as well as of books,
the biographical sketch of Schiller is appended; the
second (of the London Edition, forming vol. III. and IV.
of this Edition), of essays written in early youth, of which
the greater part originally appeared under the title of
"The Student;' with the exception of the concluding
one, not hitherto published, upon the influence of Love
on literature and life; the third (of the London Edition*),
of essays written in mature years, and first published
under the title of 'Caxtoniana.'

TORQUAY, Jan. 28, 1868.

---

* Caxtoniana has been already published separately in vol. 692 and 693
of my Collection of British Authors, and is therefore not included in the
present Edition of Lord Lytton's Miscellaneous Prose Works.

TAUCHNITZ.

CONTENTS

OF VOLUME I.

THE REIGN OF TERROR

ITS CAUSES AND RESULTS.

[First published in 'The Foreign Quarterly Review,' July, 1842.]

THE REIGN OF TERROR:

ITS CAUSES AND RESULTS.

———

[*Souvenirs de la Terreur de* 1788 *à* 1793, par M. GEORGES DUVAL. (Recollections of the Reign of Terror, from 1788 to 1793, by Georges Duval.) Paris, 4 tomes. 1841-2.]

"*JE raconte ce que j'ai vu.*" — "I relate that which I have seen!" With this avowal M. Georges Duval opens his Recollections of the Reign of Terror. The announcement is certainly attractive. But M. Duval is one of those generous writers who are always better than their word; he not only relates what he has seen, but a great deal that it was utterly impossible for him to see, and, as revelations of the latter class are vouchsafed to us with the same detail and precision as the former, we are forced to acknowledge M. Georges Duval to be a person of that lively imagination, with which 'to moralize a song' is not always 'to stoop to truth.' The plain fact is, that our author's hatred of the actors and events of the French Revolution is so intense, that, where he cannot relate as a witness, he, by no means unfrequently, invents as a partisan. With all the naïveté of Herodotus, he gives us the particulars of interviews at which he was not present, and the exact dialogue of conversations which admitted of no eavesdropper. Besides this happy gift of invention,

1*

Nature has bestowed on M. Georges Duval a turn for
banter and raillery; and even when relating circumstances in which he was a party concerned, his love of
ironical humour and his benevolent desire to amuse the
reader lead him into sundry witty exaggerations and
travesties, which, while they prove his agreeable qualities as a writer, detract from our faith in him as a
historian.

These allowances made, there however remains to
the volumes before us much to instruct the student in
his survey of the men and the times of which they
treat. M. Duval confesses in his Preface the indignation with which he "regards the numerous books that
have been written under the fallacious title of Histories
of the Revolution, being in truth nothing better than
impudent apologies for that epoch of ruin, of blood,
and of tears."

It is easy to conceive the feelings of irritation and
disgust with which an honest man who had actually
lived amidst the horrors of Paris in the Reign of Terror,
who had seen the tumbrils passing his windows to the
Barrière du Trône, who had beheld the infuriated mob
butchering a gray-haired man discovered to be a Christian pastor, and shouting round the gory head of a
woman convicted of pity for her benefactor, — must
regard the philosophizing excuses and argumentative
dogmas which some would-be Friend of Liberty, and
Lover of the People, issues from the security of his
closet.

It is unquestionably true, indeed, that in the vices
of the old *régime* we must seek the causes of the re-
volutionary crimes. To nations yet more than to individuals must be referred the awful menace that the

sins of the fathers shall be visited on the sons. But no less true is it to all, whom philosophical refinements have not besotted, that humanity itself is endangered if we allow the circumstances that conduce to guilt to steal away our natural horror of the guilt itself. Rigidly speaking, all guilt is but the result of previous circumstance. To neglected education, to vicious example, we may trace the crimes which send the thief to the hulks and the murderer to the gibbet. But we do not therefore hold excused Jack Sheppard and Daniel Good. What education and example are to the man, government and legislation are to the people. We shall do right if we blame the causes which make a demon of the multitude, but wrong if we regard the demon itself only as the suffering angel.

It is not our intention, however, to go over the beaten and hackneyed ground of the hateful time commemorated by M. Duval. We propose rather to cut a rapid and somewhat irregular path through the mighty field before us, in search only of those facts and principles which appear to us to suggest something new and not unimportant in the philosophy of history.

The era of Modern civilization, as distinct from the Feudal, begins in France with the large and determined policy of Cardinal Richelieu. And it is from this period that we are to date the primary causes of the Revolution of the Eighteenth Century.

A high churchman and an absolute monarchist, the twofold object of Richelieu was carried out with the rigidity of a strong mind thoroughly in earnest. To reduce Dissent into the One Church — to change the functions of Aristocracy from the check upon Monarchy into the ornament of a Court; for these objects he lived,

and these objects he accomplished, upon the whole,
with rapid and singular success. He had the qualities
necessary to his purpose. That which he himself called
his mission could not have been fulfilled had clemency
accompanied his sense of justice, or cowardice occa-
sioned his vigilant circumspection. His severity, never
capricious, though often cruel, was conducted on a
broad and intelligible system: it never invaded the
lives and properties of the masses; it more often secured
their properties and lives, by terrible examples amongst
the nobles, whose struggles were nearly always associated with the criminal designs of a civil war. In
his aim at absolute monarchy he was far too comprehensive a statesman to meditate the erection of an
oriental despotism, for he loved France even better
than Monarchy. He desired to make France secure
and integral. For this he humiliated Austria — for
this he dislodged the Huguenots from Rochelle (that
harbour of the disaffected) — for this he crushed every
subject powerful enough to disturb the peace of the
country. And for this he effected a change which Le
Clerc properly notices as of great importance in the
consolidation of the monarchy. Hitherto the principal
strongholds had been held by governors for life; he
swept away at one stroke offices so dangerous in a
time when the nobility could still struggle against the
throne, and substituted governors whose tenure was
too short to allow them to be other than the servants
of the Executive. But in consolidating monarchy his
policy tended to create subjects — not slaves. He
favoured commerce and trade. He gave greater security
to justice, and more impartial regularity to law. He
desired — so far as his wretched literary taste, and, his

literary jealousies yet more wretched, would permit — to encourage and circulate the refinements of intellectual cultivation. To him France is indebted for the Academy, which, if not productive to literature, at least raised literature into honour. An eminently practical man, he was aware of a truth so obvious that it is incomprehensible how the governments of Europe so commonly fail to observe it, viz. that no state is secure where the expenditure is disproportioned to the revenue: and he bequeathed an immense treasure, and, with due allowance for the notions of the time, a sufficiently effective system of finance, as a legacy to that throne, which he had found the weakest, to leave the most powerful, in Christendom. The effects of Richelieu's policy were immediately apparent in the society of France, under the reign of Louis XIV. The descendants of the turbulent barons of the League became the courtiers of Versailles. The provincial castles were deserted; retainers had passed into peasants, the old ties between the highest and the lowest order were rent away. And there already yawned a far wider gulf between the gay gentleman of Paris and his tenant harassed for rent, than existed in a ruder generation between the rural noble and his village neighbour familiarized to each other by habitual intercourse.

With the struggles of the House of Valois had commenced that spirit of nationality which united all Frenchmen against the foreigner — with the complete ascendency of the House of Valois-Bourbon commenced that disunion of classes which will always follow the establishment of Absolute Monarchy, when accompanied by the progress of the middle class and the decline of the noble.

The main characteristics of their nation and their class were still retained by the *gentilhommes*, howsoever modified by the changes of circumstance and time: they preserved the same light-hearted and daring gallantry, so distinct from the stubborn fortitude of the Anglo-Saxon, and the steady and stern valour of the Anglo-Norman. Corrupted by the life of a capital and a court, the love of pleasure degenerated into the passion for debauch; strictly honourable towards men according to the chivalric notions of honour, they deemed all meanness, duplicity, and ingratitude justifiable in regard to women. The sanctity of married life will usually be found more or less respected in proportion to the ease or impracticability of divorce for offences against fidelity. The Catholic Church, by which divorce was forbidden, left to the husband no option but connivance at his dishonour, or the ridicule of impotently proclaiming it. The vanity of the French nobles, and that experience of the salons which they termed *savoir vivre*, made them regard as the height of ill-breeding, and the consummation of absurdity, that jealous respect for the chastity of their wives which in all nations is the attribute of men to whom custom or law gives the power to preserve it — whether the Mahometan, who can drown, or the Protestant, who can divorce the delinquents. Pecuniary considerations, which are invariably the great cementers of established wrong or conventional right, tended to reconcile the injured party to his conjugal infelicities. Marriages were those of convenience; if the bridegroom knew nothing of the bride's character beforehand, he made himself thoroughly acquainted with the extent of her dower; and the fortune of the wife, while it gave her a right

to an insolent independence of conduct, consoled the
husband for the loss of a heart which he had never
wooed. But the most marked distinction between the
French aristocracy and the English, and the one which
operated the most fatally to their downfall, arose (and
this has never been sufficiently considered) from the
early extinction of the Representative System. That
safeguard of modern society, though always liable to
great abuses, necessarily clumsy in its machinery, and
perhaps hereafter, in some distant age, to be laid aside
for calmer modes of legislation and government, has
this immense advantage, — it opens a healthful field
for the energies and ambition of the great, and a field
that can be only cultivated by familiar intercourse with
their inferiors. An election brings all classes together,
unites them in common links of passion and interest;
— there can be no dangerous and prolonged separation between classes where elections are popular and
frequent. What the Feudal system was in binding
together the baron and the vassal, the Electoral is in
binding together the great proprietor and the husband-
man — the great merchant and the artisan — the rich
and the poor: there is a link of iron ·between the most
ambitious statesman and the meanest voter. It was
just at the time when the Representative System was
most needed in France, that is, in the dissolution of
the old forms and usages which cemented the different
ranks, that it was extinguished by the ambition of the
Executive.

The education of men insensibly adapts itself to
the objects of ambition open to their future career.
The rich gentleman or the powerful noble in England
has before him the one ambition of public life — and

to this a large proportion of the higher class is imperceptibly trained: hence, in spite of much that may be false and prejudiced in the intellectual cultivation through which they pass, it is impossible but what the minds of the English aristocracy should become more manly, practical, business-like, and robust, than the members of a correspondent class in a country where public life, properly speaking, existed not — where ambition had no opening, except in the army or the saloon — where a graceful person, a charming manner, a happy *bon-mot*, were the best passports to a place at court, a celebrity in society, a rich marriage, nay, a colonelcy in the army. Hence, on the other hand, was formed that peculiar polish of civilization for which the French *noblesse* were remarkable, and of which the history of the world has probably no correspondent example. Grace, manner, wit, conversation — all that could amuse, interest, fascinate their equals or superiors — these were, to the French patricians, what knowledge of business and the art of speaking, and the hard qualities of public life, were and are to the English. Habits consequent on such accomplishments were necessarily those of generosity and ostentation, — in other words, of *expense*. The expense was supplied by the most grinding exactions on a peasant tenantry, or the most flagrant jobs on the public resources — additional reasons for the separation between ranks. It is astonishing how completely unfit these brilliant personages were for any other existence than that which they corrupted and adorned. While the army was entirely officered by the nobles, while the nobles alone seized or sold every place at the court, and filled the church with odious sinecures — their unpriestly *Abbés* monopolizing the benefices of dignitaries, and leading openly the lives of *roués* — the administration of the country, the power, the business of the state, were left, for the most part, without an effort, to the members of the *bourgeoisie*, or the bar. While in England the administration of affairs was more and more falling into the aristocratic hands which have since wielded it, in France the administration became more and more the monopoly of the *roturiers*. It was not from the highborn *fainéants* that such men as Colbert and Turgot could arise.* The French gentleman, contented with the brilliant flutter of the butterfly, had none of the vulgar industry of the bee.

It was impossible that, as time went on and ripened reflection — it was impossible that such a class could long retain an established power in the state. Of the state they made no part, and they were only visible in legislation by the intrusion of privileges equally insulting to common sense, and obnoxious to common justice. Rapidly, too, in their reckless prodigality they were destroying the sole foundation on which an aristocracy can rest — property! When the baron can no longer awe by the number of his followers, the noble can only impose by the extent of his rent-roll. It is true that as a body the Aristocracy still shared with the Church the possession of the far larger portion of the lands; but agriculture declined, mortgages

---

* Even in the Revolution itself, it was not among their Prelates and their Dukes that the privileged orders could find the energy and intellect of defenders — it was left to a Maury and a Cazalès to represent the Nobles and the Church.

increased, and the lands rather served for the oppression of peasants, than for adequate resources to the extravagance of the lords. About the middle of the reign of Louis XV., along the Seine and along the Loire, dismantled chateaus, starving serfs, untilled fields, were the visible signs of a fastly falling order. Thus, in the following reign, the French seigneur became not only unpopular, — he became despised. If a Leveller of our own time and land were to paint the English Aristocracy according to his prejudice or opinion, he might describe them as hateful, but certainly not as despicable. Men never can despise the powerful. The power of the English aristocracy is everywhere and in everything — power in wealth — power in lands — power in the state — power in the affections they command from large classes not belonging to them — power in the intellect which enables them, in the open contests of party, to bear comparison with men of the highest attainments in inferior grades, and to justify by their talents the offices they aspire to from their birth. The English aristocracy have few privileges and much power; the French had many privileges and no power. Yet unquestionably the latter, with all their faults, were a sparkling, accomplished, and charming race. And it is impossible to contemplate their life as it is seen, still living and ever imperishable, in the countless Letters and Memoirs which form the most unrivalled part of the French literature, without that admiration which is extorted from our taste in despite of our severer judgment. Though ruthless as seigneurs, they were affable as masters. Between the cavalier and the servant there was in reality the same familiar affection that we see in their old comedy. If insolent in prosperity, in adversity they were always gallant. Lauzun, almost a scoundrel in the court, is almost a hero in the prison. The exquisite polish of their breeding so contributed to the cheerfulness of the society in which they moved, so sought to bestow pleasure and shun the infliction of pain, that they were scarcely wrong when they gave to Manners the title of "The Minor Morals." Though but indifferently educated, they had an enlightened affection for letters and art. They were not good men, but they were certainly fine gentlemen.

In the mean while was growing up that Middle Class, fostered and encouraged by the policy of Louis XI. and the master intellect of Richelieu. From an early period the ambition of this class was visible; but as it could not show itself on the floors of a Parliament, in the English sense of the word, * it thrust its way into the meaner openings afforded by the boudoir and the saloon. The comedy of Molière exhibits that desire of the *bourgeoisie* to ape the manners, to vie with the follies, and to court the company of the nobles, which was not a very prominent feature in English society till a much later period. The power to purchase titles, which were in fact annexed

---

* The supreme courts of justice were called parliaments, as the inferior were called seignorial. The officers of the supreme courts, or parliaments, actually became so *by purchase*, and were not removable even for malpractices! Hence the *noblesse* of the gown. It may easily be imagined how despotic, how tyrannical, and how corrupt, were such administrators of the laws. A man indeed bought the right to break you on the wheel, — and to take fees from your adversary for doing so!

to certain lands, and which no less than 4000 places or offices could confer, necessarily aided the *roturier* in a rivalry which the *gentilhomme* treated either with complaisant raillery or freezing disdain. And the sore affronts which the *roturier* received in this competition with the *gentilhomme* could not fail to engender all the bitterness of wounded self-esteem. How many an honest bourgeois, after having enjoyed a hearty laugh at the expense of Monsieur Jourdain or George Dandin, would, in graver moments of his own actual life, think with deep resentment upon the pitiable light in which the class thus satirized was regarded by the gay Dorantes and the gallant Clitandres! What! was the honest man, entertaining the natural ambition that his son should rise above the class in which he was born — was he to rear his son to more elevated spheres solely to make him a cully and a butt — ridiculous, when desiring to be accomplished — the cuckold and slave of a noble wife who did him the honour to stain his name and waste his fortune? It was easy to say that the ambition was absurd and misplaced. But was it so in reality? What other openings from his own state were left to the man whom civilization had made too wealthy to remain contented with obscurity? Parliament did not exist. Even the bar had formed a nobility of its own. Posts at the court and distinctions in the army were only to be obtained by the noble. The son of a *bourgeois* might have the valour of a Bayard, but he must become a *gentilhomme* before he could be made a captain. By a law even so late as the reign of Louis XVI. four generations of nobility were necessary to qualify a man for the rank of a sub-lieutenant. If his hard-won gold could purchase an estate with a marquisate attached to it, was the citizen despicable because he desired to enjoy what he had bought and paid for? Was there, in short, to be an eternal wall of odious distinction between his own class and that which scattered upon him the mud of Paris from the wheels of carriages which were bearing the last louis of their owners to the brothel and the gaming-house? a class not respectable for virtues, not formidable from intellect, and whose members had exchanged the sharp sword of their ancestors for the weapon, less powerful and more irritating, of the polished sarcasm.

Thus insensibly all the habits of society co-operated with all the disparities of law, to hoard up against the day of reckoning a profound sentiment of hatred on the part of the moneyed and middle class against the higher.

Meanwhile the state of the rural population was precisely that which was to be expected. The peasantry were sold like cattle with the soil; even, in many parts of the kingdom, personal servitude was abolished but a few years before the Revolution. All hereditary ties of affection were not only weakened by the absence and exactions of their lords, but utterly annihilated by the frequent transfer of property, according to marriages and sales. They had no education, but they had that gaiety and gregariousness of disposition which led them on every holiday to meet, to associate, and to pick up and to circulate in their vivacious talk many of the popular notions which the abuses of law and the works of thinkers began to scatter throughout the world. The gossip of a holiday was often to them what a news-room is to the mechanics of England.

There is no education more dangerous and more superficial than that which is exclusively oral. It needs the liberty of the press to correct the influences which belong to the licence of talk.

We have said that one object of Richelieu was the formation of Absolute Monarchy, the other that of an Absolute Church. As regards the first, — in forming its strength, he prepared the causes of its downfall. The endurance of a monarchy, where the growth of society is not absolutely stopped, will always be found in proportion to its checks; for the checks compress, and adapt, and mould the monarchy from age to age, according to the altered wants and circumstances of the time. The annihilation of popular national assemblies, and of solid power in an aristocracy, left monarchy to all the excesses into which the impunity of power is sure to pass; hateful prerogatives, wasteful ostentation, disordered finances, and subsequent weakness, were the inevitable results. The great Cardinal was not more permanently fortunate in the maintenance of his Absolute Church. For while all may allow that in the checks to monarchy exist its strength, it has never been sufficiently noticed and insisted upon, especially by French historians, that as checks are to a monarchy, so dissent is to a church. The destruction of what the Cardinal called heresies and schisms left to the bulk of the population no option but Gallic Catholicism on the one hand, or absolute irreligion on the other. Now, in a country like England, which obtained from the Wit of France the distinction "of enjoying a thousand sects, and one sauce," — the Christian religion happily proffers shades in worship, form, and faith to all varieties of enthusiasm, passion,

character, belief. If a man be revolted by any abuses
in the church, real or supposed, in the same street
lives the dissenter ready to convert him; hard at hand
rises the chapel open to his prayers. If some tenet in
one faith startle his conscience, another form of worship equally founded on scriptural authority and promise satisfies his scruples and presents a refuge from
infidelity or indifference. And this copious and wise
diversity of permitted opinion, while beneficial to Religion, is the best safeguard to the Establishment, inasmuch as the necessary effect of the competition is to
preserve a certain wholesome vigilance in the heads of
the church, an energy in education and learning, a
care for general purity of life and morals, — while,
though it may not obtain the reform of all abuses, it
creates a public prepared to correct whatever may be
obviously scandalous or oppressive. But in France,
after the expulsion of the Huguenots, the unity of the
church was so complete that the wide varieties of discontent had no practical opening but in the school of
the scoffer and the sceptic. True that some Dissenters,
chiefly Calvinists, still survived all persecution — for
tyranny can never wholly extirpate opinion — but
their number was too scanty, their zeal too suppressed,
to have any influence on the masses. Sullen and dissatisfied, they were rather dangerous as politicians than
useful as sectarians. We do not find them counteract-
ing the Philosophers, but we find them, at the first
explosion, rushing to the aid of the Revolution. Did
the reason of one man oppose a doctrine, was the sense
of another scandalized by the crime of a pastor, was
the hearth of a peasant invaded by a libidinous monk,
or the son of an honest trader corrupted by the ex-

ample of a profligate *abbé*, not only the Church, but
Religion itself, lost reverence and affection. And no
more earnest and decorous clergy were at hand to
support the tottering faith, and rescue the reason from
incredulity. Where dissent flourishes, a man often
secedes from an established church to become more
religious than before; where dissent is inactive and
suppressed, his secession from the church is the retire-
ment from religion itself. Here, an abuse drove the
Episcopalian to Wesley; there, the Papist to Voltaire.
And hence, as, in the absence of all check and all
competition, abuses multiplied through every department of the church, so rapidly and generally the entire
mass of the population were ripened for that fearful
state of contempt for all Christianity which ended in
the frantic Atheism of Clootz, or the frigid Deism of
Robespierre. Nor, in making the church supreme,
was it in the power of man to make all its priesthood
of one mind. To disqualify dissent was not to prevent
schism. Accordingly the scandalous disputes between
Jesuit and Jansenist, while producing none of the good
that arises from dissent, produced all the evil that
comes from division. They opened a breach to contempt, but no vent to dissatisfied opinion. We are
convinced that it was to the confirmation of the one
absolute church in France that we may trace the principal cause of the irreligious spirit which desecrated
the land under the Reign of Terror.

Thus then the very policy of Richelieu, in its
completeness and vigour, followed up as it was, in
either object, by Louis XIV., prepared the downfall
of the two Institutions it had been devoted to establish. The agencies of civilization to which absolutism

gives birth are always destined to destroy their parent. When Richelieu favoured commerce, and encouraged letters; when a middle class and a thinking class were permanently established — two powers were called into active life utterly incompatible with that suppression of opinion which is the essence of absolute power. And therefore, as M. Guizot well observes, at the close of the reign of Louis XIV., monarchy was as decrepit as the monarch. The splendid progress of art and mind which characterized that noble reign, announced the anomaly which always ends in gigantic innovation, — viz., a restless population and a stationary government.

But to return to our view of the Anti-religious and Republican spirit that was abroad, the intellect of the time naturally directed itself against the abuses of the time. Religion having ceased to maintain its holy and reverent influences in France, having left little or nothing except the mere husk and shell of a corrupt church, at once detested and despised, the intellect of the age became material and sceptical: monarchy unchecked, and supporting its antiquated pretensions no longer by arms and treasure, but by the Lettre de Cachet and the Bastille, presented features which no one could defend, and which the intellect of the age attacked by the common consent of men. The masses were the last, perhaps, affected by these attacks. For amongst the intellectual, intellect must first find its audience. Accordingly in the educated (comprehending the highborn) classes, infidelity and liberalism found the earliest favour. The discontented courtier became naturally a believer in the *Contrat Social;* the unbeneficed *abbé* was naturally

2*

more familiar with the Encyclopedists than the
Fathers.   Nay, more than half the nobility were disaffected by the nature of their own position.   For
there was the most invidious distinction between the
old noblesse and the new.   To enjoy consideration it
was not enough to be a marquis; the question was,
"Had your ancestor been a marquis 200 years ago?"
Legally, the new noble shared the privileges of the
old; socially and morally, he was still a *parvenu;*
thrust from preferments and honours, mortified and
galled by the contempt of the circle he had sought
to enter, while obtaining the envy and the hatred of
that which he had deserted.   It was, in short, the
unhappy condition of the French government and
constitution to engender and arm against them the
two most irresistible foes, viz., the wealth of commerce,
and the energy of intellect.   For these very powers,
which are ever struggling for distinction, were the
very powers to which all legitimate avenues of ambition were beset with difficulty and humiliation.
The doctrines thus fostered and necessitated gradually and imperceptibly descended from the higher and
more learned to the lower and less educated classes:
and from the saloons of the royal Orleans, and the
learned Malesherbes, and the respectable Bailly, passed
those sentiments which never become finally dangerous and destructive till incorporated with the
interests and animated by the passions of the popular
body.

It will often happen that the qualities of individuals, in an attacked and imperilled party, will stave
off, nay, perhaps, counteract and defeat the dangers
by which they are surrounded.   But as the storm

gradually gathered round the throne, with which
every sinister interest, whether of aristocracy or of
church, was connected, it became obvious that these
qualities were not to be found in Louis XVI. His
excellent heart, his sweet and amiable nature, were
as wholly lost and thrown away in the turbulence of
the time, as were the virtues somewhat similar of our
own Henry the Sixth in the convulsions of a civil
war. His domestic peculiarities — his innocent but
mechanical tastes — his stolid heavy countenance
smeared with the smoke of his forge — even his first
frigidity, his subsequent uxoriousness, to his queen —
were all matters that, repeated through the infinite
gossip of Paris, covered his very name with ridicule.
His amiability of disposition, too often yielding in
the wrong place, provoked insolence and disheartened
loyalty. His aversion from blood had, on imminent
occasions, the worst effect of cowardice; and while
the man had all the meekness of a saint, the system
he represented exposed him to all the odium of a
tyrant. By a people contented with Reforms, such
a king would have been adored. For Louis XVI.
was by nature a Reformer — and happy had it been
for France had her population possessed half the virtues of her king. But amongst a people less desirous
to reform than eager to destroy, the safety of the
ruler depends little on the qualities that beget affection, unless he has also those which inspire awe.
Louis was never more insecure than in those periods
of his reign when he was most popular. To add to
his dangers, his queen, more brilliant and more prominent, had contrived to be the most detested person
in the kingdom. Though possessing many fine qua-

lities, they were as little suited to the times as those of her husband. A decorous gravity of life, coupled with mild firmness, might have won for her a respect which would have gone far to rally the middle classes around the throne; but her imprudent levity daily and hourly exposed her to the coarsest suspicions, and her sarcastic humour, coupled with passionate haughtiness, multiplied the number of her personal enemies amongst those who could best have defended her from slander.   Ignorant of the people and of the times, she was perpetually grating against both. Now bullying a minister as with the power of a Catherine, now going incognita in a hackney-coach to a public masked ball as with the recklessness of a Messalina. Granting her to have been inviolably faithful to Louis, she contrived to hold him up to public scorn as a cuckold.   Granting her to have been thoroughly attached to the people of her adoption, no belief was more common than that of her hatred to them as an alien.   In stormy times, no matter what the great are, their fate depends upon what they are believed to be.

No popular revolution, according to Lord Bacon and to universal experience, was ever successful unless headed by the aristocracy; the victims lead the procession that conducts them to the knife.   Royalty, nobility, learning, and the clergy, appeared at the opening of the French Revolution as the leaders of the movement that had for its goal the bloody grave of all.   Unquestionably that commencement of the DEATH MARCH, the first assembling of the *tiers-état*, presented much to dazzle the sight and awaken the hopes of the world.   Whatever a mighty nation

seemed to have best and noblest, all united in the
cause of national reform, each party vying with the
other in the surrender of unjust privilege and the
study of the public good! And the most touching
feature ¦in the whole is the evident and enthusiastic
sincerity, the gallant and fearless earnestness of each
party of the entire public. It was a fever of patriotism,
— yet, unhappily, out of this very fever, an acute
observer might have perceived, would arise the ultimate delirium, the violence, and the frenzy.

It was, in reality, an assembly of people who
knew nothing about business — setting themselves
down to transact the most complicated affairs in a
fit of drunken inspiration. There were not twenty
practical men in the whole number. The habits of
society had been for ages against all practical experience. In England, since the revolution of 1688,
the Representative System has accustomed the minds
of every class, and every party which it embraces,
to the consideration of political affairs — to the weighing of means and ends — to distinct and intelligible
objects. Even the wildest chartist amongst us has
a thorough perception of the ends he desires to effect:
he wishes a broad democracy, and he sees clearly
that annual parliaments and universal suffrage are
the most direct means to the consummation of that
wish. But the French patriots, ardent to destroy,
had no experience of state affairs whereby to reconstruct; their policy was a confused mass of heated
theories, social dogmas, and political maxims, heaped
chaotically together: "English constitution" — "Athen-
ian republic;" — "Majesty of Roman virtues" — "Pri-
mitive simplicity of savage state;" — "Austere morals"

— "Rights of women;" — "Universal peace" — "France, the armed regenerator of Europe!" Out of these, and a myriad other incongruous medleys, rose the popular enthusiasm — what to end in but popular insanity? Experience affording no guide, religion no check, it was clear that all the strife of parties must merge in the sanguinary struggle of each for power; and that the predominant policy intended to create a government founded — so ran the jargon — "on Immutable Justice," would be but the adaptation of the shifts and expedients of the day to the passions of the populace. "There is but one step," roared Mirabeau from his stormy tribune, "from the Capitol to the Tarpeian Rock!" And on that step stood, from the taking of the Bastille till the fall of Robespierre, all the philosophers, legislators, philanthropists, dreamers; with the certainty that for him who lost the Capitol, there was no destiny but the Rock.

The two prominent figures in the early part of the revolution, Mirabeau and Lafayette, were the more suited to the exigencies of the moment inasmuch as they formed a link between the decaying state and the advancing; both noble by birth, and both with certain definite notions of a limit to destruction, they served to soften the shock of the transition. There was something aristocratic even in the Revolution, so long as the white steed and lofty plume of Lafayette were visible amid the riot, rolling back the carnage; or while the dominant genius of Mirabeau kept in awe the inferior spirits who represented the Mob the more faithfully from the absence of whatever was clear in the object, or rational in the pursuit.

The manners of the time underwent a change unparalleled in completeness and rapidity. A few years before, and even the Emperor of Austria shocked the nice etiquette of the court of France. Now it was enough to wear a crown, to be considered below the common dignity of man. Even in the first fair show of the Revolution, the day following the death of the Dauphin, while his remains were yet laid in state, while the royal parents were in the first anguish of grief, — the deputies from the *tiers-état* burst (in spite of remonstrance carried into prayer) upon the presence of the unhappy king: "What!" sighed Louis, "is not one of these men a *father?*" Already the lovers of liberty began to manifest their patriotism by the brutality of their manners; the politest nation in Christendom hastened to obtain the character of the filthiest and most savage. The type of that freedom which consisted in the pleasure of outraging others may be found in the anecdote of Danton at the theatre. This abode of the once formal Graces of France had always afforded a fair representation of the character of the time, partly in the nature of the spectacle, partly in the habits of the audience. In the midst of schemes for the overthrow of a throne, the leading republicans could still find time for equal energy in the intrigues of the *Coulisses*. When the play of 'Charles IX.,' the dramatic libel on kings, was forced upon the King's Company, the Political Revolution had made a vast stride. When, in the midst of the pit, a huge burly man sat sullen, intercepting the view of his neighbours, and shocking the *bienséances* of polished life by wearing his hat nailed to his head — when the cry of displeasure arose, and that one man, clapping the hat firmer on his head, shouted forth in his deep roar, "C'est moi,

Danton!" — and when the audience at once submitted
to the sentiment that the one freeman had the right
to annoy and insult all other freemen — the Social
Revolution was gone far into the slough of the *Sans
Culottes*.

And yet Danton himself was more genial, more
even of the old French gentleman, than most of his
compeers.   His convivial qualities, his love of women,
his very vices tended in some degree to humanize his
manners.   The true personation of the mobs, of what
the French call still *le Peuple*—(long may it be before
that word can be justly translated into the noble
Anglicism, THE PEOPLE!) — was Marat. Let us take
Mr. Duval's description of *him*. Our narrator accepts
an invitation to dine with Danton.

"*On dinait bien chez Danton*, one dined well with Danton.
Politics were not always spoken; at his table one laughed
often, and one was bored rarely. • • • • We passed
from a very elegant saloon into a dining-room looking upon
the Cour du Commerce. At this moment there entered a man.
A man — here is his portrait. He was at most from four feet
eight to four feet nine (French measure), his head a little inclined to the left shoulder, like Alexander the Great; the
limbs were crooked, the complexion yellow and bilious, the
face marked with the small-pox, the lips thin, the eyes gray
and rolling continually in their orbits, the eyelashes red, and
the white, so called, of the eyes nearly the same colour, so
that the pupil seemed to swim in blood. He moved his head
restlessly to and fro, like a Greenland bear in his den at the
Jardin des Plantes.

"As to the accoutrements of the *ami du peuple*, behold
him from head to foot; a hat *à l'andromane*, as one then called
those hats low in the crown, with broad brims turned up,

adorned with a huge tri-colour cockade; an old coat worn out at the seams, striped stockings, red, white, and blue, and bits of string in his shoes in the place of ribbons or buckles; plush breeches, a red waistcoat, turned over, and the neck all open, lank black hair plastered to the temples, with a little *queue* fastened with a leathern knot.

" 'Danton,' said Marat, 'from afar I have smelt the savour of your roast, and I have come to see if there is a corner for me at your feast.'

" 'Why not, if we crowd each other a little? I am sorry you did not let me know, that I might have ordered something more.'

" 'Pooh! your daily fare would suffice for me.'

" 'Well, but when one invites oneself to dinner amongst persons *comme il faut*, one generally presents oneself clad a little less unceremoniously.'

" 'Ah, with a laced frill, an embroidered coat, and one's hair curled *à l'oiseau royal*, eh! Thank you for nothing. Nature is at the cost of my toilet, and the friend of the *peuple* has no need of foreign ornaments.'

" '• • • • • But patriotism does not forbid a cravat or a collar.'

" 'I never wear them, as you well know.'

" 'But at least a clean shirt and clean hands.'

"I then perceived that Marat had, in fact, his hands as black as a smith's on a Saturday night, and his shirt of the same hue as his hands. May it be said without offence to his memory," &c.

Yes, this was Marat! — And in him appeared the friend of the populace (*peuple*), because the true son of the populace. This rickety, bilious, scrofulous, diseased victim of the neglect, the ailments, and the vices of his parents, represented in himself the squalid masses who formed the procession of Jourdain Coup-

tête, or filled the gloomy pandemonium of the Jacobin
Club. But beneath all this external debasement moved
the iron springs of an indomitable, dogged, frantic
energy; a spirit of blood and vengeance which made a
virtue of crime, so honest was it, so sincere. Marat
shrieking day after day for 300,000 heads — Marat
emerging from cave and garret into a power that shook
alike court and temple — the Arch Alecto starting
from the rags and decrepitude in which the fury had
been a while concealed — Marat was as willing to be
the martyr as the hangman: those filthy hands would
have spurned the gold that sullied the ruffles of the
corrupt Danton. Nothing could soften, nothing humanize, but nothing could intimidate, nothing bribe.
For a time Marat was the *peuple* and the *peuple* Marat.

Against such a spirit that now pervaded the great
masses, what were all attempts at moderation and
compromise? In vain has curiosity speculated upon
what might have been the results, had Mirabeau lived
and struggled for the preservation of the monarchy.
Monarchy had no materials for preservation left to it.
The weakness of the nobles as an order had become
so manifest from the first, so thoroughly rotted away
from amongst them was the spirit whether of cavalier
or of patriot, that they had neither the courage to defend themselves, nor the ambition to save their country.
As the ancient warrior, who, having lost his shield,
felt spirit and valour gone, and took to his heels at
once, so, as soon as the nobles lost that mere appanage
of power, their titles, they began to entertain no higher
aspirations than those of physical safety. The first
wind that shook the trunk scattered the leaves. The
ignoble prematurity of their emigration was the basest

feature in the whole revolution, and the surest sign that the noblesse as a body had lost even the elements for the restoration of aristocracy. What then could Mirabeau have done for a throne surrounded by democratic institutions, for a head destined to be crowned by the *bonnet rouge?* What man can protect, amidst the war of public passions, that which public respect and public opinion have deserted?

It was easy, we say, to see that where power had grown the monopoly of the assailants, there was no longer the hope of compromise with the assailed. That time passed when the moderate men incurred the guilt of cheering the populace on to the siege of the Bastille and the murder of its defenders. At a later period the Girondins vainly sought to be the restorers of reason; — vainly sought, in the midst of the frenzy they had encouraged, to weigh out drachms and scruples for the adjustment of scales into which a heavier sword than that of Brennus was already thrown. The Girondins may be considered the representatives of the Middle Classes. Their leaders belonged principally to that order — they had its respectability, its honesty, its prejudices, and its fears. The Girondin mayor of Paris, Péthion, riding amidst the riots, and weeping virtuous tears (he was *le vertueux Péthion*), because, after having murdered their victim, the populace quietly withdrew at his paternal remonstrances — the orators, Vergniaud and Isnard, opposing conspiracies by sentences — Barbaroux and the fair Roland imagining a government of federalisms, that in fact would have divided France into small republics, under the control of the *bourgeoisie* and the lawyers — were equally the types of a class trained to respect for law, but thoroughly

impotent at a time when law needs other force than its
own.   In such a crisis, an active Aristocracy has its
defence in armed retainers — a Democracy in mobs —
a Middle Class has nothing but an exhorting mayor
and a decorous orator!

We have said that the Girondins were the representatives of the Middle Class: — so far their position
has been recognised.   But here follows a truth of mighty
importance which we do not remember to have seen
sufficiently noticed: So long as they kept apart from
the multitude they were safe and respected; when they
called in the multitude to their aid they rapidly became insecure and despised.   We do not mean by
keeping apart from the multitude that they neglected
the legitimate means of popularity, — on the contrary,
they were eminently popular until they connived at the
popular excesses, — we mean simply their avoidance
of using the multitude as an instrument to obtain power.
In their first position, as men desiring reform, not
violence, they carried the election of Péthion against
Lafayette as mayor of Paris — they drove out the less
liberal administration — they forced their own government, under Roland, Dumouriez, and Clavière, upon
the king.   The unhappy suspicions of Louis,. and the
intrigues of Dumouriez, who deserted his party, led to
the dissolution of their ministry.   They retired "with
the regrets of the nation," according to the declaration
of the Assembly.   Their position as yet was strong and
noble; with patience and moderation their return to
power was sure.   But they formed the resolution of
defeated placemen — they began to excite the populace
against the throne: — not that they wished as yet
France to be a republic — no, but that French mon-

archy might be their appanage and patent. They became traitors to law by their palterings with force — palterings, for they still affected attachment only to constitutional measures. They would trust to the petitions of the people; nothing more legitimate! — but they suffered the petitioners to present themselves *armed* before the National Assembly; nothing more fatal! — the speeches of Vergniaud while insidious became inflammatory; he would not call Louis a tyrant, but he *supposed a case* in which every one would call Louis traitor and tyrant both. Brissot, more bold, exclaimed that "one man paralyzed France!" — and that man her king. And all the while they set the populace on fire, they seemed to have little other design in the conflagration than the roasting of their own eggs. Their ambition prevailed — a second and a more fatal time they came into power; no longer as ministers of a king, but as delegates of a mob; no longer merely as representatives of the middle class, but as destroyers of the class above, and as mouthpieces of the class below. The date of this second rule of the Girondins commences from the celebrated 10th of August, the day of the invasion and massacre of the Tuileries. M. Duval, who was a witness and actor, describes this scene with great effect and truth.

"Péthion, the mayor, had been at the chateau at midnight, and had assured the king that the menaced insurrection should be pacified. Scarcely had the king repeated this assurance to the guard, than the sound of the tocsin, the roll of the drum, were heard. Instantly the great gate toward the Carrousel is closed. 'To your posts!' is the cry. They make us take our arms — then lay them down to pile them *en*

faisceau. The greatest confusion reigns in all the courts —
everywhere we hear the cannoniers of the guard venting im-
precations on the king and queen, and declaring they will
rather point their pieces against the chateau than against the
peuple. A little before five in the morning Rœderer comes to
us, and says, 'Gentlemen, a troop of misled citizens *menace*
this *house* and its inhabitants; if they resort to violence it is
your duty to repel force by force. Here is the law, I will
read it to you:' and he takes a little book, *bound in tri-colour
paper,* reads us the law, puts up the little book again, and is
off. A quarter of an hour after the king visits our posts —
in a violet-coloured coat, his hat under his arm, his sword at
his side — he passes before our ranks, and addresses us *d'une
voix altérée:* 'Well, they come; I don't know what they want,
but my cause is that of good citizens; we will show a good
front, eh? (*nous ferons bonne contenance, n'est pas?*') and in
thus speaking to us he had the tears in his eyes, and his air
and carriage were such as to take all courage from the intre-
pid. The queen also said a few words, scarcely articulate,
struggling in vain to suppress her sobs. In this moment arrived the two hundred *gentilhommes,* who had kept in that
part of the Louvre which now forms the museum. The queen
presented them to us: 'Messieurs, these are our friends; they
will take orders, *and show you how to die for your king.'* As
if there were not enough of ill-seasoned imprudence in these
words, a rumour was spread that the queen had said, 'They
will *give* — not *take* — orders.' This was a falsehood, but it
sufficed as a pretext for the disaffected, and instantly two
battalions of the national guard, who had just arrived, broke
rank, and marched off to take position on the Carrousel with
two cannon. There they stopped the fresh battalions arriving to the succour of the chateau, and forced them to take
part in their revolt. From that moment expired all hope in
the National Guard.

"Such was the sad and first effect of the apparition of
these two hundred *gentilhommes.* Most of them very aged,
they seemed scarcely to bear the weight of the sword, which

was their only weapon. Like the unhappy Louis they had only snatched a few moments of repose upon benches and sofas, and their hair, like his, was in disorder. Nearly all in embroidered coats, satin waistcoats, and white silk stockings, a few only in uniform, their faces pale and haggard, they rather resembled men for whom sleep was necessary than champions for their imperilled king. God forbid that I should ridicule fidelity and devotion, but the truth is that their costume, so little appropriate to the occasion, their pretensions of exclusive loyalty, made them regarded with so unfavourable an eye that their succour brought less utility than danger. And it was not with this handful of aged gentlemen, however honourable and loyal, that Pergamus could be saved —

'Non tali auxilio, non defensoribus istis.'

"To complete all, one of these personages thought fit in a swaggering tone to say to the National Guard, 'Now, Messieurs of the National Guard, now is the moment to display courage.' — 'We shall not fail in *that*,' cried an officer in an extreme rage, 'but it is not by your side that we shall give the proof of it.' And instantly he went off, and carried with him his company to join the cannon already pointed against the chateau."

And yet, alas! "this handful of gentlemen" in satin vests, and court swords, and silk stockings, were all the last relics of that gallant chivalry who had rushed against the lion of England to the cry of Mountjoie St. Denis, who had followed St. Louis to the Holy Land, who had tracked through the battlefield the white plume of Henri of Navarre, who had shaken the throne under Louis XIII., who had met the charge of Marlborough at Ramilies and Blenheim, who had filled with lance and banner that very space of the Carrousel

when it first received its name from the latest tourna-
ment held in France in the gorgeous youth of the
fourteenth Louis! There now were the ashes and
tinder of that aristocracy! What could a thousand
Mirabeaus do to restore the departed glory; and what,
without a nobility, amidst such a national guard, with
such a mayoralty, invaded by such a populace, what
hope for such a king! The rest is well known —
Louis surrendered himself to the Assembly. This was
the last day of nobility and royalty, the first of the
unhallowed union between the middle class and the
populace — the Dantonists who had led the movement,
and the Girondins who had intrigued for it. In the
midst of the pæans of the Marseillaise, and the shrieks
of massacre, arose the dynasty of Vergniaud and the
Talkers!

Truly says M. Duval (vol. III. p. 242) —

"Scarcely had the sceptre, so long coveted, devolved on
them, than their feebleness and hesitation made their de-
thronement certain. The massacres of September take place
under their eyes; they are silent, or but falter out a feeble
voice. From the installation of the Convention, the reins of
government float in their hands, and they remain impotent
witnesses of the crimes of the commune, the Jacobins, the
popular societies! Members of all the committees, possessing
majorities in every commission, they know neither to foresee
nor to prevent. If sometimes they were roused into a sudden
energy, it passed like a lightning, it vanished like a smoke.
Gladly in a critical moment would they have adopted some
vigorous measure, but it was enough to induce them to re-
linquish it, if the Commune appeared angry, or the roar of
Danton was heard from the tribune. These were not the
statesmen to intimidate the hardy conspirators with whom
they had to contend."

Such are the hackneyed complaints against this ill-fated party: and yet it is rather just to blame the Girondins for the truckling to the masses by which they obtained power, than for the feebleness displayed when they had won it. In the latter instance the want of vigour was the proof of virtue. The principles most dear to them forbade the energy which was inherent in the Democracy of the Mountain. They were still the Representatives of what little was left of order, of law, of decorum, of education, of the MIDDLE CLASS in short: — their virtues forbade the vigour of butchers and assassins. And without a ruthless execution of criminals, in whom the public saw only patriots, they could not have punished crime. In a revolution, reasonable men must always appear to want vigour. He who shares the passions of the mob, ever seems most in earnest. But the school of Vergniaud and Isnard was one to make instruments of a populace, and to despise the very instruments it used. These sages of the closet had no more sympathy with the mob than Faustus with the fiend he had invoked. Already the Cordeliers and Jacobins, Danton and Robespierre, were combined for the destruction of the Girondins. Danton, aware of the sinister and jealous hatred even at this time conceived against him by Robespierre, indeed hesitated; but his indecision was brief. He saw the impossibility of allying the unscrupulous principle on which rested his power, his popularity, his safety, with the scholastic formulæ of the Girondins. "No," he said justly, "the moderates will not trust me, and I should lose myself in confiding in them." And from that moment, uniting with his serpent foe, Maximilien the Incorruptible, he

3 *

planned the ruin of the Girondins, — and went blind-
fold to his own grave.

It was on seeing the dangers that surrounded them,
on feeling that the sole power of the state was rapidly
passing into the hands of the mob of Paris, that the
Girondins began seriously to put into practice a theory
that they had long before discussed and approved in
the saloons of Madame Roland. With more of that
statesmanship which belongs to thought, if less of that
which develops itself in action, than the rival parties,
they had the intelligence to foresee that France was
too vast a territory for prolonged duration to one single
republic. A sound and effective central government is
not, at least in ancient states, compatible with a turbulent democracy, extending over an immense area.
But if France could be divided into districts, each
district a republic — if out of the provinces of the
defunct monarchy a republican federacy could be formed
— each state thus constituted could obtain submission
for the laws it enacted. The power in each, now that
aristocracy was extinguished, must gradually and quietly
settle in the middle classes — the mob of Paris would
cease to command the destinies of the nation — one
republic would counterbalance the other. No scheme
could be better for the restraint of pure democracy,
none better suited to the domination of the middle
classes. These views were powerfully cherished and
enforced by certain Protestants of the party, who probably foresaw the establishment of their faith in some of
the departments over which they might preside. Gradually the principal leaders of the party were brought
to the same policy; and preparations were being made

to effect it, when the Girondins fell: this very policy being a main cause of their ruin, inasmuch as they forgot one reason against ever having entertained it — namely, that it was impracticable; impracticable because unpopular; for in a popular revolution, what that is unpopular can succeed!*

No sooner did Robespierre publicly arraign and denounce this "phantom of federacy," than the whole populace became furious against the insult of being parcelled out and frittered away. And with justice, not only as a populace, but as a people. At that moment, surrounded by the armed powers of Europe, had the integrity of France been once lost — had the national spirit been exchanged for the departmental — had the legions of Christendom found, instead of a mighty community animated by one passion, a nest of little republics squabbling with each other, and settling the affairs of their several municipalities — the independence of France had been gone for ever. And the sense of this it was, that gave value and zeal to that bloody phrase now originated as a battle-cry by Robespierre: "*La République Une et Indivisible!*"

Much must be excused in the Girondins. If much to be blamed, for much also they are to be admired, for much pitied; but their fall was necessary to the

* Many historians have, it is true, disputed the justice of this charge against the Girondins, and have considered their scheme for Federacy to be indeed a Phantom. — M. Duval gives very curious and minute details on the *reality* of their project, and it is entirely conformable to the character and objects of their party.

nation. Girondism would have rotted the nation itself away.

With them passed the dynasty of the Middle Class, and rose that of the Mob — the true Reign of Terror. The tone of manners became still more gross and revolting. The words "Fraternity or Death," written upon all the prisons, gave the exact idea of the ferocious philanthropy which then denounced as an aristocrat any one who used the pronoun *you* instead of *thou.* Then Atheism, the rankest and most intolerable, grew at once the safest and the most fashionable, creed. Whatever was most ignorant, most absurd, most brutal in human folly, ascended into despotism: — Naturally; — for it was the most ignorant and the most passionate class, in a moment of general frenzy, that ruled all France. But force and passion are never enthroned utterly in vain. Amidst all the crimes of the period, one virtue of immense importance when acting upon large communities was unquestionable — Patriotism. The principle of nationality endangered by the Girondins blazed up with increased fire and indomitable vigour. The foreign enemy was on the frontiers; and the same spirit that rendered life intolerable to the peaceful civilian, made the fierce soldier irresistible. The new leaders of the state, that is, the chiefs of the Mountain, who had supplanted the Girondins, carried into full action not only the vices, but equally this one virtue of the Mob. It is literally startling to see the sudden and brilliant contrast which their energetic policy presented to the vacillation of their predecessors. These butchers, so atrocious in the capital, were magnificent as statesmen and heroes the moment their minds flew to the borders, of invaded France. There, the iron will of Robespierre, the savage genius of St. Just, the reckless daring of Danton, changed at once from vices into virtues.

We hear it often said that the French republic would not have been so disastrous a failure in the experiments of liberty, had it not been for the frenzy produced by the invasion of the allies. On the contrary, to that invasion alone France owed its reentrance into civilization. Left to waste all the strength of the new passions upon internal contests, to proscriptions would have succeeded civil war; and the wild democracy of old Corcyra would have been a heaven to the Pandemonium of a society for the evil spirit of which there would have been no vent. The superior sagacity of Mr. Pitt was never more displayed than in his reluctance to enter into the war forced on him at last; a reluctance for which the Royalists never forgave him. From wrong into right — from the hell of Paris into the daylight of truth and liberty — broke the youth of France in the just and holy cause of independence and self-defence. From the bosom of the Mountain fourteen armies poured the spirit that never fails to conquer against the lukewarm hirelings of invading sovereigns. From the fires of the Mountain flashed the enthusiastic heroism of Jourdan, Hoche, Pichegru, and Moreau. Liberty common to all — promotion the right of each — every soldier was a hero: no matter the rawness of the recruits, the inexperience of the generals, — it was as the strife of the young man against the old, of vigour against decrepitude, when a whole population, drunk with liberty, marched against the time-worn sove-

reignties of the sober world.   Well may M. Duval
exclaim —

"Oh, if the Convention could be considered only in the
light of defenders from the foreigner, how noble its part in
history!"

Meanwhile at Paris three great factions were
struggling for power.   The impracticable enthusiasts
of brotherhood and atheism under Clootz, Chaumette,
and Hébert; the Cordeliers, under Danton and Des-
moulins; the Jacobins, under Robespierre.   The time
for the first was gone by.   No sooner had the vigorous measures of the Mountain arrayed the ardour of
France against the whole of Europe, than poor Baron
Clootz's declamations upon Universal Love, upon the
superiority of Philanthropy to Patriotism, were not
only impertinent but treasonable.   These men (the
Atheist-Philanthropists) had nothing in their minds
or their policy that could command more than momentary success; they appear for the most part to
have honestly believed the articles of their execrable
creed, but their very fanaticism was the proof of
their inability to govern.   They were to the more
practical and robust demagoguy, whether of Robespierre or Danton, what the Socialists of our day are
to the Chartists.   Most of them desired the entire
abolition of private property, "*La richesse nuit à la
santé et conduit rarement à la vertu.*"   The tribunes
might applaud these sentiments, but how were they
to be practised?   Such doctrines preluded the Procession (under the management of Chaumette) of the
Goddess of Reason.   Was it possible that a faction,

declaring the sole Deity of the Universe was an abstract word, represented by an immodest harlot, could exist long in any community however besotted? The most striking feature in that farce was the man ordained to convert it into a great and awful tragedy, — Maximilien Robespierre. He, the formal, the moral, the precise; he, the educated, thoughtful cynic; with what hate and scorn must he have regarded such a spectacle of human folly! M. Duval describes him graphically.

"Among the numerous deputies, resting in disdain on their curule chairs, I will cite Robespierre. He took off, replaced his spectacles, wiping the glasses, beat a tattoo with his feet, shrugged his shoulders, yawned, took notes, and from time to time whispered to St. Just seated by his side. I have not seen the notes that passed between them, but I am free to think that they furnished the exordium of the famous report on the faction of Atheists which St. Just recited four months later at the tribune, and which served as a footstool for Chaumette to ascend the scaffold."

A faction so characterized was but the representative of the ignorance and folly of the mob; it could obviously not secure its interests nor wield its passions; it had not one element of duration, one quality for the acquisition of solid power. And every observer must have seen that the real strife for the mastery of France lay between Robespierre and Danton. Of these two men, amongst most historians, especially in England, Danton is the favourite. There is indeed, to a vulgar gaze, something almost captivating in this Mirabeau of the Mob, despite his horrible ex-

cesses. He was free from all personal vindictiveness,
he was not naturally cruel; he spilt blood in torrents,
but always for a purpose and from policy; he could
not be sanguinary in detail; he had no cowardice in
him, no envy. About his character was a large rough
good-nature; he was affectionate and loyal to those he
loved (for he did love and he was loved, this master
butcher who could order the massacre of 2000 prisoners
in cold blood). He had no religion, even of atheism;
for atheism is not, like scepticism, lukewarm and hesitating, but is ardent and intolerant in its creed; he
laughed at the Goddess of Reason: he had therefore
no vestige of hypocrisy or cant. Frankly he confessed
his total infidelity, candidly he owned his theories of
Revolutions, "things not made with rose-water," in
which (as he said) "the boldest scoundrel was the
most successful actor." He was profligate, lustful,
and corrupt in money matters, but he was all these
so undisguisedly, that the vulgar, who like a frank
villain, ranked them amongst his merits. On the other
hand, Robespierre was physically timid, and hence
arose, perhaps, all his crimes. He, too, certainly was
not by nature cruel, nor even vindictive, whatever
has been said to the contrary; for it is a fact that he
took no notice of many of his early personal enemies
when their lives were in his power; but he never
spared one man who could be an obstacle to his ambition, or who could endanger his safety. He, like
Danton, was sanguinary only on a system, but his
system was one of private fear as well as public
interest. He was essentially an egotist. Danton lived
for the circle, not from faith in its interests, but
from his joyous temper; Robespierre sat wrapped in

himself. The same cause that made Maximilien cruel, made him treacherous; for personal cowardice, combined with moral energy (which last Robespierre possessed to the highest possible degree), works through craft that which the bolder villany achieves through violence.

But then Robespierre had faith in something, and Danton in nothing. Robespierre believed in Liberty, in Virtue, in a Deity, in the People, in the Revolution itself. Danton regarded all with the same careless and hardy *insouciance*. With him Virtue was a convention, a Deity a word; the People, Liberty, and Revolution, — all pretences for ambition, — counters in the game of knaves. He got wearied of the Reign of Terror, partly because he saw it made subservient to the personal egotism of Robespierre, partly because he was a man who lived for the day, and he was newly married, had amassed a fortune, and was fond of his villa.* But he wanted that earnestness and faith of purpose which could alone have enabled him to carry on the movement into order and mercy. He toyed with the time; he was wholly incapable to construct, while so marvellously fitted to destroy. With all his talents, which, though of a coarse quality, were considerable, he was a child when compared to the

* "They say," observed a patriot to Danton, "that your zeal is abated now you are rich; that you toiled to advance the Revolution till it had made your fortune; that now your fortune is made you would arrest it. This is not said of Robespierre, always poor and always zealous. Why is this?" "Because," answered Danton, without denying the charge, "I love gold, and Robespierre only blood."

concentrated will, and indefatigable industry, and
patient intellect of Robespierre.* And therefore, in
looking calmly and dispassionately at the two men,
the profound observer must feel, that if, placed in
those times, he had been constrained to take his choice
between Robespierre and Danton, had been forced to
rest his last hopes of the Revolution, of Humanity, of
Civilized Institutions, upon one or the other, Danton
would not have been his election. The more, amidst
that chaos of motives and of actors, we regard the
prominent individuals, the more we must perceive
that the only INTELLIGENCE of the time was Maximilien Robespierre. He had objects and purposes
beyond the hour; he was ever looking forward to the
time when the Reign of Blood was to cease; he only
desired to destroy his enemies in order to call into
being the new state of things in which he could reduce to system the theories he cherished. He was
engaged with David on designs for benevolent institutions a few days before he perished; he was drawing
up notes for a code of laws in which his earliest
dream of the abolition of capital punishments might
be realized, while struggling foot to foot with Barras
and Tallien for his head or their own. He firmly
believed in all the principles he professed; — a hypo-
crite in his conduct to men, but an enthusiast in his
faith in dogmas.

* Danton felt this even while affecting to call Robespierre
lache, and pretending to despise him. Latterly he shrunk
from all contest with him, all association with Robespierre's
foes, and could not defend from Maximilien's grasp even his
own friends. It is noticeable that, throughout the Revolution,

In times of convulsion two qualities are necessary, forethought to design, courage to act. Only one man in modern revolutions ever perhaps united these in the perfection necessary to complete personal success, and that man was Cromwell.* In the French Revolution Danton had more of the last, Robespierre incalculably more of the first. Historians compare Danton to a lion, and in all his qualities, noble or savage, he had much of the brute — soul in him seemed extinct. Robespierre, with all his atrocities, still had the calculation, reason, and belief of a Man. And the Man beat the Lion.

But when Danton fell, Robespierre, to survive, had no option but the choice of Augustus after the proscriptions. If the excitement arising from terror was to be prolonged, what could feed it after the death of Danton — except his own? He might have made the tragedy end with that signal catastrophe; but if the interest was to go on, if another act was to be added, all that could engage the audience was the fall of Maximilien Robespierre.

We have seen, that, as the Revolution advanced step after step, it preyed upon class after class, which it dragged up into power. As Vergniaud eloquently said, "Like Saturn, it devoured its own children." The head of Louis was destined from the moment the crowd shouted to behold it encircled with the *bonnet*

Robespierre was the only man who could protect his creatures. No one but himself could dare to lay hands on those he appeared to favour. This was an immense advantage over all his rivals.

* Another such man has risen since this was written.

rouge; the nobility were predestined the moment they
merged themselves with the commons; the middle class
were invaded, pillaged, decimated, as soon as their
dynasty fell with the Girondins. And now that the
empire of the populace was founded, the populace
began to find the fiend they had raised fixing its fangs
and talons on themselves. Sated with the blood of
nobles, priests, and scholars, the Guillotine had begun
to reek with the gore of carpenters, shoemakers, masons,
cobblers; and the eyes of the Populace opened when
they saw *themselves* the prey of their own ferocity. The
shops were shut up as the tumbrils passed to the
scaffold — Paris was sickened of the Reign of
Blood.

Amidst acclamations that came from a human
hope, Robespierre had proclaimed the existence of a
Deity; for men, believing or not in God, believed that,
the worship of a God once established, something of
mercy and goodwill to Man would mingle with the
creed. In the presence of the FATHER, the son's hand
would surely drop the blade lifted against the brother.
But no; the Deity proclaimed by Robespierre had
brought no mitigation of crime and slaughter amongst
mankind. Like the gods of Epicurus, the Being a
Robespierre could invoke seemed to disdain regard of
the affairs of earth. And they who had wept hot tears
to hear the eloquent periods in which this would-be
Prophet, this Master of the Ceremonies to Heaven, introduced the new worship, began now to ask themselves whether indeed Maximilien Robespierre was the
man to bestow Religion upon the world. Egotist in
everything, it might be said that Robespierre sought to
turn even the Almighty to his own advantage. He had

invoked Heaven to crush the atheists as political enemies, not to curb atheism as a moral evil.

At this time Robespierre was a spectacle of absorbing and awful interest. His constitution, always sickly, was sinking fast under his vigilance and his terror. He seldom slept, he never reposed. Devoured by the acrid humours of his system, his face became livid, his eyes streaked with blood. Hour after hour anonymous letters threatened him with the hand of the assassin — conspiracies gathered rapidly round him. Men, insignificant while Danton lived, took the strength of dragons from the blood of that awful head. Robespierre reigned but by his hold over the club of the Jacobins, and the hearts of the women! A strange subject for female enthusiasm! but *that* usually follows power and will. And there was something too of mystery in this cold, austere being — young in years, with the hoary cunning and hard heart of age; resisting all temptation, except that of governing mankind; and shaking Europe from a chamber over a cabinet-maker's shop.

The singular and ruthless determination of purpose which Robespierre had hitherto shown began to desert him. His energies, no longer concentrated upon the downfall of single rivals, wandered wild and indecisive over that vast field of enmity and peril which spread before his gaze. In proportion as he lost in vigour of action, he improved in eloquence of word. The common horror in which his character is held, makes us unjust to his talents. And it requires all the charity of abstract criticism to praise the orator while sickening at the man. But it would be difficult to find any-

where in the modern literature of the rostrum finer
passages than some of his principal speeches contain.
The address, delivered to the Convention, in vindication of the Deity, is full of beauties in language, and
justice of thought. But it is natural that those who
read should be so revolted at the want of harmony
between the orator and the subject, — at the character
of the butcher arrogating that of the theologian, — the
Nero assuming the Numa, — that even the finest
passages shock the moral taste too much to win justice
from the intellectual. Robespierre vindicating, in the
midst of massacre, the existence of a God of mercy, is
like our own Richard III. issuing his Proclamation
against Vice after the murder of his nephews. The
sentiments professed by either may be admirable in
themselves, but they only serve to deepen the general
abhorrence of the character they contrast. No man
ever had so complete a command over an assembly
from the mere force of mind and thought as Robespierre
long enjoyed over the Convention, and to the last over the
Jacobin Club. For, unlike most successful orators, he
owed nothing to physical advantages: a wretched person, mean features, even the fire of the eyes concealed
by glasses, a discordant voice, hoarse and indistinct in
the low tones, shrill and grating in the higher, the
words and the thoughts had nothing to set them off.
It was this faculty of genuine eloquence, cultivated
and improved till it triumphed over all physical defects, which hastened his ruin; for he was eminently a
vain man, and like vain men he attached undue importance to means that obtained momentary applause.
Yes! he would speak, he would denounce, he would
prove, he would trust his cause to his eloquence! He

thought of words at the moment when nothing could
have saved him but deeds. And of all his efforts,
never one equal in eloquence to his last speech at the
Convention! Had it been delivered by a man whose
history commanded admiration instead of loathing, it
would have been cited as a masterpiece of lucid argument, subtle thought, and fiery and earnest passion;
— for in words Robespierre had passion, and his cold
dogmas ring out as living principles. But the spirit of
the audience was gone, the speech was out of place
and season. As a sermon from Dr. Chalmers on the
hustings, as Milton's Defence of Unlicensed Printing in
a council of war with the enemy at the gates, — was
a long tirade of arguments or complaints in an assembly of men who knew that in six days France must
be the executioner of Robespierre, or his slave. And
the time lost in preparing the harangue, would have —
But no, whether in words or deeds his hour was past:
— the sense of humanity was at length awakened, and
the last Representative of the Populace fell amidst its
hoots and curses to make way for the eternal successor
of Civil Convulsion, — Military Rule. When Napoleon first pointed his cannon *against* the populace, the
final moral was given to that tale of a world's shame
and wonder: and the multitude prepared the crown for
the man who delivered them from themselves!

In looking at this distance of time over the great
Revolution of France, — even if we consent to make for
its follies and its crimes all the excuses prescribed to
us, — if we emancipate ourselves from the prejudices
(so let them be called) with which human nature must
regard its revolting incidents and details, — we must
still find it a matter of grave astonishment, that so

violent a convulsion should have produced such insignificant benefits. To those who read history with
the eyes of Mignet and of Thiers (the great masters of
the school so well entitled the *Fatalist*) history may
interest, but it never warns — once grant that events
are the things of destiny, and what signify the faults
or virtues of the actors? This is indeed to reduce
history to an almanack, nay, to an astrological almanack, and to place the horoscope of nations under
the fabulous influence of the stars. But they who see,
in the chronicles of a state, matter to make succeeding
times profit by the disaster and emulate the triumph,
must ever ask themselves that question, on the answer
to which, so much to dethrone Law or to legalize
Force must rest — "What has France gained by her
Revolution?" And we think it might be satisfactorily
shown, that whatever benefit France has derived from
the Revolution itself is a wretched recompense for the
crimes through which she waded to obtain it. Do not
let us be misunderstood. We grant, at once, that if
we compare the state of the people and the nature of
the laws, in 1785, with their existence in 1842, there
is in great and vital respects a considerable improvement; that improvement, however, is not to be ascribed
to the Revolution, *but to the spirit that preceded the
Revolution, and could have sufficed for all beneficial
changes, without it.* Until, by the siege of the Bastille,
the Populace were permitted to take the law into their
own hands, there was no fear for the safe progress of
Opinion; and the events of 1789—94 would have
changed their character, and been known by the name,
not of Revolution, but Reform. Popular principles had
only to be temperate in order to be permanently success-

ful. The king was prepared to yield; the state of the finances placed him and his hostile court at the irresistible command of the Assembly; the nobles, the church, and the men of letters, were, on the whole, pervaded by the spirit of the time. Nothing could have prevented the most lasting compromise of all interests, had, what is properly Revolution, namely, Illegal Violence, not usurped the place of Constitutional Improvement. At this period, the temper of the times, so far from being yet sanguinary, was for the extinction of capital punishment. We repeat and insist upon the truth that the Movement had only to abstain from violence in order to have carried reform to the highest point which the liberty and enlightenment of the Age could have desired: the moment that movement passed into revolution; the moment LAW, instead of being *corrected*, was *resisted;* the moment the populace were permitted to indulge passion and to taste blood; the moment, in fact, Force began, — Reform ceased. We concede all that the apologists for the excesses of the Revolution have demanded. We allow the unhappy influences of Marie Antoinette and the courtiers, the impolitic intrigues of the emigrants, and the unjustifiable aggression of the allies. But such are only the ordinary obstacles with which liberty has to contend in all stages of conflict and transition. And never, perhaps, had liberty advantages so great as those which France possessed, and threw away; viz., a population of one mind, and a king whose heart was with his country. Desèze, in his defence of Louis XVI. before the Assembly, thus summed up, and not a voice could contradict: — "At the age of twenty, Louis, in ascending the throne, carried with him the example of

4*

moral excellence — of justice and economy. The
people wished the abolition of an onerous impost —
Louis destroyed it; — the abolition of servitude —
Louis abolished it. The people asked reforms — he
made them; — their rights — he restored them; —
their liberty — he gave it. No one can deny to Louis
the glory of having been in advance of the people by
his sacrifices, and it is he whom they propose to —
Citizens! I will not conclude the sentence — I pause
before that History — which, remember, shall judge
your judgment — and hers is the verdict that endures
for centuries."

Yes, no candid man denied this praise to Louis,
and what hopes would such a king have afforded to
a People, wise to ask and patient to abide! What
better chief has been gained for liberty — in Robespierre, in Napoleon, in Louis XVIII., in Charles X.,
in Louis-Philippe? Without a revolution, unless the
mere assembling of the *Tiers-Etat* is so to be called,
without, in short, violence and convulsion, France,
under Louis XVI., and his noble son (tortured to
death by the cobbler Simon), would have had a Representative Assembly on the broadest basis, a Government managed with the severest economy, a Press carried on by the freest regulations, — and more than all,
the hearty sympathy and love of every land where
Civilization can free the limbs or elevate the mind.
Has she ever had them since? — has she got them
now?

Unquestionably the abolition of privileges, the
purification of the church, the amendment of the laws,
have been great boons to France, but those were predestined from the first meeting of the *Tiers-Etat.* For

those, no massacres, no guillotine, no regicide, no reign of terror, no revolution (such as we mean by the revolution of France), were required. It was not for those *real* benefits to France that her streets were to swim with blood. The blood was lavished *after* those benefits were obtained.

Perhaps the two greatest evils of the Revolution were, first, that it created that habit of impatience which the best thinkers of France lament as the prevalent characteristic of their countrymen in this age — an impatience equally lamentable in public and individual existence. To succeed at once, or at once to destroy — such is the maxim that makes the assassin and the suicide. The second evil was the habit of indifference to moral character in public men, which could not but be engendered by a demagoguy succeeded by a soldiery. At this moment France has scarcely one guarantee, either for permanent government or liberal institutions.* The representative chamber is so confined that it never represents public opinion; and the electoral chamber, from its constitution, is tainted with the servility of courtiers, and has never that interest against despotism which belongs to aristocracy. Even the Press, to which the French have, from the instinct of weakness elsewhere, attached such affectionate importance, is so feebly guarded by harmonizing institutions, that, while in a popular crisis it can inflame passions better appeased, in ordinary

* The reader will remember that this was written in the later years of Louis Philippe. It is beyond the limits of this essay to inquire whether constitutional liberty has obtained better safeguards since.

times it is exposed to persecutions, the virulence and impunity of which are a scandal both to the people and the crown. If we compare the real safeguards for liberty, the real strata and foundations for good government possessed now by the French, *with those at their disposal in* 1789, far from having gained, they have incalculably lost. And at this moment no man can foresee whether, ten years hence, France may not again be a democracy without education, or a despotism under a conqueror.

A twofold moral then arises from the contemplation of the Reign of Terror; the moral to Rulers, and that to the People. A terrible warning is it to a Monarchy that does not in time partake its responsibility with constitutional assemblies; to a Government that does not regard laws as its right arm, finance as its left; to a Nobility that do not link themselves with the Commons, not suddenly and violently, but through all the slow and imperceptible links of social life; to a Priesthood that forgets the duties which command reverence and attract love. A lesson is it also to rulers no less in resistance than concession; to concede early what is just, but to resist to the last what is iniquitous. The horrors of the Revolution were owing as much to the latter cowardice of all who should have opposed, as to the early obstinacy of all who should have foreseen and forestalled it. A warning equally grave, and if possible more important, is it to the People, that one step gained by law leads to practical and enduring liberty far sooner than a thousand steps gained by force; that excesses in the power they attack never justify excesses in the power they would establish; that revenge is not only as criminal in a people as an individual, but that it is as impolitic and foolish. The greatest errors, and those most fatal to our happiness, which we as private men commit in life, are those which we commit through vindictive passions. We acknowledge this truth as persons, let us enforce it as a people. Above all, perhaps, this revolution ' teaches communities that to institutions alone liberty can be confided, and that institutions to be permanent must not too materially differ from the ancient habits that innovators seek to reform. The indifference to institutions is still a characteristic of our neighbours. Gallant to overthrow, unsteady to construct, the error of their first Revolution pervaded their last; and after a movement almost unparalleled for energy and humanity (for such must the events of the Three Days ever be considered), they were contented with a dynasty and a parchment charter, without one single institution to render the objects for which they fought the heritage of their children. They have obtained a dexterous and an able king; they have won neither reform for their Laws, representation for their Chamber, nor liberty for their Press.

GOLDSMITH.

[First published in 'THE EDINBURGH REVIEW.' July, 1848.]

GOLDSMITH.

—

[*The Life and Adventures of Oliver Goldsmith. A Biography, in Four Books.* By JOHN FORSTER, of the Inner Temple, Author of the *Lives of Statesmen of the Commonwealth.* Bradbury and Evans.]

ONCE upon a time, in the pretty village of Lissoy, in the county of Westmeath, barony of Kilkenny West, a young woman, afterwards known as Elizabeth Delap, put into the hands of a little boy, "impenetrably stupid," his first book. 'Labour dire it was and weary woe' to that little boy; but not seemingly an event of much importance to the literary world. The signposts to Knowledge are not, however, like those set up before the gates at Versailles, inscribed with laconic magniloquence, "To Spain," "To Flanders." We creep into the high road, little knowing whither it will lead us, — and we have a natural curiosity to learn by what humble lanes and crossings our fellow-travellers first emerged into the great thoroughfare. The next glimpse of the small alumnus is caught through the cabin-smoke of the village school, kept by Thomas Byrne, a retired quartermaster of an Irish regiment. It is a glimpse, and no more, still of a little boy, with a manner for the most part uncommonly serious and reserved, — though when gay none more cheerful, —

listening to his preceptor's stories, whether taken from
the brisk adventures of a soldier's life, or the more
bewitching stories of fairy legend; now and then making
rhymes; now and then reading such polite aids to reflection as 'Moll Flanders' or 'Jack the Bachelor.'
From this hazy twilight we perceive our little pilgrim
emerging into somewhat clearer atmosphere, — pre-
senting to us a heavy sickly face, deeply marked with
the small-pox, and placed upon the thick shoulders of
'a stupid blockhead,' at the "superior academy" of
Mr. Griffin, of Elphin, in Roscommon. In due time,
however, this unpromising specimen of Humanity put
out to Knowledge, begins to evince tokens, erratic and
uncouth, of the culture it has reluctantly received.
Our little boy is now a lad, — still at school — though
no longer at Mr. Griffin's, — at school at Edgeworths-
town. He presumes to have likings and dislikings as
to the different authors enforced on him. His school-
fellows remember that he was pleased much with
Horace, more with Ovid, and that he hated Cicero, or
at least did not highly esteem him. His character already assumes somewhat of definite shape. From out
the crowd of boys, with their general attributes of
coarse but healthful boyhood, stands distinct a peculiar
idiosyncrasy. Our pock-marked, pale-faced, clumsy
stripling is noticed as 'sensitive,' over-sensitive. He is
quick to take offence, quicker still to forgive. He is
at first shy and backward; but by degrees he is bold
enough to be mischievous — and makes a figure at
'Fives.' He is no longer considered quite a blockhead, — nay, though indolent, he is thought not
destitute of talent; but the master thinks more highly
of him than the boys do. But school closes — Col-

lege begins — the sensitive, ugly boy is an idle sham-
bling student at the University of Dublin.

A piece of worldly luck which has befallen his
family has proved to him a bitter affliction. He has a
sister who has married above her station. His father
has encumbered his means to provide for that sister
such a dower as may satisfy his pride. And our over-
sensitive youth must go as a sizar to the university at
which his elder brother had won some distinction, nay,
had obtained a scholarship, as a pensioner. A youth
of vigorous judgment and resolute purpose, — one
exulting in what Erasmus calls *basileâ, athleticâ, pan-
craticâ valetudine*, — would have only the more steadily
exerted himself to rise superior to a meanness of circumstance, which could not forbid to industry its re-
wards, nor to genius its career. But our youth —
though not the dunce he had seemed to his early
teachers — is far from that being 'teres, atque rotundus,'
from whose surface the shafts of fortune turn aside.
That pride of his, so easily offended, is terribly in his
way here. He is more sensitive of a condition he feels
beneath him (though it would have been difficult to
say why, since his father's means warranted no higher
station, and his uncle had been a sizar before him)
than eager to establish intellectual claims to respect.
And to say truth, difficult would it have been for this
lad, so imperfectly educated, to force his way into
distinction purely academical. "The popular picture
of him in these Dublin University days is little more
than of a slow, hesitating, somewhat hollow voice,
heard seldom and always to great disadvantage in the
class-rooms; and of a low-sized, thick, robust, ungainly
figure, lounging about the College courts, on the wait

for misery and ill-luck." Hitherto his father has
scraped means to supply the niggard wants of a sizar,
not without reasonable hope that the son will exert
himself, as his brother the pensioner had done before
him, and obtain something like independence in the
way of a scholarship. But now his father dies — and
our lazy, lounging student lives as he can, by small
gifts from his uncle, or petty loans from College friends
— learning from the last that worst and surest lesson
in the Art of Sinking — the practical bathos of human
life — viz. to borrow without shame. Yet here, a
certain energy, fitful and irregular, but energy still,
breaks out; an energy that rivets our eyes to this com-
fortless picture, and interests us in this unequal battle
between Poverty and Man. He does not, it is true,
set himself resolutely to work to redeem lost time, and
wrest subsistence, by patient labour, from the resources
which the university offers to its students. But he
shuts himself up — he composes street ballads, he
runs forth to sell them at the Rein-Deer Repository in
Montrath Court, for five shillings a-piece. And now
comes his reward — he steals out of the College to
hear them sung!

With pathetic eloquence exclaims the last biographer, whom this stupid child and idle student has
contrived to find, "Happy night — worth all the
dreary days! Hidden by some dusky wall, or creep-
ing within darkling shadows of the ill-lighted streets,
watched and waited this poor neglected sizar for the
only effort of his life which had not wholly failed!
Few and dull, perhaps, the beggar's audience at first;
more thronging, eager, and delighted when he shouted
the newly-gotten ware. . . Gentle faces pleased,

old men stopping by the way, young lads venturing a purchase with their last remaining farthing: why, here was a world in little with its fame at the sizar's feet. 'The greater world will be listening one day,' perhaps he muttered, as he turned with a lighter heart to his dull home." And this poor poet of the ballad-singers, this truant student with his morbid sensitive-ness — and his pride, no less unhealthy perhaps in the false direction it had taken — still has something, which does not always accompany over-sensitiveness, and is very rarely found in company with false pride: He has ready sympathy for others. Those five shil-lings which his ballads have brought him will in all probability not reach home undiminished. That audi-ence listening to his muse comprises many more desti-tute than himself, and pleasure and pity both unlock the poor poet's hand, and careless easy heart. "To one starving creature with five children he gave at one time the blankets off his bed, and crept into the bed-ding for shelter from the cold."

It is not to be denied by any one of right prin-ciple, that our youth would have been much better employed on the legitimate studies for which he was sent to college, even on the "cold logic of Burgers-dicius, or the dreary subtleties of Smiglesius," than in writing street ballads sold at five shillings a-piece; that his generosity would have been better evinced in paying the loans he had borrowed; and that his sensi-tiveness would have been more praiseworthy, had it reminded him that he had no right to this looseness of sympathy, while he himself was dependent upon others. It is indubitably wrong, while abridging per-haps the decent wants of some generous benefactor, to

indulge the luxury even of doing good. We cannot
blame those who take the more rigid view of amiable
weaknesses and charitable errors. But good or ill, we
describe our student as we find him. And were we
to set him up as a model, few we suspect would be
his imitators. Thus, then, our very unexemplary sizar
scrambles his way through college, making small progress in mathematics, but able, he himself boasts, "to
turn an ode of Horace into English with any of them."
And as this is the best he can say of his classical
acquirements, so we must suppose them to be far from
deep or extensive. He gets into various scrapes, the
worst of which is, the aiding and abetting a memorable
college riot; and this, or the serious admonition it
entails, spurs him up into a laudable attempt at self-
retrieval. He tries for a scholarship, and actually gets
an exhibition. Seventeenth out of a fortunate nineteen! last but two on the list. This exhibition brings
him in thirty shillings.

> "Nunc est bibendum, nunc pede libero
>   Pulsanda tellus."

Seventeenth on the list, and thirty shillings in his
pocket! it is too much for human nature — at least,
for *that* human nature — to support with dignified
equanimity! He gives a dance in his rooms, —

> "Accipiter velut
> Molles columbas,"

a cross tutor, who bears him no good will, pounces
upon him and his guests. Caught in the act, the
punishment is condign; but considering that both the

parties were Irish, and that the offence, in an English
university, would have entailed rustication at the least,
we are not inclined to be very severe on the exas-
perated tutor, who knocks down the sizar. Next day
the sizar sells his books, leaves his college, lingers in
Dublin till he arrives at his last shilling, and then sets
off for Cork. His brother relieves him from famine,
clothes him, takes him back to the Mater — who to
that rude son scarcely deserves the epithet of Alma, —
and patches up a hollow reconciliation between disciple and master. At last our sizar takes his bachelor's
degree, lowest in the list. And now behold him a
man! He is twenty-one! The law asserts that he is
arrived at years of discretion. He resolves to prove
that the law never more flagrantly indulged in its privileges of legal fiction. The charming biographer
before us says, "this is the sunny time between two
dismal periods of his life." Sunny, no doubt, it
seemed by contrast to our emancipated sizar, for he
often recalled it with a regret which we believe to be
sincere. "If I go (he wrote in after years), if I go
to the opera, where Signora Columba pours out all
the mazes of melody, I sit and sigh for Lissoy's fire-
side, and 'Johnny Armstrong's last good Night,' from
Peggy Golden!" But whatever sunshine he found
here, little sunshine he brought to his mother's cottage. By fits and snatches he helps his respectable
praiseworthy brother in the irksome drudgery of teacher
at the village school; but more often we find him
sauntering into the village inn: there, entering with
him, we see the scapegrace in full glory, presiding
over lesser scapegraces, as thoughtless as himself, at
a kind of club, playing whist, singing songs, and

parading the scraps and remnants of Latin he has
brought home from that feast of learning where he sate
last at the table.   Now and then, in Protean varieties
of idleness, we may see his clumsy careless figure
bending over the banks of the Inny, the rod in his
hand, or the flute on his lips; or hunting otters in the
Shannon; or throwing a sledge-hammer at the fair of
Ballymahon.   His friends entreat him to take orders.
But this rude creature, so little favoured by the
Graces, is not without a strange love of personal
finery: the black coat revolts him; perhaps other and
better reasons concur in making him set his face
against the church.   Later in life, he thought himself
not good enough to read prayers in a private family.
He may have thought himself not good enough to read
them to a congregation and to enforce the lesson by
example.   Nevertheless, — for our vagrant is docile
in his own way, — he yields to the wishes of his
family; whether he reads for orders is not quite clear;
but he certainly applies for ordination, and as certainly
is rejected: some say because he is too young, others
because he has been too wild at college; one worthy
witness believes because he presented himself to the
bishop in scarlet breeches!   Again, new phases of this
disorderly existence present themselves.   We see our
friend, whom nothing hitherto has sufficed to teach
what at least we desire our sons to learn — in the
capacity of a tutor.   Poor pupil, what became of thee!
Soon lost to that occupation, we greet him in setting
out to Cork on a good horse with thirty pounds in his
pocket, intent, it would seem, on the El Dorado of
America, and returning home without a sixpence on a
lean beast, to whom he has vouchsafed the name of

Fiddleback, wondering "that his mother is not more rejoiced to see him!"

But what matters the insensible evaporation of thirty pounds, or the metamorphosis of plump horses into skeleton Fiddlebacks? Be it remembered that our hero has an uncle, — an uncle rarely seen, except in the old comedies, — an uncle precious, placable, inexhaustible. Into those pockets whence thirty pounds have just vanished, the uncle sinks fifty more, and sends off the nephew to study the law. Arrived in Dublin, with that propitiatory offering to Themis, our youth thinks proper to pay his first respects to Fortune, — is allured into one of her temples, called by mortals a gaming-house, and the *Diva præsens* benignantly appropriates to herself the sacrifice designed for an austerer goddess. Our unfortunate adventurer this time has some natural compunction: it is long before he owns what has happened. He is then invited back to the country, forgiven (but that of course) by his uncle; stays a few months with his brother, with whom he unfortunately quarrels; and then his friends exert themselves once more to push him on in the world. The project of the law as a profession is however abandoned. It seems to be tacitly acknowledged, that a calling, which our social infirmities ordain for the protection of the pockets of others, is little suited to one who can take such poor care of his own. Failing Church and Law, what is left? Medicine. Again the uncle opens the elastic purse-strings, and, in 1752, our adventurer starts for Edinburgh, as a medical student. There he distinguishes himself highly — as a capital singer of Irish songs. He varies this occupation by some kind of employment (probably as

5*

tutor) at the Duke of Hamilton's, where "he is liked more as a jester than companion." His pride takes offence, and this employment, whatever it be, lasts little more than a fortnight. He visits the Highlands on a hired horse, "about the size of a ram, who walks away (trot he cannot), as pensive as his master." But if no promising student in medicine, those with whom this strange creature corresponded must have been aware that under all defects of character there was now clear and distinct proof of something to justify, both in the youth himself, and in his more indulgent friends, that "knack of hoping" which belonged to his own facile nature. In his letters there are signs of a humour original and exquisite; — evidences of an observation, not deep, perhaps, but keen; a command of style, peculiar at once for chastened grace and for lively ease. The letters were worth paying for; — they generally *were* paid for. Meanwhile, the Law that our medical student had deserted, pursues him revengefully in the shapes of its wonted Eumenides — the bailiffs. With his usual goodnature he has been security for one friend, and, with his usual readiness of resource, he meets the penalties of the security by borrowing from others. Thus possessed of thirty-three pounds, he prudently leaves Edinburgh, and embarks for Bordeaux. Fortunately he goes on shore at Newcastle-on-Tyne, and is making very merry with seven men, when in march a sergeant and twelve grenadiers with their bayonets screwed, and arrest him as a Scotch Jacobite; his seven boon companions being Scotchmen in the French service. He remains a fortnight in prison, while the ship sails on without him, and sinks at the mouth of the Garonne. At

last, *per varios casus*, our medical nomad arrives at
Leyden.

Here, perhaps attending lectures, and certainly
playing at cards, he remains nearly a year without an
effort for a degree; he thinks it then time to leave the
university, and for that purpose borrows, *more suo*, a
small sum from a friend. Whatever the faults of our
hero, we have seen that at least he was generous (bor-
rowers mostly are so); he passes a florist's garden, and
expends the greater part of the loan he has received in
purchasing costly roots, which he sends to his uncle.
Thus relieved of unphilosophical superfluities, he sets
off from Leyden, one guinea in his pocket, one shirt
on his back, and a flute in his hand; that flute — we
beg pardon for so cursory and slighting a mention of
that flute; what was our friend without it? That flute,
dear mischief, had been his solace and perdition. Woe,
and thrice woe to any man, constitutionally indolent,
with his own way to make in this hard life, who takes
to the flute! Slow will be his advance in the world
with his fingers on those fatal stops! — that flute,
deadliest of all the friendships the sizar had made at
college — at every new insult he had received from
man, at every fresh disaster he had provoked from
fortune — that flute had furnished inauspicious vent
for 'blowing off,' what otherwise might have been
salutary 'excitement.' It was as much as Ulysses could
do, what with stopping the ears of his seamen and having himself lashed to the mast, to save his ship from
the Sirens. But when one is not Ulysses, and when
one carries a Siren always about with one in one's own
pocket, shipwreck must be the habitual incident of life!
With this flute he then sets off on a tour — the man

who had tried in vain to be a scholar, a clergyman, a lawyer, and ought now to be hard at work in qualifying himself for a doctor! Travelling on foot, the flute (*fiat justitia*, for once not all perfidious) opens to him the hospitality of humble roofs. He sees the world to the sound of his own music.

Through Flanders, France, Switzerland, and parts of Italy, he pursues his wanderings, and boasts that "he examines mankind and sees both sides of the picture." So at last he fights (or rather flutes) his way towards England, and steps on shore at Dover. No more flute-playing now, poor vagrant! — No doors open here to that disreputable Siren. There is reason to suspect (thinks his last biographer) that, on the journey from Dover to London, he attempted a comic performance in a country barn; and at one of the towns he passed through (Heaven knows how, and curiosity would in vain guess where), he is said to have received from some homicidal university the physician's formal authority to slay — he yet implores to be hired assistant in an apothecary's shop.

In the middle of February behold him wandering, "without friend or acquaintance, without the knowledge or comfort of one kind face, in the lonely, terrible London streets."

Whether he picks up crumbs as an usher; whether he lives among the beggars of Axe Lane; whether he spreads plaisters and pounds in mortars for an apothecary at the corner of Monument Yard; he contrives, however, to elude famine; and we see him at length physician in a humble way in Bankside, Southwark, feeling the pulse of a courteous and credulous patient, and, in spite of all entreaties to be relieved of his hat,

hugging itight over his breast to conceal a patch in
the second-hand velvet.

Of all earthly means whereby man can live by the
sweat of his brow, there was none which our friend so
utterly detested, none for which he was so unfitted, as
teaching the young idea how to shoot, — he whose
own ideas had hitherto shot up all ways but the right
one; yet this was precisely the lot which Fate in her
malice had always hitherto insisted to obtrude upon
him. He could never stretch out those loose, unretain-
ing, awkward hands of his for bread, but what some
sinister chance thrust into them the birch and the horn-
book. And suddenly, from the unprofitable employment of feeling the pulses of patients who are more
likely to be feed by him than to fee him, he is wrenched
aside into that of assistant at the academy at Peckham.
"May I die by an anodyne necklace," saith he (speaking out of his own heart though through the lips of
another), "but I had rather be under-turnkey at New-
gate!" With the most morbid desire that man ever
had to be treated with respect, our poor friend sets to
work to command it in a way peculiarly his own. "He
plays all kinds of tricks on the servants and the boys
(of which he had no lack of return in kind), tells
entertaining stories, and amuses everybody with his
flute." That accursed flute!

> "Ille venena colchica
> Et quicquid usquam concipitur nefas
> Tractavit, agro qui statuit suo
> Te, triste lignum!" —

·But here at length that goal, which those wandering, blundering, luckless feet were ordained to reach,

appears, though still dim and distant. Dr. Milner, the
principal of the Academy, is an occasional contributor
to the 'Monthly Review.'   Griffiths, the bookseller,
parent of that periodical, dines with Dr. Milner, and
meets the usher at the board. Talk turns upon the
'Monthly Review,' and its new rival the 'Critical,' set
up by Archibald Hamilton, assisted by Smollett. Pub-
lishers have a peculiar instinct for discovering those
who can help them. With scent more than canine,
under beeches the unlikeliest to the common eye, they
detect the hidden truffle. Something said by this thick-
set, pale-faced usher, arrests the attention of Mr. Griffiths; he asks to be favoured with a few specimens of
criticism. The specimens are sent and approved; the
usher leaves Dr. Milner's, and binds himself to Mr.
Griffiths for one year; to board and lodge with the
bookseller, receive a small salary, and devote himself
to the 'Monthly Review.' Here, then, this desultory,
roving spirit — hitherto one foot on land and one on sea
— settles at last. He has found out, as calling after
calling has slipped from him, his true profession. Never
more will he be indolent now — the gay holiday of life
is over. He is to be an author. And so first emerges
from all the disguises of unsteady, fickle, vagrant youth,
the immortal effigies of OLIVER GOLDSMITH.

Thus far, we have done little more than avail
ourselves of the striking pictures which Goldsmith's
last biographer has placed before us: Pictures necessary
to impress upon our recollection when we come to
examine the peculiar characteristics of a writer whose
popularity equals his renown. For, indeed, under all
these distractions from the regular course of education,
the education which made Oliver Goldsmith what he

was, proceeded steadfast, uniform, and distinct. From the early stories and rhymes of Thomas Byrne, the soldier schoolmaster, to the wanderings, flute in hand, by the murmuring Loire, Goldsmith was emphatically a writer from experience. What he had seen, what he had felt, that he reproduced. Comparatively with his other gifts, his imagination was not vivid nor comprehensive. Not of him could it be said that he "exhausted worlds and then imagined new." It is astonishing that an author who wrote so much, who skimmed over so vast a surface of reading, should have ventured so little, in his creations, beyond the pale of his personal observation. His favourite characters are notoriously variations of the same forms; most of them, indeed, are but likenesses of the author himself in different positions. Now he appears almost at full length in the Philosophic Vagabond (George Primrose) to tell his own adventures, to utter his own sentiments; now, in a character meant, one would think, to be wholly dissimilar to his own — that of Sir William Thornhill — all which is really natural and interesting, is the *silhouette* of Oliver Goldsmith. In the Mr. Burchell, who is presented to us as the strange gentleman, "who had been two days in the inn and could not satisfy the hostess for his reckoning, though no later than yesterday he had given three guineas to the beadle to spare an old broken soldier that was to be whipped through the town for dog-stealing;" "who had carried benevolence to an excess when young; whom the slightest distress, whether real or fictitious, touched to the quick; who grew improvident as he grew poor; who travelled through Europe on foot; who still preserves the character of a humourist, and feels most pleasure in eccentric virtue; who was

fondest of the company of children, and was famous
for singing them ballads and telling them stories;" —
in this Mr. Burchell who does not recognise at once the
author? And, in proportion as in the other attributes
of the character we lose sight of Goldsmith, the character
itself becomes artificial and incongruous. Even in his
plays, we find our author sitting to himself in Marlow,
with a caricature of his own youthful festivities as Tony
Lumpkin at the head of the table in the alehouse.
Honeywood, who calls his extravagance, 'generosity,'
and his trusting everybody, 'universal benevolence,' is
still more transparent. Again, in 'The Citizen of the
World,' the Philosopher of China perpetually reminds
us of the features of Goldsmith; and, as if that were
not enough, he appears *in propriâ personâ* as the Gentleman in Black. By some extraordinary perversion
of judgment, there are persons who still believe that
Lord Byron depicts himself in his heroes. Though we
concede that Lord Byron may, in his earlier poems,
have depicted heroes whom he was willing the world
should think like him, — yet if all we know of that
great poet, out of his works, were cancelled and forgotten, there is not one of his creations by which we
could form the remotest conjecture of what the Poet
really was. But every impression of Goldsmith's mind
is stamped with a likeness of himself. Where he depicts other characters, he is felicitous only when his
experience is at home. His portrait of a profligate
English gentleman in young Thornhill is but a disagreeable and odious caricature; it is the worst specimen of
an Irish squireen dressed up as an English squire. But
his 'Vicar of Wakefield,' and its counterpart the Village
Preacher of Auburn, drawn from his kinsman (with

sundry lively traits of himself in the first), are not
more exquisite than truthful. Characters completed
with a fainter genius, but still admirable, such as Lofty
and Croaker, were precisely those which our poor
poet's life must have thrown constantly across his way;
and even in their mouths he puts sentiments all his
own.

His conception of character was, in short, masterly
beyond praise, wherever it was drawn from actual observation, not from creative invention. And it is precisely this which renders his satire so inimitably truthful in the most consummate, though the briefest, of all
his works of character, the 'Retaliation.' Goldsmith
could never have written a Rape of the Lock; but, in
his later days, he could have illustrated Horace with
modern examples more life-like than Pope's. It is the
same with ideas as characters; — Goldsmith's range
was limited. Every one familiar with his writings
knows how he loves to repeat the same thoughts,
especially the same images, in almost the same expressions. Even in the 'History of Greece' the meta-
phor used in a 'Life of Parnell' is repeated; even a
familiar letter to Mr. Hodgson is embellished with the
polished ornaments of 'The Vicar of Wakefield.' Mr.
Prior is right when he says, "No man seems to have
written more immediately from himself, or to owe less
obligation to classical sources." Indeed there is but
one instance we can remember in Goldsmith of an
imitation from another poet so direct, that, being unacknowledged, it amounts to plagiarism. This instance
occurs in the famous lines which end the description
of the Country Clergyman in the 'Deserted Village;'
and as no one, we believe, has hitherto detected the

source from which the noble simile in those lines is borrowed, we will annex to Goldsmith's imitation the original, which is to be found in a poem by the Abbé de Chaulieu: —

GOLDSMITH.
"As some tall cliff that lifts its awful form,
    Swells from the vale, and midway leaves the storm,
    Though round its breast the rolling clouds are spread,
    Eternal sunshine settles on its head."

CHAULIEU.
"Tel qu'un rocher dont la tête,
    Egalant le Mont Athos,
    Voit à ses pieds la tempête
    Troubler le calme des flots,
    La mer autour bruit et gronde;
    Malgré ses émotions,
Sur son front élevé règne une paix profonde."

Chaulieu was the poet most in fashion when Goldsmith travelled on the Continent, and his verses were quoted in all literary societies. But as he only allowed them to circulate in private during his life-time, they could not have been known in England, and might certainly be copied with little chance of detection. But every one must own that, in copying, Goldsmith wonderfully improved the original; and his application of the image to the Christian preacher gives it a moral sublimity to which it has no pretension in Chaulieu, who applies it to his own philosophical patience under his physical maladies.

Perhaps it might be wished that the sentence we have quoted from Mr. Prior were not so truthfully applicable to Goldsmith, and that he had written less "immediately from himself." A man who writes immediately from himself, that is, from his own personal experience alone; who does not appropriate, remodel, and re-create the results of his reading and reflection; who does not travel out of himself and live in others, must necessarily have a range narrow and circumscribed. That characteristic proves the defect of imagination, using the word in the higher sense in which alone it should be applied to so eminent a writer. Shakspeare does not write from himself when he creates Ariel and Macbeth; nor does he disdain to owe obligations to other writers, when he takes plot and incident from novelist, chronicler, historian, and by his imagination infuses its peculiar life into every character which conduces to the plot, or animates the incident. We may detect this comparative want of imagination in Goldsmith's critical tastes. A man of large imagination is always peculiarly susceptible to beauty whatever form it takes; he cannot cripple his judgment to any particular school, though he may reasonably prefer one to another. Goldsmith cannot appreciate Gray. In spite of Mr. Forster, we must think that Goldsmith's praise of his brother poet was as niggard and cold as it could well be; while his indirect sneers imply unequivocal disdain; and he actually thinks Parnell's 'Night Piece on Death,' which we fear Death has long since kindly accepted, "might be made to surpass all the churchyard scenes that have since appeared." He clubs up Gray with Hurd and Mason, and, if we believe Mr. Cradock (and there is no reason why we should not), he actually proposes to amend the famous 'Elegy' by leaving out an idle word in every line, as thus: —

> "The curfew tolls the knell of day,
> The lowing herd winds o'er the lea,
> The ploughman homeward plods his way;" —

and here, in full career "to leave Gray and the world
to darkness and —" he is fortunately stopped; having
contrived, by amendments that may rank amongst the
most ingenious of his literary efforts, — amendments
confined to the skilful omission of three words, — to
strip the stanza of all the music which redeems its
real blemishes, while of the blemishes themselves he
has evidently no perception!* Goldsmith's systematic
aversion to epithets is indeed a sign of defect in the
imaginative faculty. For the epithet is often (and in
no poet more than Gray) precisely that word in a verse
which addresses itself most to the imagination of the
reader, and tests most severely that of the author. A
good epithet is always an image. Shakspeare has a
line made up of epithets —

> "The gaudy, babbling, and remorseless day."

Goldsmith would have thought he rid it of impertinent
superfluities by reducing the line to —

> "The day!"

The beauties of Sterne, which certainly do not lie
most on the surface, and consist in perpetual, indirect
appeals to the imagination, appear to have been perfectly incomprehensible to Goldsmith. He spoke with

* For those blemishes, which are in truthfulness of picture,
see the subsequent article on Gray, p. 164.

absolute contempt of Milton's prose works; he under-
valued the Elizabethan dramatists; and fell into
the most prosaic and unimaginative of all possible
criticisms upon Shakspeare, whose beauties, he says,
"seem rather the result of chance than design, and
who labours to satisfy his audience with monsters and
mummery."

Having shown what Goldsmith did not admire, it
is just to show what he did. And it will be readily
seen that the poetry which most pleased his taste made
the smallest demand on his imagination. In the brief
criticisms introduced into a compilation from the English
Poets, edited with his name, he says of Tickell's poem
on the *Death of Addison*,' "this elegy is one of the
finest in the language." Of a *Letter from Italy to
Lord Halifax*,' that, "had its harmony been equal to
Pope's versification, it would be incontestably the finest
poem in the language." Of Rowe's song, *Despairing
beside a clear Stream*,' "this is better than anything of
the kind in our language." Of *Cooper's Hill*,' "This
poem, though it may have been exceeded by later
attempts in description, yet deserves the highest applause, as it far surpasses all that went before it."
While of the *Penseroso*' and *L'Allegro*' he cannot say
more than that "it is certain the imagination shown in
them is correct and strong; the introduction to both in
the irregular measure is borrowed from the Italian, and
hurts an English ear:" nor of Thomson's 'Palemon and
Lavinia' than that, "though Mr. Thomson is generally
a verbose and affected poet, he has told his story with
unusual simplicity, but that it (the extract) is rather
given for being much esteemed by the public than by
the editor."

Goldsmith wrote more than two acts of a tragedy, which he appears never to have finished, and, indeed, to have destroyed. We cannot but think the loss fortunate for his fame. We suspect that tragedy would have been precisely the composition in which, next always to criticism, this charming writer would most have failed. Master of a pathos, exquisite of its kind, it is the pathos intimately allied to humour, and touching upon the tears that lie nearest to our smiles. Of that depth of thought, that loftiness of conception, which a tragedy worthy his fame would have required, he could not have been capable. With the passions necessary to the elements of tragedy, love and terror, he nowhere shows himself familiar. The last, indeed, he does not attempt. The former he touches with a delicate but feeble hand, and rather plays over the surface of the passion than throws any light upon its depths. The loves of Squire Thornhill and Olivia, the nearest approach to the graver aspects of the emotion which he has ventured to make, are among the least satisfactory parts of his immortal novel. We suspect the reason to be that Goldsmith was never seriously in love himself.

From the same deficiency of imagination, he cannot paint a bad man with consistency and power. As his good men have always some of his own foibles; so his bad men, with whom he could not identify himself, are little better than sharpers, of whose villany his goodnature seems scarcely conscious.

But it is in the narrowness of his range, and in the close identity of his characters with his own heart and experience, that we are to find the main cause of Goldsmith's universal and unfading popularity. He

had in himself an original to draw from, with precisely
those qualities which win general affection. Loveable
himself, in spite of all his grave faults, he makes loveable the various copies that he takes from the master
portrait. His secret is this — the emotions he commands are pleasurable. He is precisely what Johnson
calls him, "*affectuum lenis dominator*" — *potens* because
lenis. He is never above the height of the humblest
understanding; and, by touching the human heart, he
raises himself to a level with the loftiest. He has to
perfection what the Germans call *Anmuth*. His muse
wears the zone of the Graces.

There is another peculiarity in Goldsmith. Precisely because his ideas are not numerous, he has the
most complete command over them. They have all
the versatility of a practised company. He can make
them do duty alike in a poem, a comedy, a novel, an
essay. Like Bobadil, he selects "but nineteen more to
himself — gentlemen of good spirit, strong and able
constitutions, teaches them the special rules — your
punto, your reverso," and may then boast, with more
truth than Bobadil, that he can make them a match
for "forty thousand strong." Various, in the larger
sense of the word, as we apply it to Goethe or
Shakspeare, he was not; but he was wonderfully ver-
satile. He always addresses the same feelings, presents the same phases of life, the same family of
thought — but then it is in all ways, which are rarely
indeed at the command of the same man. Whether
you read 'The Deserted Village,' 'The Vicar of Wakefield,' 'The Goodnatured Man,' or 'The Citizen of the
World,' you find at the close that much the same
emotions have been awakened — the heart has been

touched much in the same place. But with what pliant
aptitude the form and mode are changed and disguised!
Poem, novel, essay, drama, how exquisite of its kind!
The humour that draws tears, and the pathos that provokes smiles, will be popular to the end of the world.
That these merits imply an extraordinary charm of
style, is self-evident. "The style is the man," says a
French authority; — at all events, the style is the
writer. But where in this irregular course of study —
where in his college associations or his village festivities — did this man, with his rustic manners and Irish
brogue, pick up a style so pure, so delicate? How
comes it that, in all the miry paths of life that he had
trodden, no speck ever sullied the robe of his modest
and graceful muse? How, amidst all that love for inferior company, which never to the last forsook him,
did he keep his genius so free from every touch of
vulgarity? What style in the English language is
more thoroughly elegant and high bred — more impressed with the stamp of gentleman — its ease so
polished, its dignity so sweet? Johnson says that
"Goldsmith was a plant that flowered late." This is
not strictly true. In the earlier letters of Goldsmith,
those, for instance, written from Edinburgh, we see
(as has been before implied) the same peculiar graces
of diction, the same happy humour, with its undercur-
rent of tenderness, which make the works of his ma-
turity so delightful. On examining narrowly the
character of Goldsmith, we find, even in what are commonly regarded as its defects, and served to render
him ridiculous in the circles of London, some clue to
the enigma of the contrast between the habits of the
man and the style of the writer. Goldsmith never,

from the period at which he lounged at the college-
gates as a sizar to the time when his peach-blossom
coat attracted the mirth of Garrick, divested himself of
the notion that he was a gentleman. This conviction
was almost the strongest he possessed; the more it was
invaded, the more he clung to it. He surrounded it
with all the keenest susceptibilities of his sensitive nature. Nothing so galled and offended him as a hint to
the contrary. To be liked as a jester, not companion
— to be despised for his poverty — to be underrated
as a sizar — to be taunted by a schoolboy with a
question of his gentility — were cruelties beyond all
others that fate could inflict. This conviction, and its
concomitant yearning for respect, could not influence
conventional manners, formed under auspices the least
propitious. It could not invest with dignity the stunted
and awkward figure; it could not check the lively impulses of a quick blundering Irish temper; but in that
best and most sacred part of him, his genius, it moulded
his taste to instinctive refinement. Here he was always
true to his ideal. There is something to us inexpres-
sibly touching in the jealous religion with which this
man, exposed to the rough trials and coarse temptations of life, preserved the sanctity of his muse. The
troops of Comus in vain "knit hands and beat the
ground" by the stream in which that pure Sabrina
"commends her fair innocence to the flood:" —

> "Summer drouth or singed air
> Never scorch those tresses fair,
> Nor wet October's torrent flood
> The molten crystal fills with mud."

To judge by Goldsmith's early letters, we are in-

6*

clined to believe that Le Sage was one of his first
models in diction. When we read them, with their
naïve accounts of his own credulity — the amusing
adventures they recite — their mingled simplicity and
shrewdness — we seem to be opening a new chapter
in the youthful history of Gil Blas. Goldsmith, indeed, was in himself a kind of Irish Gil Blas, ter-
minating in a Fabricio instead of a minister's secretary
and retired statesman. But if Le Sage did really influence his earlier mode of description and his easy
views of life, he added in his maturer years the grace
of a sentiment and the softness of a pathos all his own.
He never attained to that wonderful knowledge of the
world, that careless comprehension of external character
in its widest varieties, which render Gil Blas the wisest
novel that man ever wrote; but with much of Le Sage's
polished facility of narrative he combined a command
over emotions which Le Sage never aspired to reach.
He added poetry to the Frenchman's prose, — for
Goldsmith was a poet, Le Sage was not.

While the character of Goldsmith tends to illustrate his genius, so, on the other hand, we may find
in certain idiosyncrasies of the genius the clue to the
most remarkable foibles of the character. We have
seen how much the range of Goldsmith was confined
to his personal feelings and experience, how constantly
he was possessed with the sense of his own individuality. And this consciousness of self, which imparts
so indescribable a truthfulness to the happier creations
of the writer, gives the appearance of a fidgety and
restless vanity to the man. Goldsmith carried that
self-consciousness with him into all societies; and
forgetfulness of self is the only secret of social ease.

Aware of merit, which he uneasily felt he was not able to make manifest when the pen was out of his hand, Goldsmith was always in Goldsmith's way; to borrow his own line, there was —

"Nobody with him at sea but himself."

The popular stories of his envy and jealousy we know now to be exaggerated — some of them wholly untrue; but with that candour which almost invariably belongs to over-sensitive men, with whom self is prominent, every passing shade of such emotions, from which minds the kindest and spirits the noblest may not be always free, he was apt at once to betray. He had not, as Boswell opines, "more envy than other people," but he talked of it more freely. Mr. Forster says truly, in the course of his temperate but subtle vindication of Goldsmith in this respect — a vindication evincing very profound acquaintance with some of the most intricate chords of human nature, — "This free talking did all the mischief. He was simple enough to say aloud what others would more prudently have concealed."

To the same self-consciousness we must ascribe the peculiarities more external. Goldsmith could not think of himself without many causes for distrust. He was aware of his defects of person, of "his ugly face," of his brogue, of his deficiency in the conventional manners of cultivated society. "Too little self-confidence," says Mr. Forster, well and pithily, "begets the forms of vanity." But how could he be possibly blind to his immeasurable superiority in genius, over almost all with whom life could bring him into contact? And

we must remember, that, at all events in the earlier
stages of his career, that genius was not recognised.
He thus entered the social world both proud and bash-
ful. "Society," says Mr. Forster, "exposed him to
continual misconstruction; so that few more touching
things have been recorded of him than those which
have most awakened laughter. 'People are greatly
mistaken in me' (he remarked on one occasion). 'A
notion goes about, that when I am silent I mean to be
impudent; but I assure you, gentlemen, my silence
proceeds from bashfulness.' From the same cause proceeded the unconcealed talk which was less easily forgiven than silence." Grasping at that respect of which
he was so tenacious, he resorts to fine clothes to set off
his homely person — to paradoxes in conversation to
enforce attention; he gives breakfasts and suppers he
can ill afford; he apologises for lodgings beneath his
dignity. He is always keeping the hat off his head,
to hide some patch on his coat. This sensitiveness,
proceeding from intense self-consciousness, is mixed up
with the most amiable attributes of his nature, and has
subjected even his lavish generosity, his cordial charity,
to the imputation of a want of true feeling. There
seems certainly some neglect of his nearest kindred,
not very satisfactorily explained, and not very consistent with his kindly nature. The household relations
with all are, however, so complicated and so little to
be judged fairly by others, that it is both just and prudent to extend to the dead that tacit acquiescence in
their mysterious sanctity which we accord to the living.
It is too much the fashion to parade a man's Lares in
his funeral procession, and to claim them as public
property the moment they have left the hearth. Per-

haps, however, we may get some clue to a secret that has attracted so much loose conjecture, in the letter which Goldsmith himself addresses to his brother Maurice: — "Dear brother," he writes, "I should have answered your letter sooner, but in truth *I am not fond of thinking of the necessities of those I love, when it is so very little in my power to help them.*" Distress was so painful to Goldsmith, that, at whatever cost, he must get it out of his way. He will give it the coat from his back, the blankets from his bed, the last guinea in his pocket. In one of the most pleasing anecdotes recorded of him, Goldsmith himself illustrates this sympathy of the nerves. He throws down his cards when playing at whist, runs out of doors, and says, on his return, "I could not bear to hear that unfortunate woman in the street, half singing, half sobbing; her voice grated painfully on my ear, and jarred my whole frame, so that I could not rest till I had sent her away."* Such was his ready tenderness to distress — the pity that gave ere charity began. But if he could give nothing to the distress — if he could not send it away, — then he must hide from it, — put it out of his thoughts. The suffering that was present was thus always usurping the juster claims of the suffering that was absent. The beggar or impostor was constantly intercepting the resources of the day from

* Nevertheless we suspect the genuineness of this anecdote: it seems to have escaped Goldsmith's biographers that a very similar story is told (containing the main idea "of the voice between singing and crying") of the Black Gentleman, in 'The Citizen of the World,' published many years before the date of the anecdote.

their better channels towards relations, of whose necessities "he is not fond of thinking." He cannot bear
to write to them and give nothing; and to think of
them is a pain to be shunned. But never must we
forget, in justice to Goldsmith, that, with all his consciousness of self, he was the least selfish of men —
that his sensitiveness, if morbid, was at least genuine.
He had not that fineness of nerves which permitted
Rousseau to leave his friend in a fit in the street, nor
that tenderness of disposition which could have dropped
his children into a foundling hospital. Like Rousseau,
he felt self to a disease; but, unlike Rousseau, the
feverish sensitiveness was contagious, and embraced all
that came within his reach. Irritable, sore, justly provoked as he often was, he shrunk from inflicting the
pain he received. No wound to his vanity, no outrage
to his pride, ever made him malignant and revengeful.
He did not smile and hate, he writhed and forgave.

Something of Goldsmith's facility to distress is to
be found in the boyhood of Schiller. Similar anecdotes are told of both — in stripping themselves of
clothing to relieve some more destitute object. Their
fates, at the onset of life, were not very dissimilar;
but Schiller settled into the firm virtues of manhood—
Goldsmith remained to the last with the spontaneous
impulses of the child. Schiller, however, had two
great advantages denied to Goldsmith. First, his genius
was recognised early and liberally. Secondly, he was
fortunate enough to make a happy and congenial marriage. But Goldsmith's youth was without renown,
and his manhood without a home. If any man ever
could have been improved by the domestic influences,
that man would have been Goldsmith. Had it been

his fate to meet with a woman who could have loved him despite his faults, and respected him despite his foibles, we cannot but think that his life would have been much more in harmony with his genius, his desultory affections would have been concentered, his craving self-love appeased, his pursuits been more settled, his character more solid. A nature like Goldsmith's, so affectionate and so confiding — so susceptible to simple innocent enjoyments — so dependent on others for the sunshine of existence, does not fairly flower if deprived of the atmosphere of home.

We have left our author in his twenty-ninth year, a man of letters at last; an author by compulsion, with "the hope of greatness and distinction, — day-star of his wanderings and privations, — more than ever dim, distant, cold." We will leave our readers to trace in Mr. Forster's graphic and instructive pages the process of his apprenticeship; — his task-work at the Review; his quarrels with the proprietor; his translations from the French of the 'Memoirs of a Protestant condemned to the Galleys of France for his Religion;' his despondent retreat to the Peckham academy; his return to the town and the pen; "in a garret writing for bread, expecting to be dunned for a milk-score;" his hopes of a medical appointment to a factory on the coast of Coromandel; their mysterious frustration; his examination at Surgeons' Hall as mate to an hospital, and his rejection as not qualified; his labours in the Critical Review; and his Memoir of Voltaire: we pass over the delicate and subtle transition marked with fine discrimination by Mr. Forster, from "authorship by compulsion" to "authorship by choice;" when the "Bee" begins to gather honey in a spring yet too raw and

premature; when "the Citizen of the World" yet finds
the world reluctant to admit him to the franchise; and
pause to behold 'the Literary Drudge,' "as *we* at the
club" (says Sir John Hawkins in all the pomp of his
"shoes and *stankins*") "considered him," having gained
entry to the learned festivities at the Turk's Head,
formed his first acquaintance with Johnson, and been
presented (if Goldsmith would here allow the epithets
to be more than expletives), to "the gaudy, babbling,
and remorseless" — Boswell. — But the Poet had arrived at the foot of the Hill, "Là ove terminava quello
valle." He might say, with the great pilgrim who had
preceded him through the *selva selvaggia*,

> "Guarda in alto, e vidi le suo spalle
> Vestite già de' raggi del pianeta."

As yet Goldsmith had never prefixed his name to
his publications, and had done comparatively little to
make the world aware of the powers he possessed; but
Johnson's acute eye had detected, in the anonymous
essayist, a master in composition. "Sir," said he to
the wondering Boswell, "Goldsmith is one of the first
men we have now as an author."

The period of obscurity is passed. Through all
the drudgery for bread, works worthy of fame, worthy
to make known to the world the name of its author,
had been silently accomplished. "One day," says
Johnson, "I received a message from poor Goldsmith
that he was in great distress, and, as it was not in his
power to come to me, begging I would come to him
directly." The scene is well known: the arrest by the
landlady; the violent passion of the poet; the bottle of

madeira on the table, which Johnson corks up; the inquiry into the means by which the poet may be ex-
tricated; the production of a novel ready for the press;
Johnson's glance at the MS., his perception of its
merit, and his sale of the copyright for 60*l.* But this
is not all: "on the very day of the arrest," says Mr.
Forster, "'The Traveller' lay completed in the poet's
desk;" and on the 19th of December, 1764, the first
work bearing the name of Oliver Goldsmith, 'The
Traveller,' was published.

From this time the author's fame is established: the
rest of his career is, so far as literary achievement is
concerned, a succession of triumphs. The effect produced by 'The Traveller' was not instantaneous; but
in eight months it reached its fourth edition. His
essays were republished in three volumes and acknowledged. 'The Vicar of Wakefield' followed, and,
though not much helped by friend or critic, reached
its third edition in a few months. Poet, essayist,
novelist, already; he aspires to the fame of the drama.
He had always been a passionate lover of the stage:
in the worst hours of poverty he had contrived to escape
from his own life, to that fair illusion on the boards.
With much difficulty, humiliation, wear and tear of
mind, he at length succeeds in getting 'The Goodnatured Man' upon the stage. On the 29th of January,
1768, that comedy appeared: its success seems to have
been equivocal on the stage, and its run limited to ten
nights, with an eleventh night a month later for the
benefit of Shuter, whose inimitable acting of Croaker
saved the play; but, no doubt, it served to render the
author's name more generally known. Its sale proved
the interest felt in it by the public. Judicious readers

could not but ratify, at least, the praise of Johnson,
that "it was the best comedy since the Provoked Husband." And the profits had a sensible influence on
Goldsmith's mode of life. Passing (and, alas! pass-
ingly) rich, with 300*l.* for the performance, and 100*l.*
for the copyright, he descended from his attic story in
the staircase, Inner Temple, and purchased chambers
in Brick Court: a purchase which consumed the 400*l.*
he had received. Thus the increased means were but
the prelude to difficulties on a larger scale. Money
thus continues to be the necessary object; and for
money he writes his Roman History; but it is to his
honour, that no necessities can compel him to write for
money only. 'The Deserted Village' proceeds with
the Roman History: in 1770 that poem appears: Gray
hears it read aloud to him, and, juster to Goldsmith
than Goldsmith to Gray, exclaims, "That man is a
poet!" In 1773 appears 'She Stoops to Conquer:' it
is received throughout with the greatest acclamations;
its effect was signal, — it completed the revolution
which 'The Goodnatured Man' had too prematurely
commenced: it annihilated, for the time at least, 'the
Sentimental Comedy.'

We are now in the meridian of that fourth sub-
division of his life which Mr. Forster has described:—
Goldsmith is at the height of his renown. Even his
Histories, though really not better than elegant com-
pilations, were regarded with respect by his contemporaries. Johnson sets him above Robertson as an
historian. What wants our Author? that for which he
has pined all his life — the personal consideration he
feels to be his due. All the more eminent of his associates had remembered him but as 'little Goldy,' and

'little Goldy' they persist in considering him still. We acquit Boswell of the more unamiable motives for depreciation, which are uncharitably assigned to him. But Boswell was evidently unable to measure the genius of Goldsmith, or comprehend that in 'The Vicar of Wakefield,' 'The Deserted Village,' and 'She Stoops to Conquer,' posterity would venerate an excellence, equal at least to the merits of 'Rasselas,' 'London,' and 'Irene.' The concurrent mass of testimony is too strong to permit us to doubt that there was something in Goldsmith's manner and conversation, which, if it did not justify contempt, tended inevitably to his disparagement. And what that something was is sufficiently evident in the uneasy consciousness of self to which we have referred. Peculiarities of dress, even if amounting to foppery, are common among eminent men, and are carried off from ridicule by ease in some, or stateliness in others. We may smile at Chatham, scrupulously crowned in his best wig, if intending to speak; at Erskine, drawing on his bright yellow gloves before he rose to plead; at Horace Walpole, in a cravat of Gibbon's carvings; at Raleigh, loading his shoes with jewels so heavy that he could scarcely walk; at Petrarch, pinching his feet till he crippled them; at the rings which covered the philosophical fingers of Aristotle; at the bare throat of Lord Byron; the Armenian dress of Rousseau; the scarlet and gold coat of Voltaire; or the prudent carefulness with which Cæsar scratched his head, so as not to disturb the locks arranged over the bald place. But most of these men, we apprehend, found it easy to enforce respect and curb impertinence. Many great men are silent, or, what is worse, dull in conversation, and are yet not

despised for it. The talk of Addison and Gibbon was
very inferior to their books. The talent of conversation is one not to be lightly rated; carried to a high
degree, it implies and necessitates the possession of
many rare faculties. But while the gift proves a clever
man, the want of it is no proof of a dull one. "Conversation," says Mr. Forster, truly, "is a game where
the wise do not always win." That Goldsmith often
talked foolishly, there is sufficient authority to induce
us to believe. Indeed, when we consider that two-
thirds of the conversation among literary men are composed of criticism, and that Goldsmith was, perhaps,
the very worst critic that any man of ability ever was,
he would only have had to talk much the same as he
wrote in his remarks upon the poems admitted into
"the Beauties of English Poetry," to have seemed
either an envious man or a shallow one. Yet, after
all, we have few records left to us of the foolish sayings: on the contrary, most of the sayings which come
down to us as specimens of his table talk, when upon
persons or things, not books, are among the best in a
circle which comprised the best talkers of the age.
And we incline to think that his vindicators are not
far wrong in supposing that much of what passed for
silly, was drollery in disguise. It was not, we apprehend, so much the words as the manner that provoked ridicule. With his acute self-consciousness,
Goldsmith was never at his ease in the society of
learned wits and sarcastic men of the world. Too well
aware of his inclination to levity, he is thus often
"solemn," as Warton found him. He plays a part in
those ungenial circles, and plays it ill. There is a
grotesque incongruity about him, which strikes us even

at this distance, and through the medium of the tender
reverence he commands. The peach-blossom coat
Topham Beauclerk could have borne away on his well-
bred shoulders as an elegant audacity; but it is out of
all keeping on the form which Goldsmith himself in-
dignantly suspects has been taken for a tailor's. Mr.
Forster says, "that insensibility was what he wanted
most, and it is amazing to think how small an amount
of it would have exalted Dr. Goldsmith's position in
the literary circles of his day." This is true; but it is
just that we should here discriminate: there are various
kinds of sensitiveness. Keen susceptibility to sneers
upon honour or assaults on character, is no weakness
— it is the noble jealousy of a noble heart; sensitiveness to the perfidy of false friends, affection trifled with,
and trust betrayed, is not morbidity — it is the healthful action of a generous nature. But it was not on
these matters that Goldsmith's susceptibility was over
acute. He could boast that there was not a country
in Europe in which he was not a debtor; and he could
turn into philosophical merriment the tricks that had
imposed on his credulity. Goldsmith's sensitiveness
was as to his person, his dress, his manners, his *gentility* — the attention he sought to exact, the effect
that he laboured to create; and sensitiveness of this
kind can only be characterised as the epidermis of self-
love in a state of chronic inflammation.

To have seen and heard Goldsmith to advantage
one should have followed him from the Turk's Head
— escaped with him from the polished sneer of Beauclerk — the arch malice of Garrick — the imperious
domination of Johnson — the affluent resources of

Burke — the conceited condescension of Boswell —
one should not have sat next him at a table where he
is stopped, when talking his best, by a "Hush! the
Doctor (Johnson) is going to say something;" or where,
politely thanking a pedantic schoolmaster for an invitation he supposes meant for himself, he, the unsur-
passed writer of a great age, is crushed with a "No
— no! 'tis not you I mean, Doctor Minor — 'tis Doctor
Major there." One should have seen him presiding
over the banquet where he himself was Mæcenas —
his gay spirit released from restraint, and the "two
great wrinkles between the brows" smoothed at sight
of the happy faces he loved to contemplate; — singing
songs, cracking jokes: — or, better still, one should,
like the young adventurer whom he found reading
Boileau in the Temple Gardens, have crept into his
confidence by its open gate of benevolence. Had the
biographer before us lived in that day, we are sure we
should have received very different impressions of
Goldsmith's conversational eloquence. We can well
conceive how an admirer so delicate and earnest would
have soothed to sleep the self-distrust, broken the solemn
spell of artificial restraint, by the homage of due respect,
— have led the frank poet, too happy to "tell of all
he felt and all he knew," to converse of his own early
wanderings and light-hearted trials, when the pony
walked away with him into the Highlands; — when the
Carinthian shut the door in his face; — when he lived
with the beggars in Axe Lane, or pounded in the
apothecary's mortar. Here, we believe, his talk would
have been worthy of his books; full of that experience
in which lay his wisdom, — of gentle pathos, and

bewitching humour. "Vates caret vate;" the poet wanted the poet's heart to understand, the poet's tongue to speak of him.

But we left Goldsmith at the height of his renown. His likeness is in the print-shops — his name in the journals — complimentary poems rain upon him — imitations abound — and the higher the front he raises, the more conspicuous the butt he presents to his relentless friends. In the confession of Johnson, "the partiality of his friends was always against him; it was with difficulty we could give him a hearing." His necessities increase with his fame and his new dignity, for "dignity," says a certain sage, "requires a great deal to keep up!" He pauses from works that yield the fame, to drudge on works that will keep up the dignity. He toils at a Grecian History, knowing, we suspect, as little Greek as a man who has been last at a college examination can well know. He pursues undaunted his way through 'Animated Nature,' with the doubt of Dr. Johnson "whether he could distinguish a cow from a horse" — but with a certainty more strong than the doubt that "he would make a very fine book of it." He forms a plan for a Dictionary of Arts and Sciences, to which he brings but the art of composition, and the science taught in Laputa of extracting sunbeams from cucumbers. But the thick robust form begins to give way, the careless spirits to flag. Cradock, one of the kindest, perhaps because one of the most recent, of his friends, and not knowing him till after little Goldy had become great Goldsmith, finds him much altered; his usual cheerfulness "all forced." He suggests a subscription edition of the 'Traveller' and 'Deserted Village.' But Goldsmith's difficulties were probably

too great to be met by such relief. "He rather submitted than encouraged, and the scheme fell to the
ground." Amidst these cares he appears at the St.
James's Coffeehouse, and, for his comfort, hears read
a series of satirical epitaphs upon him; of which Garrick's, the only one preserved, is perhaps a mild specimen: —

> "Here lies poet Goldsmith, for shortness called Noll,
> Who wrote like an angel, but talked like poor Poll."

This is the latest tribute offered to the man whose life
had been one struggle for social estimation! And the
latest effort of the sensitive genius is a characteristic
(it is his single) revenge; — the unfinished poem of
'Retaliation.' No trace of malignity embitters this satire;
perhaps, so far as it goes, the most perfect in the
English language. Kindly and grateful to those who
had been kind to him; blending the happiest praise
with the justest blame to those who had so mercilessly
galled his vain, proud, large, loving heart. The hand
rests in the midst of that exquisite tribute to the one
friend who saw, even in the talk like poor Poll, but
"excess of conviviality," — which gives the surest immortality to Reynolds himself. An old local disorder
returns to him, "brought on by neglect," and "continued vexation of mind arising from involved circumstances." He arrives in London the middle of March,
struggling with symptoms of low nervous fever. He
obstinately persists, against the advice of his medical
attendants, to dose himself with James's powders; the
disease takes root, becomes alarming; sleep deserts him.
Yet at times, even in dying, that light uncomprehended

spirit can become cheerful; but the cheerfulness, we fear, was on the surface, as it had been when feeling "horrid tortures" at the supposed failure of his first play, and when, while none "could imagine to themselves the anguish of his heart," he sang his favourite song. IIis physician says, "Your pulse is in greater disorder than it should be from the degree of fever you have,—is your mind at ease?" "It is not," answered Goldsmith; and "these" says Mr. Forster, "are the last words we hear him utter in this world." On the 4th of April, 1774, and at the early age of forty-five Oliver Goldsmith died.

We shall not pursue the more obvious moral to be drawn from the life thus closed. The world satisfies itself too easily when it dismisses the memoir of one of its benefactors with some trite maxim drawn from the errors of genius. In spite of all Goldsmith's faults, we will not dispute Mr. Forster's assertion,

"that he worthily did the work that was in him to do; proved himself in his garret a gentleman of nature, and left the world no ungenerous bequest. . . . Nor have posterity been backward to acknowledge the debt which his contemporaries left them to discharge; and it is with calm, unruffled, joyful aspect on the one hand, and with grateful, loving, eager admiration on the other, that the creditor and his debtor at length stand face to face."

To what follows we invite a closer attention.

"All this is to the world's honour as well as gain; which has yet to consider, notwithstanding, with a view to its own larger profit in both, if its debt to the man of genius might not earlier be discharged, and if the thorns that only become

invisible beneath the laurel that overgrows his grave, should
not rather, while he lives, be plucked away. It is not an act
of parliament which can determine this . . . it must flow
from a higher sense than has at any period prevailed in England of the duties and responsibilities assumed by the public
writer, and of the social consideration and respect that their
effectual discharge should have undisputed right to claim.
The world will be greatly the gainer when such time shall
arrive; and when the biography of the man of genius shall
no longer be a picture of the most harsh struggles and mean
necessities to which man's life is subject, exhibited as in
shameful contrast to the calm and classic glory of his fame."

These eloquent reflections are pertinent to the subject. Goldsmith, indeed, was one whom, perhaps, no
social consideration which the world can pay would
have lifted into the personal respect of his associates,
or out of the "mean necessities" which, in his later
life at least, his own improvidence in some degree
wantonly created. But the observations apply to a
large class, the majority of whom have his just pride
without its concomitant foibles, and are exposed to the
same harsh struggles, without the same aggravations
in their own errors. The evil complained of is patent,
and but seldom denied. The remedy, however, is
difficult, and admits of too much dispute to allow us,
now and here, to discuss it. We content ourselves
with a few passing observations.

That the present pension-list, intended as a relief
to all the science and literature of the British empire,
is miserably inadequate, is incontestable. It is somewhere about half the sum which a country squire, with
economy, devotes to the maintenance of a pack of
fox-hounds. It may be a question whether there

should be any pension-list whatever for men of literature and science; there can be none, that, if it is to
exist, it should be worthy of the nation that bestows
the bounty. It is dangerous to provoke comparison
between the salary of the Master of the Buckhounds
and the sum apportioned to the aggregate intellect
which the Monarchy of Great Britain (in the act itself
of the donation) professes to foster or reward. But the
principle of a pension-list is not one that dignifies the
community of letters, nor does it meet the questions
at issue. Even in a pecuniary point of view, a sum
might often be necessary for a limited period in the
production of a particular work, which it would not
be necessary to continue for life, and which need not
be applied to the mere relief of positive distress, or
the support of infirmity and age. Schiller was in the
prime of his life, and quite capable of being a bookseller's drudge, perhaps of writing Grecian histories,
and works on Animated Nature, when two noblemen,
thinking that his genius was meant for other things,
subscribed to endow him with a pension for three years,
to enable him to do that which he was calculated best
to do. It came to Schiller at the right time of his
existence. It served, we believe, not only to aid his
genius, but to soften his heart. Some help of a similar nature, a national fund, in connection with the
pension-list, might not unprofitably bestow.

Perhaps, in any comprehensive system of national
education which the conflicting opinions and prejudices of party may permit the legislature ultimately
to accomplish, means may be taken to render the
Mechanics' Institutes (many of which are fast decaying, and cannot, we believe, long exist upon resources

wholly voluntary) permanent and valuable auxiliaries
to popular instruction; and endowed lectureships or
professorships, at the more important of these in our
larger towns, might be devoted to men distinguished
in letters and science, connect them more with the
practical world, occupy but little of their time, and
yield them emoluments, if modest, still sufficient to
relieve them from actual dependence on the ordinary
public and trading booksellers.   •

Perhaps, too, in the point of social consideration,
it may be well to reflect whether it is wise or just
that England should be the only country in which
men of letters are deprived of the ordinary social
honours, which tend to raise literature to its proper
place in the estimation of the crowd. Hereditary
distinctions (a peerage or a baronetcy) require the
possession of a wealth that it would be absurd to
expect in the class of which we treat. Even where
the government might overlook such requirement,
the author, if prudent, could not suffer himself to do
so; and Dr. Southey wisely refused the baronetcy
offered to him. But there are honours in this country,
as in others, which are not hereditary, and are supposed to be assigned to merit. It may be well to talk
of orders and badges as unphilosophical; but if they
are objects of emulation, proofs of desert, or symbols
of social dignity in the eyes of others, we do not see
why literature and science should be excluded from
their attainment. They may not elevate the possessor
in the eyes of the few; but that is not the question.
They may elevate the cultivation of literature in the
eyes of the many, and insensibly train the opinions of
"the world" to regard with honour those to whom the

state accords the outward distinction it bestows on di-
plomatists and soldiers. An order created solely for
men of science and letters, as has been more than once
suggested, would wholly fail in its object. There is no
reason why they should be separated from others who
deserve well of their country. On the contrary, it is
to amalgamate them with their fellow-citizens in
honours as in labours that we desire; and to suffer
them to rank (where their reputation so entitles them)
with whomsoever be the other claimants to social consideration. There is not a city knight who would not
jeer at an order consisting only of authors, to whose
united rentroll he would prefer even half a dozen rail-
way debentures. If any practical honours ever be
accorded to authors, philosophers, or artists, agreeably
to the usual principles of an aristocratic monarchy, we
fear, strange though it may appear to sages, that they
must be honours shared with dukes and earls, ambas-
sadors and generals.

That some abuse, favour, and partiality would
attend such distinctions, we readily concede. These
attend all honours. But public opinion would operate
perhaps more strongly on the class we refer to than
on any other in resenting unworthy selection or
illiberal exclusion. Briefly, — in a country in which
both the constitution and the popular modes of thinking are essentially aristocratic, should those of our
countrymen whom foreign nations the most esteem,
to whom we ourselves are under obligations of the
highest kind, and in whom posterity will regard the
loftiest representatives of the age that they adorn, be
the only men in pursuit of distinction to whom the
honours of aristocracy are denied? — the only men

living under a monarchy to whom the austere philosophy of a republic is to be applied; a republic, indeed,
in which they are admitted to the equality of the old
villeins; all equal in being equally shut out from the
lists of knighthood; and enrolled in the fraternity of
Esau's, who have lost their birthright, but without receiving the pottage.

We must now turn more directly to the very remarkable and delightful biography which has induced
this recurrence to an author whose life always interests, and whose books always charm. We know
of no man more fit for the task he has undertaken
than Mr. Forster. He brings to it a mind habitually
critical, subtle, and inquiring; that strong sympathy
with men of letters which the life of Goldsmith especially demands; a large practical knowledge of the
infirmities and misfortunes, as well as the virtues and
solaces of the class, with which kindred pursuits must
have made him familiar; an extensive store of general
information; a style, not always equal it is true, but
never bald nor insipid; often weighty with earnest
thought, often coloured with eloquence, animated or
touching.

Mr. Forster's "Lives of the Statesmen of the
Commonwealth," — a work of high merit, and especially so for the qualities such an undertaking most
needs, — have habituated him to the difficulties of
one of the most difficult departments in literary art;
viz., the biography of men with whom the author was
unacquainted, and the main facts of whose lives are
already generally known. It is no ordinary talent
that can make a biography of this kind both interesting and important; give not only a seeming but a

genuine originality to materials with which we had thought ourselves familiar; and supply a gap in previous researches of which we were scarcely aware, till the ingenuity which detected the gap had durably repaired it. Mr. Forster has treated the subject before us with a judgment correspondent to the ability. That he is more lenient to his hero than we always are, is natural. The duties of a reviewer are sterner than those of a biographer. But Mr. Forster does not vindicate Goldsmith from all his errors with the violent effort of Mr. Prior; and, by candid if guarded admissions, turns aside that reaction from wilful indulgence to rigid justice which Mr. Prior could not fail to create. He concedes all that we demand, though we may have enforced the concessions somewhat more stringently than he intended, when he says, "It is not an example I would wish to inculcate. It would be dangerous to try any such process for the chance of another Goldsmith." What follows is truly said, — and in the patient care with which Mr. Forster follows out his proposition, consist much of the originality and value of his work: — "The truth is important to be kept in mind, that genius is in no respect allied to these weaknesses, but, when unhappily connected with them, is in itself a means to avert their most evil consequences."

It was impossible to write a thick volume on Goldsmith, and not use the facts which others had used before. Facts are open to all men. They are the brick earth upon the common land, from which, by right immemorial, each man may build his castle or his cottage. It is not because one man has used bricks before us, that we are to confine ourselves to mortar

and rubble. Mr. Prior has published a letter in which
he seems to claim an exclusive property in Goldsmith,
and to regard Mr. Forster's biography as a trespass
upon his rights. Mr. Forster's reply is complete as to
the details upon which Mr. Prior justifies so extraordinary a claim. Upon the principle of the claim itself, it would be idle to waste many words in controversy. The matter lies in a nutshell. Mr. Prior
mistakes the whole question at issue, when he com-
pares a wholesale plagiarism from works of imagination, to the adaptation of facts in a work of biography.
In the former, the author creates materials that did not
exist before; — he not only discovers the ground, he
makes it. In the latter, he does but apply to his individual use, that which not only before existed, but
which the public have a paramount interest in regarding as public property. If anything belongs to a nation, it is the lives of its great men; if anything 'lies
out of the pale of a patent, it is historical truth. Fact
is always improveable — Fiction not so. Facts belong to science, — Fiction to art. Every year some
cultivator of science borrows the facts of another. Are
we to have no Histories of England because Hume
wrote a History of England? or is any new writer of
that History to avoid the facts which Hume disburied
from the chronicles? Goldsmith himself, in his History
of England, takes pretty largely from Hume; but
Hume's warmest admirers cannot assert that Hume's
rights are invaded. All they can say is, that Goldsmith does not supersede Hume. The only immunity
a writer who deals with facts can find against rivals
and successors is to do his work so well that the public
will either think all further labour on the same subject

uncalled for, or prefer the old work, whatever its defects, to the new. Even in Fiction itself, we fear that an author cannot guard himself from a pretty extensive invasion of what may be regarded as the facts of fiction, viz., the characters the author invents, or the new ideas he calls to life. Let a Corsair or a Childe Harold be famous, and before the year is out we have Corsairs and Childe Harolds enough to people a colony. They die off;—and the old Corsair and Childe Harold live on — because the original poems are both the first and the best of their kind. If they were not the best, it would not be sufficient to be the first. Many of Shakspeare's subjects were taken before him. But the world leaves it to antiquary and critic to hunt out the crude original. That is the true original — the permanent and standard development of any given idea — which improves the most what went before, and cannot be improved by what comes after. It is not in the disinterment of facts, but in the manner in which they take life and colour, that originality consists. Stones are on all the high roads, every man may throw them into the midst of a crowd, but every man is not a Cadmus who by throwing a stone gets rid of the pre-existences useless to his purpose, and retains only those that aid him in building up his city. Had Mr. Forster borrowed infinitely more largely from Mr. Prior's facts than he has done, the mode in which he has selected, arranged, and applied them, would not leave his biography less peculiarly his own. Indeed, we do not know any work of the kind more distinctly original. And, since Mr. Prior provokes the observation, we remember few instances in the lists of literary chivalry, in which the shield of a rival has been

touched with more courteous forbearance: — Not till
Mr. Forster's self-defence was extorted, had the public
been called upon to notice what errors had been corrected, — to what anecdotes, marred in the telling, the
point had been restored. While obligations were acknowledged with frank respect, blunders were removed
with generous silence.

The subdivisions of Mr. Forster's work are philosophical and effective. In the first, he presents to us
the childhood, the youth, the desultory adventures,
which prepare us for the second — Authorship by compulsion; he leads us on, through the Authorship by
choice, to the time when labour and inclination, both
combined, place his hero where we now behold him,
amongst the constellation of imperishable names —
"the novelist, the dramatist, the poet."

Without that eternal attempt at stage grouping and
stage effect, by which some of the French writers have
distorted the even course of history, our pleasant biographer has quietly contrived to render picturesque
and touching all the more interesting positions of the
poet. Nothing can be more artful than the pause from
ungenial and dreary studies, which invites us to contemplate the poor sizar listening to his own ballads; —
or, before we see in full length the snubbed and de-
rided butt of the London coteries, bids us halt to greet
Nature smiling on her darling in the garret of "Garden
Court;" — nothing more impressive for Goldsmith's
vindication, than the steady enforcement of those scenes
in which, what elsewhere might be warning, assumes
the nobler lesson of example — scenes in which distress
is met with sunny spirit, poverty endured with manly
courage, and labours that startle us to contemplate,

cheerfully undertaken by one constitutionally indolent, in the double aim, both noble, of independence and renown.

In the multiform groups, which, at different stages of Goldsmith's life, Mr. Forster presents to our view, we have some reproach to make perhaps, especially in the later portions of the work, that he deals too summarily with certain of the great shapes he invokes, and occasionally treats, with an air too "eager and nipping," some of the political and incidental events which he rather decides than discusses. But a portrait-painter assumes a kind of prescriptive right to use the background as may best set off the figure; and we readily confess the skill with which Mr. Forster has placed his hero in the midst of every circle, in that position he really occupied, while suggesting temperately that which was more his due. One main difference between Mr. Prior and Mr. Forster, in fine, is this, — the first gives us the facts, the last the man; the one has compiled a *mémoire pour servir*, the other has composed a discriminating and intellectual biography.

In the criticisms which Mr. Forster introduces, he betrays the subtlety of an accomplished intellect, and the sympathy of a kindred taste. And it is not a little to his praise that he has contrived to say much that is new upon 'The Vicar of Wakefield,' and to point out the graver benefits to society, the moral effect on later authors, which that delight of all ages has indirectly bequeathed. When, after quoting Dr. Primrose's unpretending boast, "that in less than a fortnight he had formed them (the felons of the gaol) into something social and humane," Mr. Forster adds, "In how many hearts may this have planted a desire which as yet had become no man's care?" we instinctively turned to the distinguished writer* to whom Mr. Forster has appropriately dedicated his book, and asked ourselves what Oliver Twist may have owed to Oliver Goldsmith.

Here, then, for all else, whether in praise or in qualification, we dismiss Mr. Forster's book to the judgment of the public — a fitting, and, we think, a permanent companion to the works of the author whose career it commemorates: — a gentle but a manly apology for the life which it tracks through each pathetic transition of light and shadow: written in that spirit of which Goldsmith himself would have approved — pleasing while it instructs us, mild without tameness, earnest without acerbity.

* Charles Dickens.

C H A R L E S   L A M B

AND SOME OF IIIS COMPANIONS.

[First published in 'The Quarterly Review,' January, 1867.]

CHARLES LAMB

AND SOME OF HIS COMPANIONS.

———

[1. *Final Memorials of Charles Lamb, consisting of unpublished Letters, with Sketches of his Companions.* By SERJEANT TAL-FOURD. London, 1848.
2. *Charles Lamb; a Memoir.* By BARRY CORNWALL. London, 1866.]

AMONG the modes of expression by which philosophers have sought to classify the divisions of our species, the nickname is obviously the most convenient. It condenses the tediousness of description into the tersest compactness of epigram; and finds ready acceptance with the facile ill-nature which the learned Huet assures us is the prevalent characteristic of an intelligent public. According to that venerable authority, there is nothing which men in polite society enjoy more than unflattering representations of their fellow-creatures. This, he asserts, is the main reason why Tacitus is so popular with scholars — displeasing likenesses of humanity being especially pleasant to the cultivators of humane letters.

To a certain set of writers who flourished at the earlier part of this brilliant century, and who were supposed to live in close intercourse with each other,

and to have many attributes of mannerism in common,
one of the wits of Edinburgh applied the unalluring
denomination of the Cockney School. It was a name
sufficiently significant of ridicule to frighten away bash-
ful admirers, and had just so much of that kind of one-
sided justice which belongs to satire, as not to seem to
the ordinary public an unfair definition.

We know not how it is that among civilized nations
England stands alone in imputing to that development
of the national intellect more peculiarly metropolitan,
the defective liberality, whether in the culture of letters
or in the survey of men and manners, which in other
countries is rather ascribed to the denizens of provinces.
Cicero finds a want of "urbanitas" in those writers
who lived remote from the Roman capital, and narrowed
their views of the world to the limited range of a
coterie.   It is praise to a French author to say that on
life and manners he writes like a thoroughbred Parisian;
it is the reverse of praise to an English author on such
subjects to say that he writes like a thoroughbred Londoner.   To him we impute exactly the same spirit of
clique — the same partial estimate of himself and the
privileged few with whom he lives in sympathy of taste
and reciprocity of compliment, which are the alleged
characteristics of a provincial genius.   The Cockney is
the archetype of the Londoner east of Temple Bar, and
is as grotesquely identified with the bells of Bow as
Quasimodo with those of Notre Dame.   In the men on
whom this metropolitan distinction was conferred, including writers not less remarkable than Hazlitt, Leigh
Hunt, and Charles Lamb, we cannot honestly affirm ·
that there was no element of cockneyfication.   Though
differing much from each other in character and in

direction of intellect, they agreed in this — they all
so far rejected the urbanizing tendencies of a great
metropolis, that they moved in as small a circle as if
they had lived in a country town. In their publications
they quote and praise, quarrel and make it up with
each other, as if, like the Chinese, they confined the
map of the civilized world to their celestial empire, and
inscribed on the space left outside of the circle, "Corners of earth inhabited by barbarians." The Waverley
Novels can excite no interest in Lamb: it is a matter
of doubt whether he was ever seduced into reading
them. Hazlitt, indeed, succumbs to their enchantment,
but atones for such praise as he bestows on the fictions
by declaring that "he despises their author as the
meanest of mankind." Lamb has a lofty disdain for
so comparative a pigmy as Byron. Hazlitt does not
openly share in that disdain, but he implies it by the
sneer with which he accompanies the stinted measure
of his praise. According to him, Byron "seldom gets
beyond force of style," and "his poetry consists mostly
of a tissue of superb commonplaces." With the contemporaneous literature of the Continent the professors
of this school reject all acquaintance; among the rising
generation of writers in England it is only their own
Alumni whom they deem worthy of notice. Those,
they regard with indiscriminate favour — equally kind
to a Sheridan Knowles and a Janus Weathercock.
Hunt, the least exclusive of the coterie, in vain commends Shelley and Keats to the cordial welcome of his
associates. Hazlitt speaks of Keats, indeed, when
Keats was dead, with a certain civility, such as a
strong man compassionately bestows on a promising
though sickly child. But of Shelley, in Shelley's life-

5*

time, his criticism is that of stern contempt. According to him, Shelley "is not a poet, but a sophist, a theorist, a controversial writer in verse; he gives us for representations of things rhapsodies of words; he paints gaudy, flimsy, allegorical pictures on gauze, on the cobwebs of his own brain" (Hazlitt's 'Plain Speaker: On People of Sense') — an estimate of Shelley, from which Lamb does not greatly differ. In fact, when the chiefs of this oligarchy commend to our reverence the men of their own day, they compliment each other — Hunt praises Hazlitt, Hazlitt praises Hunt; Lamb praises both, and by both is praised. We must make one honourable exception to this exclusive co-admiration. The Cockney School acknowledged the genius of the Lake School, and paved the way to that appreciation of Wordsworth and Coleridge which the pertinacity of critics has at last wrung from the passive assent of the general public. But this so-called Cockney School was, in much, an offshoot from the Lake School. Wordsworth and Coleridge exercised a predominant power over the minds of Hunt, Hazlitt, and Lamb, and served greatly to determine the point of view from which the two latter regarded the form and substance of contemporaneous poetic creation. And perhaps they found in the homage they rendered to the great Poets of the Lake School an excuse for the depreciation of other contemporaries more popularly admired. It is but just to the Public of that day to preface remarks intended to do equal justice to the merits of the writers referred to, with this admission of their characteristic failings; because it was but natural that the Public should hesitate before confirming the reputation which the members of a coterie so dogmatically bestowed upon each other.

The Public has always a certain interest in guarding its judgments from the dictations of a critical clique.

Of the three eminent writers to whom this unlucky appellation of Cockney was popularly assigned, Hazlitt deserved it least in the literal sense of the word, and most in the symbolical. In the literal sense of the word he did not indeed deserve it at all. Hazlitt was no Londoner. By origin he was Irish; he himself a native of Shropshire. But in the symbolical sense of the word, he was the most obnoxious to the ridicule it conveyed, partly because, once identified with the set of writers to whom it was applied, he stood forth the most aggressive and the most provocative, and carrying out into the fullest display the sins attributed to the Cockney School. He of the three best answers to his own sprightly and accurate definition of Cockney: "Your true Cockney," saith Hazlitt, "is your only true leveller. Let him be as low as he will, he fancies he is as good as anybody else." The faults of Hazlitt were the more disagreeable because the man was one of those warm-blooded creatures whom we wish to like if they will but let us. And though he does his best to prevent our liking him, it is not in his power to prevent any one who knows the English language from admiring. The admiration is uneasy, chequered, qualified, but it is admiration still. If Hazlitt lacked the poetic genius of his two gentler friends, he was gifted with an eloquence more masculine. The fibre of his brain was less fine than theirs, but it was of stronger tissue. He had in early youth cultivated his reasoning faculty with a patient study unknown to those playmates of the muse, and that faculty was sufficiently acute to have achieved no mean repute in metaphysical speculation,

or in the more practical domain of judicial criticism,
had it not been constantly obscured and perverted by
passions fiercely combative, which, accompanied with
an arrogant self-esteem, and a very limited knowledge
of the world, too often deprived his judgment of value,
because they robbed it of charity and candour.   And
it was exactly where his knowledge of the world was
the most deficient that his passions and his arrogance
led him to parade his defect with the loftiest ostentation.
He delighted in analytical comments on the public
characters of his time; and it is difficult to conceive
any man, of letters with so profound an ignorance, not
only of the characters thus superciliously depicted, but
of the estimates formed of them by persons the most
competent to know. What can be more ludicrously unlike the speaking of the late Marquis Wellesley (in his
most brilliant day; the date of the criticism is April 13,
1813, and on his special subject, Indian affairs) than
the following attempt at description which heads the
collection of Hazlitt's 'Political Essays'? "We confess
those of his (Lord Wellesley's) speeches which we have
heard appear to us prodigies of physical prowess and
intellectual imbecility; the ardour of his natural temperament stimulating and controlling the ordinary faculties of his mind; the exuberance of his animal spirits
contending with the barrenness of his genius, produce
a degree of dull vivacity, of paraded insignificance and
impotent energy, which is without any parallel but itself."   Who does not here see a man in love with his
own style, and exulting in smart impertinences about
an orator of whose attributes of mind and speaking he
was ignorant as a babe unborn?
    This is but one instance out of the many we

might quote, not of caricature (for in caricature there is something of truth), but of utter dissimilarity between the original man and the fanciful image which the student of Titian would have us accept as a portrait. And we select this special instance, because elsewhere we might suppose the common sense of the artist distorted by private vindictiveness or political hate. But Mr. Hazlitt could never have had his feelings hurt by Lord Wellesley, nor could there have been anything calculated to stir up his gall in a speech upon our Indian Empire. Hazlitt never pretended to be a cosmopolitan reformer. No man ever ridiculed with a keener irony the affectation of universal benevolence. He cared about the Indian Empire as little as he did about Lord Wellesley. He would have resolved both into limbo for the head of any wrinkled old hag on the canvas of Rembrandt. Hurried away by a temperament thus vehemently aggressive, there was scarcely a section of opinion or a class of fellow-subjects that William Hazlitt did not, at one time or other, go out of his way to offend. A bitter politician, though without giving us the slightest idea what he would destroy, except the principle of hereditary monarchy, or what he would reconstruct, except universal suffrage; equally a fanatic against constitutional kings and for Napoleonic autocracy, he smote with the same unexpected swing of his flail Tory, Whig, Radical, Reformer, Utopianist, Benthamite, Churchman, Dissenter, Free-thinker. He believed in nothing but Hazlittism *plus* Napoleonism. There was but one Hazlitt, and Napoleon was his prophet. That which he recognised in himself was unscrupulous force. Unscrupulous force had been crowned in Napoleon. Such amiable disciples as the late Ser-

jeant Talfourd tell us that Hazlitt viewed in Napoleon
the principle of force opposed to the legitimate Right
Divine. Napoleon commenced his career not by de-
throning the legitimate Right Divine, but by cannonad-
ing King Mob. And a man must know very little of
Hazlitt's works who is not aware that, though he
speaks of legitimate kings with the hate of a French
sans-culotte, he speaks of the common people with the
scorn of a Venetian oligarch. In fact, Hazlitt's judgment is so constantly coloured by his spleen, that he
is scarcely more consistent in his likings than in his
dislikings. Even in literature, the few contemporaries
for whom at one moment he professes the deepest
reverence, to whose publications he ascribes, not un-
truly, the deepest obligations in the forming or de-
veloping of his own intellectual powers, are addressed
with the same disdainful insolence with which, perched
on the wall of his small enclosure, he crows scornful
defiance to such foes afar off as the Wellesleys and
Cannings, — if these guides, philosophers, fathers,
friends, do but exercise their liberty of thought in a
way disapproved by William Hazlitt. He tells us
himself of the marked kindness with which, in his
earliest youth, he had been distinguished by Coleridge,
and of the lasting effect on his own mind produced
by his first contact with that vast and luminous intelligence: —

"I was at that time" (he says in his own picturesque and
vivid diction) "dumb, inarticulate, helpless, like a worm by
the way-side, crushed, bleeding, lifeless. But now, bursting
from the deadly bands

       'that bound them
     With Styx nine times round them,'

my ideas float on winged words, and as they expand their plumes catch the golden light of other years. My soul, indeed, has remained in its original bondage, dark, obscure, with longings infinite and unsatisfied; my heart, shut up in the prison-house of this rude clay, has never found nor will it find a heart to speak to; but that my understanding also did not remain dull and brutish, or at length found a language to express itself, I owe to Coleridge." *

One might suppose that such reminiscence would have sufficed to induce a man of feelings so warm to soften any blow which he might afterwards feel it a painful duty to inflict upon the greatest of his intellectual benefactors. To suppose this would be to misjudge William Hazlitt. The Lay Sermon of Mr. Coleridge displeases him, and he exhausts all his powers of sarcasm for expressions of contempt best fitted to cut into the heart of the sensitive man of genius, through whom his own understanding "had found a language to express itself:"

"No one," he says, "ever yet gave Mr. Coleridge a penny for his thoughts." . . . "He is the secret Tattle of the Press. . . . . He is the dog in the manger of literature; an intellectual Marplot, who will neither let anybody else come to a conclusion nor come to one himself " . . . "He lives in the belief of a perpetual lie, and in affecting to think what he pretends to say," &c. &c. **

Nor is this ferocity of censure confined to the poli-

---

* Hazlitt's 'Literary Remains,' vol. ii., on 'My First Acquaintance with Poets.'
** Hazlitt's 'Political Essays:' on Coleridge's 'Lay Sermon.'

tical articles of a newspaper, to be palliated by the hot
blood of spontaneous debate. In one of his most elaborate
compositions ('On the Prose Style of Poets') he com-
pares the prose style of Coleridge "to the secondhand
finery of a lady's maid:" —

"With bits of tarnished lace and worthless frippery he
assumes a sweeping Oriental costume. . . . He is swelling
and turgid, everlastingly aiming to be greater than his subject, filling his fancy with fumes and vapours in the pangs
and throes of miraculous parturition, and bringing forth only
stillbirths."

Wordsworth, whom elsewhere he exalts to the
seventh heaven, he treats with the same measureless
contempt when Wordsworth takes the liberty to say
something which Hazlitt disapproves. Then thus doth
the idolater fustigate the idol: —

"The spirit of Jacobin poetry is rank egotism. We know
an instance; it is that of a person who founded a school of
poetry on sheer humanity, on ideal boys and mad mothers,
and on Simon Lee the old huntsman. The secret of the
Jacobin poetry and the anti-Jacobin politics of this writer is
the same. His lyrical poetry was a cant of humanity about
the commonest people, to level the great with the small; and
his political poetry is a cant of loyalty, to level Bonaparte
with kings and hereditary imbecility. This person admires
nothing that is admirable, feels no interest in anything interesting, no grandeur in anything grand, no beauty in anything beautiful. He tolerates nothing but what he himself
creates" —

and so on.

Strangely enough, after so flattering a description of Wordsworth, Hazlitt actually quarrels with Lamb because, when receiving Wordsworth at his house, he does not specially invite Hazlitt to meet him!

We do not adduce these violent breaches of that "comity" which, between those who aspire to represent the literature of nations, should form the same unwritten law which it does between nations themselves, in any spirit of undue harshness to the memory of the passionate offender; but partly because without noticing them it would be impossible to arrive at a fair critical estimate of the genius and character of William Hazlitt, and partly because they suffice for answer to the complaint made by Serjeant Talfourd and other enthusiastic partisans of this powerful writer that Hazlitt was assailed and misrepresented in his own day, ignored by dignified reviewers, or libelled by malevolent critics. How could it be supposed that much courtesy would be shown to a man who displayed so little? One does not readily make room in any decorous society for a visitor who slaps everybody's face and treads on everybody's toes. And certainly, were there not very great merits to set off against faults so grave, and which we can survey with a calmer eye now that Time has become "the beautifier of the dead," we should scarcely be tempted to rescue the writings of William Hazlitt from the neglect into which, with the mass of the reading public, they have fallen,

But amidst all these intolerant prejudices and this wild extravagance of apparent hate, there are in Hazlitt from time to time — those times not unfrequent — outbursts of sentiment scarcely surpassed among the writers of our century for tender sweetness, rapid perceptions of truth and beauty in regions of criticism then but sparingly cultured — nay, scarcely discovered — and massive fragments of such composition as no hand of ordinary strength could hew out of the unransacked mines of our native language.

Nor is it without a melancholy and softening interest that we detect sometimes, amidst the very lucubrations that most displease the taste by virulent personalities, some excuse for the writer's indulgence of hate in the sorrows of his private life, the mortifications of his literary career; and imagine that we can trace that bitterness of spirit which taints the current flow of his mind to its springs in disappointed affection and baffled aspiration. For it is one of the peculiarities in the egotism of this writer to launch into savage diatribes on the faults to which his acute self-consciousness made him aware that he was most subjected. He would insist on the virtue of courtesy, denounce the vituperation which comes from envy at another's success, call before him the phantom of his own mind, arraign it, and condemn. Surely there is something of the soured philanthropy of Alceste in the burst of wild declamation with which he concludes his ironical Essay 'On the Pleasure of Hating:' —

"Mistaken as I have been in my public and private hopes, calculating others from myself, and calculating wrong; always disappointed where I placed most reliance; the dupe of friendship and the fool of love, have I not reason to hate and despise myself? Indeed I do; and chiefly for not having hated and despised the world enough."

This is not the writing of a cynical hate, but of a

passionate despair; and, unless we mistake, of such
despair as is never wrung from a strong man except
where the heart is constitutionally warm and the
aspirations originally noble. Such a despair the best
and greatest have conceived when, walking in the
Valley of Shadow, they forget that the visibility of
shadow is the evidence of light.

In his Thoughts on the Intellectual Character of
William Hazlitt (prefixed to his Literary Remains)
Serjeant Talfourd says, with commendable brevity of
distinction, —

"As an author, Mr. Hazlitt may be contemplated principally in three aspects, — as a moral and political reasoner,
as an observer of character and manners, and as a critic in
literature and painting." Serjeant Talfourd adds, "It is in
the first character *only* that he should be followed with caution."

Only in the *first* character! The shade of Serjeant Talfourd must pardon us! We think that in
each of the three aspects those who did not follow
William Hazlitt with caution would be led into innumerable bogs and pitfalls. We have already sufficiently implied how little he is to be trusted, not
only as a political reasoner, but as an observer of
character. For an observer of manners apart from
character he had some marked advantages in his
early study of metaphysics, and his passion for connecting the outward manners of society with the in-
ward motives of man in the abstract; nor less in a
command of many varieties of style, but especially in
the epigrammatic terseness which makes the excellence of the French writers upon manners. But one

has only to glance over the leading features of his biography to perceive how exceedingly limited was the range permitted to his observation. The son of an Unitarian minister in a small provincial town, intended originally for the profession of a painter, relinquishing the hope of that calling, to which he was ardently attached, from the conviction that in it he could not attain to his own standard of excellence, but to the last, with eye and heart ever turning from the "full tide of life in Fleet Street," to dwell enamoured on the likenesses of humanity limned upon canvas; thrown a stranger upon London, inexperienced and raw; forcing from "that stony-hearted mother of orphans" a diploma to practise upon "public characters," first as a newspaper reporter, and next as a newspaper contributor; in proportion as, feeling his own powers, he stormed his way onward — rather contracting than expanding his commerce with mankind — quarrelling, as he himself tells us, with the very friends he had at first made, and even those friends, for the most part, of minds bookish and eccentric as his own; selecting his favourite resort in a sequestered village inn, with half a dozen volumes of authors a century or two old; studying the humours of no class, with a fastidious refinement that shunned the vulgar, with a pride that kept him aloof from the great, it is difficult to conceive any man less adapted by circumstance and habit for the comprehensive delineation of contemporaneous manners. And it is when he attempts to vie with the Horace Walpoles and La Bruyères, when he aims his satire at polite society, and illustrates his page with such newspaper anecdotes of what passed in courts and "gilded saloons" as a wit about town would invent as a hoax, but no man about town would repeat as a truth, that with all his native elevation of intellect, all his intuitive perception of poetic grace and beauty, we are reluctantly compelled to admit that he becomes vulgar, and vulgar according to his own true analysis of the elements in vulgarity, — vulgar from affectation, the affectation of knowing intimately things which he could not possibly know at all.

His mistake was aggravated, because it was a kind of knowledge which, as a wise man, it was not necessary he should possess, but the pretence to which any fool could detect. When, in criticising Molière's great comedy, "L'Ecole des Femmes," he speaks of Arnolphe as the *husband* of Agnes, not many of his English readers would be sufficiently familiar with the play to perceive how hastily the critic had read or how imperfectly he remembered it — Agnes being, of course, unmarried, and the whole comic conception of her character lost if she were a wife. But when Hazlitt parades as a matter of fact on which to ground argument or declamation some scrap of servants' hall gossip about kings and statesmen, Sir Fopling Flutter can look down on his ignorance, and Benjamin Backbite moralise on his malice. On the other hand, when, as an essayist on contemporaneous manners, Hazlitt writes from his own personal experience as observer, and in good humour with the subject selected, he can give grace and dignity to things commonplace or coarse. Of this, the essential faculty of genius, his description of the prize-fight between Hickman and Neate may suffice for example. It is with very felicitous art that he adapts to a description

of one of the rudest and most violent scenes admitted
into civilized life that character of style most associated with our notions of classic serenity and decorous
grace.   In the choice of words, in the rhythm of
period and cadence, we seem to read a paper in the
"Spectator." It reminds us both of Addison and Steele
— the exquisite neatness of the one, the spirited ease
of the other.

It is, however, as a critic, not of manners, but
of books, of pictures, and of the stage, that Hazlitt
chiefly excels; though even here we have need of all
"the caution" which Serjeant Talfourd implies that
we no longer require when this writer quits the
ground of moral and political controversy. For, as
we have before observed, Hazlitt's judgment is never
so beyond the control of the mood of temper in which
he writes as to keep him consistent in praise or blame.
And we shall find in one passage the most direct contradictions of opinions he has advanced in another.
Even in his criticism on pictures or on actors, where
his mind is least disturbed by passion, he cannot
demand our admiration for one of his favourites, but
what he must wantonly immolate some rival renown.
If he does justice to Reynolds, he must depreciate
Gainsborough; if he expatiates on the humour of
Hogarth, he must deny that Wilkie has any humour
at all.   If he extols Kean, he must degrade Young.
Acd because Madame Pasta was a grand actress, poor
Mademoiselle Mars must be abased into an artificial
machine.   There is nothing more adverse to the true
spirit of criticism than these invidious comparisons
between persons who essentially differ.   In art as in
nature varieties cannot be illustrated by opposing in

a hostile spirit things that are of dissimilar genus. We grant this truth at once in the objects of nature, and we sin against criticism if we do not recognise it in art. No man, if he would praise a racehorse, thinks it necessary to abuse a lion; no man who calls on us to admire the rose asks us to despise the violet; no man who invites the eye to the shimmer of the ash-leaves thinks we cannot adequately enjoy the sight unless we point a finger of scorn at the stolid repose of the cedar. But in objects of art it is the trick of commonplace critics to insist on comparisons or contrasts, not for the purpose of showing the beauty appropriate to each, but in order to make the beauty of the one a reason why there must be something deformed in the other. That Hazlitt descended to this trick was in itself enough to depose him from the highest rank of critics. Criticism stops where injustice begins. In criticisms on literature his faults of caprice and temper become much more glaring than they are in his discourses on pictorial art, and are expressed with infinitely more presumption, because with infinitely less knowledge of his subject. Not knowing a word of German, he calls Goethe's "Faust" a mere "piece of abortive perverseness, and not to be named in a day with Marlowe's." Telling us that Ford only wrote one play either acted or worth acting, he adds, and "that would no more bear acting than Lord Byron and Goethe together could have written it."

These examples, which might be multiplied *ad nauseam*, suffice to show how little we can dispense with that caution which Serjeant Talfourd invites us to dismiss in seeking intercourse with this powerful

but irregular intellect, even on its happiest ground.
It is not as a guide that Hazlitt can be useful to any
man. His merit is that of a companion in districts
little trodden — a companion strong and hardy, who
keeps our sinews in healthful strain; rough and iras-
cible, whose temper will constantly offend us if we do
not steadily preserve our own; but always animated,
vivacious, brilliant in his talk; suggestive of truths,
even where insisting on paradoxes; and of whom when
we part company we retain impressions stamped with
the crownmark of indisputable genius. We have said
that Hazlitt cultivated his reasoning faculty as a meta-
physician; and his earliest work, on the 'Principles of
Human Action,' is a very extraordinary performance,
considering the early age at which it was conceived
and composed. To the abstract principle upon which
it is grounded Hazlitt remained faithful to the close of
his life; that principle pervades the best of his writings,
colours many of their lovelier beauties, and throws a
redeeming light upon many of their gloomier faults.
The warmth of his heart revolted at the doctrine which
traced the springs of all human virtues to an enlightened
self-love. It was less with the austere disdain of a
Stoic than with the cordial detestation of a lover of art,
in whom romance in sentiment was inseparable from
worthy conceptions of truth and nature, that he regarded
that old Epicurean philosophy which, brought down to
the drawing-room by Rochefoucauld and Helvetius, had
of late been familiarized to the counter and adapted to
the hustings by the utilitarianism, positive and political,
of Jeremy Bentham. Hazlitt's work on the Principles
of Human Action is intended to prove the natural
disinterestedness of the human mind. Weapons in

plenty against the Epicurean system may be taken from antique armouries, repolished, and whetted anew; and we may observe, in passing, that perhaps no arguments in confutation of the philosophy of self-interest are more popularly adapted to a plain understanding than those to be found in Seneca. But Hazlitt was little acquainted with the labours of predecessors in the same cause; he conducted his argument as if it had been untouched. Where he says something that has been said before, it is in his own way, and ideas which, taken singly, had occurred to other minds, form themselves, when conceived by his, into original combinations. The fundamental principle in his metaphysical creed, that "we are naturally interested in the welfare of others, through the same way, the same motives, the same mental operations by which we naturally pursue our own;" that, in a word, benevolence is as elementary as self-love in the principles of human action, is certainly a noble and generous doctrine, and enforced by Hazlitt with all the earnestness of his vigorous and fervid nature. And it was his faith in this doctrine that not only kept him aloof from those democratic reformers who exercised prevailing influence over the more educated members of the movement party, viz., the disciples of Mill and Bentham, but directed against their school of philosophy the instincts of his heart and the bias of his tastes, as well as the convictions of his reason.

We must notice, as briefly as possible, the most ambitious of Hazlitt's numerous writings, and the one upon which he and some of his admirers most counted for enduring fame — 'The Life of Napoleon.'   "He lived," says the writer of the preface to that history,

9*

"to complete the 'Life of Napoleon,' and then laid down his own."

We can say little or nothing to redeem this work from the oblivion into which it has already passed. It was altogether a mistake. Whatever intellectual qualities Hazlitt possessed, they were not those of a historian. He was naturally impatient of details; neither had he the temper nor the discipline of mind essential to comprehensive generalization. Even his proper beauties of style, when happiest, are but brilliant impertinences in historical composition. He sentimentalizes, digresses, declaims, in the wrong spirit and in the wrong place. He lacks the simplicity of a narrator. He lacks still more the impartiality of a judge. But were his History far better than it is, it could not have stood its ground against histories of the same stormy epoch and the same marvellous man written since Hazlitt's time.

It is, then, as a critic of Art in painting and in poetry that Hazlitt principally demands our admiration — demands and generally deserves, not indeed when he censures, but when he praises; when on those beauties which had so long elevated his thoughts and vivified his fancies he expatiates with all the enthusiasm of reverential love: — it is then that he deserves the eulogy bestowed on him by Leigh Hunt, and "throws a light on Art as from a painted window."

Still more than as a critic Hazlitt excels as a writer of the Essay of Sentiment; when, in the spirit of his favourite Montaigne, he abandons himself fairly to self-commune and self-confession; when he unfolds to us, with a frankness at once melancholy and genial, the record of his early impressions, and makes us partners in the joys and the griefs of genius. For in essays of this kind the self-obtrusion to which we give the name of egotism is not a fault; it is the essential quality, infusing into desultory reveries the distinct vitality of individualised being. It is in this portion of his works that the most striking instances of Hazlitt's eloquence are to be found: an eloquence which, though retaining the form of prose, approaches near enough to poetry to bring before the reader's eye "fantastic heights or hidden recesses" in the enchanted border-land. Then, worthy of the praise he bestows on his favourite Poussin, "words start up into images, thoughts become things. He clothes a dream, a phantom, with form and colour, and the wholesome attribute of reality." (Hazlitt's 'Table-Talk,' vol. ii. On a Landscape by Nicholas Poussin.)

Hazlitt's style, when at the best, is not that of a rhetorician, but in much that of an orator. It is spontaneous, varied, and glowing, full of illustrations that are rarely superfluous embellishments of fancy, but rather arguments lighted up. For between the rhetorical and the oratorical style there is the distinction which Mr. Pugin makes in architecture between constructed ornament and ornamental construction. The first (as recently observed in this Journal*) is merely for show, and does not affect the substance of the framework if removed; but the last, as in the columns and entablature of a Grecian temple, is part and parcel of the building itself, and to remove it would be to destroy the fabric.

To pass from Hazlitt to Leigh Hunt is like passing

* 'Quarterly Review' for October, 1866, p. 443.

from a rough landscape sketch by Salvator, in which,
according to Coleridge, the rocks take vague likeness
of the human figure, to a garden scene by Lancret,
with a group seated round a fountain engaged in
dining off peaches, and listening to a gentle shepherd
who is playing a guitar or telling a pleasant story.
Leigh Hunt is as constitutionally gay as Hazlitt is
constitutionally saturnine.   He has a sprightly sense
of enjoyment which he communicates to readers who
will give themselves up to him, take him for what he
is, and not frown or pish because he is not something
else.   He has a feminine love for pretty ornaments,
and gets together quaint little trinkets, arranged so
neatly and paraded with so amiable an air that he
wins our goodnature to his side.   We admire as curiosities in his collection things which might seem trifles
in that of a ruder man.   The neatness and delicacy
of his style are not achieved without some apparent
affectation; but the affectation is only apparent.   To
no writer can be more truly applied the saying attributed to Buffon — "the style is the man."   A certain
gracefulness in his plastic temperament made him love
to associate his actual existence with small elegancies,
which cheered his eye and gladdened his heart.   He
covers the walls of his prison-room with a trellis paper,
and can imagine that he is with Ariosto in Tuscan
bowers.   He goes into the poetic heaven at sight of
"an old-looking s ucer with a handle to it."   "Its
little shallow circle overflows for him with the milk
and honey of a thousand pleasant associations." "This,"
he exclaims, "is *one of the uses of having mantel-pieces!*
You may often see on no very rich mantel-piece a
representative body of all elements, physical and in-

tellectual, — a shell for the sea, a stuffed bird or
some feathers for the air, a curious piece of mineral
for the earth, a glass of water with some flowers in it
for the visible process of creation, and underneath all
is the bright and ever-springing fire running up through
them heavenwards, like Hope through materiality.
We like to have any little curiosity of the mantel-
piece kind within our reach and inspection." A reader
who feels himself inclined to scorn the amiable
idiosyncrasy of mind which not only delights in these
small adornments of our work-day life, but calls us
off from our anxious cares or our vaulting aspirations
to share in its harmless delight, is not a reader fitted
to appreciate the genius of Leigh Hunt. "Since
trifles make the sum of human things," Hunt, with
no irrational philosophy, seeks to make trifles pleasant,
and with no profitless poetry to extract from them
an ideal happiness. Like the butterfly described by
Spenser —

> "He pastures on the pleasures of each place,
>   Now sucking of the sap of herbe most meet,
> Or of the dew which yet on them does lie,
>   Now in the same bathing his tender feet,
> And then he percheth on some branch thereby,
> To weather him and his moist wings to dry."

With a writer of so sunny a temperament it would
be but a crabbed philosophy to provoke cause of
serious quarrel. We cannot bring ourselves to look
on Leigh Hunt in his character of rabid politician. His
are not the wings that ride on the whirlwind and direct
the storm —

" Now this, now that he tasteth tenderly,
Yet none of them he rudely doth disorder."

Nor, in recognising the general kindliness of disposition which characterised the man, are we unwilling
to regard with lenity, as an exceptional aberration
from his better nature, the ill-advised work on Lord
Byron. And we are reconciled to this forbearance
with a quieter conscience because we have reason to
believe that Leigh Hunt himself sincerely regretted
that he had been ever galled by a skin-deep wound
to too sensitive a self-love into a breach of those hospitable laws which involve obligations upon personal
honour.

Of all Leigh Hunt's writings we like best his
prose essays, and of these we like best the light and
varied lucubrations contained in the 'Indicator.' Than
this we do not know a more agreeable book in its own
way, nor one that can be read more often with renewed pleasure in re-perusal. Hunt wanted breadth
of colour and strength of hand for the filling up of
any large canvas, and in such attempts he lost his own
peculiar merits, which consist in smoothness of tone
and delicacy of finish. He tells a short story of
mingled fancy and sentiment with much grace and
animation. 'The Hamadryad,' in the 'Indicator,' is
beautifully conceived and composed. He can illustrate
with a light not indeed very large nor searching, but
of "ray serene," many little nooks and corners in the
mind and heart of man, many minor beauties of form
and expression in the authors he loved to study. But
when he attempts a five-act drama or a prose fiction in
three volumes, we become aware of his deficiencies.

He has neither the art of constructing a sustained fable, nor the power of creating new characters of life-like size; above all, he wants passion, perhaps because he abounds in fancy. This last defect is transparent in 'Rimini,' a poem which has nevertheless many strik-ing detached beauties, and, in spite of its disagreeable subject, is the best of his more ambitious works. In the same way, as a critic, he is worthy not only of praise but of study in detached observations upon what by the German Aristarchus* are called "particulars," but he seems to us somewhat feeble in his grasp of "generals." He feels sensitively, and explains with lucid eloquence the poetry which lurks in a form of expression, in an artful cadence, in a combination of melodious liquids. But we cannot grant that he has adequate comprehension of that highest form of "im-perial poetry" which retains its imperishable substance even when stripped of its felicitous expressions and de-frauded of its original music; that which, though sub-jected to the baldest translation, can never be reduced to prose, but, passing from land to land, varies its "singing robes" in each, and secures its privilege of royalty in all.

In one of his most delightful essays, entitled 'My Books,' Hunt, speaking of the great writers who were book-lovers like himself, exclaims, "How pleasant it is to reflect that all these lovers of books have them-selves become books!" And after pursuing that thought through "links of sweetness long drawn out," con-cludes with a modest pathos, "May I hope to become the meanest of these existences?" .... "I should like

---

* Hegel.

to remain visible in this shape. The little of myself
that pleases myself I could wish to be accounted worth
pleasing others. I should like to survive so, were it
only for the sake of those who love me in private,
knowing, as I do, what a treasure is the possession of
a friend's mind when he is no more."

We think few can read this very lovely passage
and not sympathise cordially in the wish so nobly conceived and so tenderly expressed. Something not to
be replaced would be struck out of the gentler literature of our century, could the mind of Leigh Hunt
cease to speak to us in a book.

Charles Lamb has been more fortunate in propitiat-
ing friends and disarming enemies than either of the
contemporaries whose names are popularly associated
with his own, and to whose attributes we have devoted
the preceding pages. His reputation, never angrily
contested, has taken a deeper root than theirs, and
spreads at present over a far wider surface. He needs
not, as they yet do, the aid of the critic to take his
rank among standard and popular writers. For this
elder brother's share of favour he is indebted partly,
no doubt, to a genius singularly sweet and concilia-
tory, partly also to the idiosyncrasies of a personal
character in moral harmony with the genius, and so
uniting our love with our admiration that it pleases
ourselves to praise him, and it almost becomes an act
of ingratitude to blame.

Lamb is one of those rare favourites of the Graces
on whom the gift of *charm* is bestowed — a gift not
indeed denied to Hunt, but much more sparingly
granted to him and much more alloyed in its nature
— while it is almost the last attribute we can as-

sign to the irritating and aggressive intellect of Hazlitt.

He is not without something of charm, even in those compositions in which his genius appears to the least advantage. As a Drama, 'John Woodvill' has almost every defect that a Drama can have, and it is only in very rare passages that some happiness of expression or grace of versification atones for the general tameness of the language and the dissonance of the rhythm — yet still the work leaves a pleasing impression. We are not moved by the action of the play, but we are contented to enjoy in repose and calm the contemplation of that amiable mind which reflects itself in the current that quietly flows before us. 'Rosamond Gray' is a story which in ruder hands would have been disagreeable and painful, and, brief as it is, while aiming at the simplest form of narrative, it wants the truthfulness of incident essential to genuine simplicity. The victim meets her fate by an accident which seems highly improbable. A girl of sixteen, brought up as strictly as Rosamond Gray, does not leave her home in the depth of night without any motive stronger than a fancy that she should like to retrace the scenes through which she had walked all day with a female acquaintance, to wander amidst "lonely glens, into a lonely copse, out of the hearing of any human habitation." Or, if it be said this might possibly have happened in real life, the Natural which belongs to Art forbids the construction of a tragic story upon an impulse so exceptional, an accident so unusual. This is not the breach of a merely conventional rule in artistic narrative. It argues a want of the intuitive faculty requisite for constructing a well-told tale. Accident, as the cause of a tragic *dénouement*, is as inadmissible in narrative fiction as it is in dramatic; and the author who employs in either such an agency cannot achieve a genuine success, — a success that satisfies intellectual requirements. The punishment of the guilty man, Matravis, is an accident again: it is no consequence of his crime, it has no connection with the incidents in the story. He is wounded in a duel, with whom we know not; his wounds "are unskilfully treated," and so he dies. Other defects in the elementary requisites of "story-telling," scarcely less grave, might be pointed out in 'Rosamond Gray.' But we have said enough to show that Lamb's special genius was as little adapted to romantic narrative as it was to dramatic character and passion. Yet, with all its faults, 'Rosamond Gray' has an attraction which many a good novelist might envy, because there is in it that nameless sweetness of sentiment which constitutes the master-spell of the author.

But neither in these departments of literature nor in those minor poems — which are rather evidences of an exquisite poetic sensibility than achievements of poetic power — did the true genius of Charles Lamb find its natural scope. It is not on these that he rests the enduring reputation of "Elia." Happily for us and for him, he found in the pages of a Magazine precisely the field best suited to exercise, without over-straining, the faculties in which he excelled. As an Essayist, following the bent of his own mind — stamping on all that he wrote the vivid impression of his own rare individuality — he gave to the varieties of mankind a new character, and left to his language a

new style. As the character given was his own, so
the style bequeathed was, with all its mannerism, perfectly natural to the man. It was no style invented
and built up for a literary purpose. We have only to
read his delightful correspondence to see that the quaint
diction of "Elia" was that in which he habitually expressed himself in familiar commune with his friends.
Hence, artificial though it seem at the first glance, he
is much more at his ease in it than when he writes in
a style more natural to other men. In the last he for-
feits originality, and gains nothing to compensate in
exchange. The brevity to which he was compelled by
the limited space that a Magazine allots to a contributor
was favourable to Lamb's peculiar genius. It forced
him to concentrate his thoughts, and out of that con-
centration comes the pause of reflection which is propitious to felicity in wording; so that his essays are
really marvellous for terseness of treatment and nicety
of expression. "Elia" is never verbose, yet never incomplete. You are not wearied because he says too
much, nor dissatisfied because he says too little. In
this inimitable sense of proportion, this fitness of adjustment between thought and expression, the prose
of "Elia" reminds us of the verse of Horace. Nor is
the Essayist without some other resemblance to the
Poet; in the amenity which accompanies his satire;
in his sportive view of things grave; the grave morality
he deduces from things sportive; his equal sympathy
for rural and for town life; his constant good fellow-
ship and his lenient philosophy. Here, indeed, all
similitude ceases: the modern essayist advances no
pretension to the ancient poet's wide survey of the
social varieties of mankind; to his seizure of those

large and catholic types of human nature which are
familiárly recognisable in every polished community,
every civilized time; still less to that intense sympathy
in the life and movement of the world around him
which renders the utterance of his individual emotion
the vivid illustration of the character and history of
his age. Yet "Elia" secures a charm of his own in
the very narrowness of the range to which he limits
his genius. For thus the interest he creates becomes
more intimate and household.

Humour in itself is among the most popular gifts
of genius; amiable humour among the most lovable.
The humour of Charles Lamb is at once pure and
genial; it has no malice in its smile. His keenest sarcasm is but his archest pleasantry. It is not of the
very highest order, because the highest order necessitates the creation of characters self-developed in the
action of romance or drama. Lamb is not Cervantes
nor Molière; nor could he have created a Caleb Balder-
stone or a Major Dalgetty. Yet, if it be not of the
highest order, its delicacy places it among the rarest.
A proverb has been defined to be the wisdom of many
in the wit of one. There is much in the humour of
Charles Lamb, and the terseness of style into which
its riches are compressed, that would merit this definition of a proverb. As Scott's humour is that of a
novelist, and therefore objective, so Lamb's is that of
an essayist, and eminently subjective. All that he
knows or observes in the world of books or men becomes absorbed in the single life of his own mind, and
is reproduced as part and parcel of Charles Lamb. If
thus he does not create imaginary characters, Caleb
Balderstones and Major Dalgettys, he calls up, com-

pletes, and leaves to the admiration of all time a character which, as a personification of humour, is a higher being than even Scott has imagined, viz. that of Charles Lamb himself. Nor is there in the whole world of humorous creation an image more beautiful in its combinations of mirth and pathos. In the embodiment of humour, as it actually lived amongst us in this man, there is a dignity equal to that with which Cervantes elevates our delight in his. ideal creation. Quixote is not more essentially a gentleman than Lamb. How we respect his manhood while we are charmed by his gentleness! What strength in the firm resolve, during his early stage of poverty and privation, to secure inviolate that independence from debt and pecuniary obligation which is almost inseparable from the maintenance of personal honour! To effect this object, with what noble cheerfulness he makes a jest of every minor sacrifice! Nor do we know in fiction anything more touching, and yet more heroic, than the devotion with which he gives up his life from youth till age to the discharge of such a trust as the bravest nature, not made by love brave beyond the ordinary instincts of nature, could scarcely have dared to undertake. In a moment of insanity his sister stabs her mother to the heart. To use his own words in his letter to Coleridge: "I was at hand only time enough to snatch the knife out of her grasp. She is at present in a madhouse, from whence I fear she must be moved to an hospital." His father was imbecile. He alone takes care of the old man; when the old man dies, he alone takes charge of the unhappy sister.

"For her sake at the same time," says Serjeant Talfourd,

"he abandoned all thoughts of love and marriage" (all hope
of "the Fairhaired," whose image yet flits here and there
across his page in later years, glimpses of a bygone dream),
"and with an income of scarcely more than 100l. a year derived from his clerkship, aided for a little while by the old
aunt's small annuity, set out on the journey of life at twenty-
two years of age, cheerfully with his beloved companion, en-
deared to him the more by her strange calamity, and the
constant apprehension of a recurrence of the malady which
had caused it." .

We add nothing to the picture conveyed in these
few words; the words suffice to show the strength
and the greatness in this man's nature; they account
for the reverential affection he inspired, and for that
subdued and serene melancholy which rarely saddens,
but often sweetens, the music of his gentle laugh.
The resolve to secure pecuniary independence with
which Charles Lamb commenced life, aided by the
simplicity of his tastes, gradually worked out its own
success. And as we glance over the record of himself and the companions most associated with his
literary career, he seems to stand out as the rich man
among them — the host around whom they gathered
every week as welcome guests.   True that the board
is sufficiently Socratic, but it is pleasant to think how
little the hospitality of a man of genius need cost him
when he adds to "the cold joint and the foaming
tankard" the eloquence and the wit not to be found
at the board of Dives. Most of Lamb's familiar associates were brilliant talkers. Leigh Hunt was always
animated and lively; he talked as he wrote. Hazlitt,
painfully shy before strangers, was easily drawn forth
by the first jest of Lamb into confident display of his

singular powers of language. Godwin was considered
a dull proser by these quick wits and vivid declaimers;
but we are old enough to have heard Godwin talk in
the society of ordinary mortals, and there he was
well worth hearing, nor without a grim jocularity of
sarcasm. A later guest in those symposia was the
charming poet from whom so much was then expected,
and whose sweet note will be more clearly heard
hereafter, when noisier singers are hushed in night:
he who, himself a veteran, has just recorded the
pleasant recollections of his youth, and added to the
Amenities of Literature, Barry Cornwall's Reminiscences of Lamb. There too, on rare occasions,
Wordsworth might be seen and heard; but of his
visits the records are brief and scanty. If somewhat
in the background, still conspicuous amidst and
bending over, all, we behold the vast front of
Coleridge. For ever there, when absent in the body
he is visible in the spirit. From his intellect Hazlitt's
took light and warmth. To his imagination Hunt
was indebted for his happiest illustrations of poetic
art. To Lamb he was more than philosopher and poet
— he was the dearest of friends, the most spiritual
of teachers; and as we could form but an imperfect notion of Lamb if we abstracted from his life its
intercourse with Coleridge, so we should but superficially comprehend the intellectual character of our
own time, if we saw but in Coleridge, as we are
commonly invited to see, a man of incompleted and
desultory genius, purposing much and performing
little. This erring estimate of the peculiar properties
of Coleridge has been founded perhaps on his own
modest self-reproaches. He could not consummate

the whole of that which he designed; and he therefore speaks of himself as a painter of outlines, a
sculptor of fragments. In this he did but confess
that distinction between ideal excellence and practical performance which cannot fail to be inly felt
by every man who unites in a high degree imagination and intellect. For though the intellect suggests
to the imagination the conception of any given
work', and sustains the imagination throughout the
doing of it, nothing which the imagination can
do quite satisfies the intellect when done. Hence,
judging by the Sonnets in which he intimates his
disdain of the works on which his life was spent, and
by the indifference with which he left those works to
their fate among the other properties of the Globe
Theatre, Shakspeare would probably have told us that
he never fully wrought out that which was in him, and
that we saw of his genius but outlines and fragments.
Hence Descartes, the most imaginative of mathe-
maticians, sought, at the very outset of his career,
for modes to prolong human life to the age of the
patriarchs, because within the limits of threescore years
and ten it seemed to him impossible to accomplish
more than outlines and fragments of the designs he
conceived as wholes. A man of superior genius does
not require critics to show him his defects; if he is to
correct those defects and approach nearer to his ideal,
he may need critics to reassure him as to his merits.
This was not the good fortune of Coleridge. Of the
men to be named in the same breath with him, some
were enthusiastically lauded, some vehemently abused;
Coleridge was ignored: and in those lauded and those
abused, equally, through praise or censure, made famous

in their time, could be distinctly traced the informing
genius of the man ignored. For here we come to the
special idiosyncrasy of Coleridge, and that which makes
his grand life, not — as his duller disciples would at-
tenuate it into — a dreamy abstraction, but a strong,
an enduring, and a colossal entity. The distinguishing
attribute of his genius is this; it was not merely original, it was originating, it penetrated the genius of
others, it originated their originality — and this in
ways not only so many, but so diverging and so opposed. In 'Christabel' and the 'Rhyme of the Ancient
Mariner,' he originates the lyrical narrative as it afterwards expanded in 'Marmion' and the 'Siege of
Corinth.' In other poems, more devoted to musical
contrivance, to sensuous glow of description, to human
passion chastened and spiritualised, he originates the
poetry that succeeds to Scott and Byron, from Shelley
and Keats to Tennyson. All that he originates, fused
into other minds, becomes in those minds original. But
Coleridge's influence does not limit itself to poets, it
extends to reasoners, and abides with us at this day in
the thoroughfares of positive life. To comprehend, in
this, the influence of Coleridge, we must contrast with
it the influence of an antagonistic genius — also originating as well as original — the influence of Bentham.
We remember well, in our own green college days,
the effect which Bentham produced on the mind of the
then rising generation. There was something captivating even to the poets — whom, still more rigidly than
Plato, Bentham would have banished from his republic
— in the brevity of his royal roads into political
science — in the sparkle of his aphorisms — in the
decision with which he trampled under foot not less

the vulgar commonplaces of radical fustian than the
foil and tinsel of courtly adulation; something captivating, too, even in his scholar-like wit and raciness of
style, when (as in his 'Essay on Usury') Bentham himself completes his own designs, and does not, as in
most of his later works, merely present the sinew and
bone of his ideas to the Frankensteins who construct
into a shape so portentously unhandsome the giant
intended to be an improvement on the standard form
of mankind. The sole great thinker of the time who,
with but little direct reply to Bentham, on special
points, stood opposed to him in substance and spirit,
and intellectual mastery over earnest minds, was this
mighty Coleridge, of whom sciolists talk as of a moon-
stricken dreamer. Rich in the learning of the schools,
richer still in a treasury of thought on which his own
sovereign mintage is stamped, it is Coleridge who has
shown how little the liberty of human reason and the
requirements of human life can be pent up within the
close wall-works of Bentham. On young men of genius,
who, the more they are by impulse poetical, are the
more, by the poetry within them, constrained to examine
into "truths severe," the intellect of Coleridge flashed
like a ray from heaven. He did not so much furnish
special weapons against a school essentially material as
he fitted the reason of intellectual man, taken as a
whole, to strike down the arguments which appealed
to him as a material atom, confused and lost amidst a
perishable conglomeration of atoms, with as little of
freedom and as little of soul as an emmet at work in
an ant-hill.

It would have been enough for the completeness of
any individual life to have originated in the poetic and

the ratiocinative forms of truth a millionth part of the
ideas which owed their origin to Coleridge. It is
Coleridge who first made England aware of the riches
of German philosophy and German song; and in him
originate whatever influences the higher spirit of German genius has exercised upon the English mind. And
how much of that earnestness of aim which signalizes
the clergy of the younger generation, and brings to
the service of the Church a scholarship so enlarged,
and an enthusiasm so chastened from sectarian bigotry,
is to be traced to the new spirit which Coleridge in-
fused into theological learning, exalting the mission of
the preacher, as Fichtè exalted the vocation of the
scholar! It was much, too, in that day — it would
have been much in any day, for such effect, on minds
hesitating between belief and disbelief, as belongs to
authority and example — that the ablest and the
boldest investigator of truth which the age could boast
gave to revealed religion no qualified adhesion, no
conventional acquiescence, but the deep-felt, clear-
spoken convictions of an intellect subtler than Hume's,
more eloquent than Rousseau's, more comprehensive
than Voltaire's. In fact, Coleridge exerted so large an
influence over so many of those minds which are in
themselves reproductive, and yield in the sheaf what
they receive in the germ, that if we were asked "What
he had done in his life?" it might be enough to answer, "He has lived." We might almost suppress re-
ference to his own writings, we might point to the
writings of others; to recognise the true worth of that
life in its vivifying power over other lives, we must,
indeed, look around, but we must also look upward,
searching for its traces wherever some fertile eminence,

dominating the level table-land of thought, expands to a nearer sunbeam the purple of a richer vintage or the gold of an ampler harvest.

It is true that the vast effect which the genius of Coleridge has exercised on our age was not produced only by the suggestive character of his written compositions, in which, as Pliny says of Greek master-pieces of art, "more is felt than understood." Much is due to the charm and the power of his oral eloquence. He left impressions that endured through a lifetime on those who met and heard him in his more felicitous moments. So that, if he had written nothing, he would still have done much of that work which we commonly ascribe to writers. It is not absolutely necessary that a man should write in order to inspire, to harmonize, and to perpetuate ideas, out of which systems arise and schools are formed. Socrates himself wrote nothing; but "Socrates taught Xenophon and Plato." The minds of Xenophon and Plato were the works he left behind him. It is only, however, a very superior genius in whom ideas thus spontaneously cast off in familiar discourse can set into movement the genius of great writers, and wing in others the words by which those ideas are borne on through space. There is in this power something beyond even the eloquence of public orators. For it is the business of orators not so much to suggest new ideas to writers as to give warmth and force to ideas which writers have already expressed.

We have submitted to our readers these views of the peculiar genius of Coleridge, and of the large results it achieved, in order to suggest to some critic more competent than ourselves to estimate and apportion the multiform capacities of a man so munificently endowed, some slight hints for the refutation of the fallacious charge of "wasted powers" popularly urged against him.

We think that in this accusation there is a complete misconception of the real nature of Coleridge's genius, and that, obeying the customary law of genius, he actually did that which he was mentally best fitted to do.

It is true that in his visionary moments Coleridge drew up prospectuses, as it were, of vast designs never fulfilled, that he sketched maps of the El-Dorados he desired to colonize and declined to visit. But if in schemes so projected his imagination deceived his understanding, we hold it fortunate that his understanding subsequently triumphed over his imagination. For, in the fine thought of Cowley —

> "Life did never to one man allow
> Time to discover worlds and conquer too."

Any critic of sound common sense has only, first, to glance at the programmes of the works Coleridge proposed to write, and, secondly, to examine fairly the generic characteristics of the things he did write, in order to be quite sure that he *would* have wasted his powers had he seriously toiled to realize the vision in 'Kubla Khan' —

> "Reach the caverns measureless to man
> *   *   *   *   *
> And build *his* dome in air."

Of the eighteen works which Mr. Joseph Cottle says, with reproachful groan, "Mr. Coleridge intended

to write, and not one of which he effected," how many
are there for which we would exchange 'Kubla Khan'
itself, fragment though it be? "At the top of the list,"
says Mr. Cottle, "appeared the word 'PANTISOCRACY,
Quarto.'" Who much deplores the loss of that quarto?
Who laments as a privation to posterity the non-com-
pletion of a 'Book on Morals in answer to Godwin;' a
'Treatise on the Corn Laws,' or on 'The Principles of
Population'? Even the only work among the eighteen
that advanced somewhat beyond the land of dreams,
viz. a 'Translation of the Modern Latin Poets,' in two
volumes, it seems to us that Coleridge showed his good
sense "in putting off." It is with a shudder that we
find among these eighteen projects of prospective labour
an idea of "finishing Christabel;" finishing 'Christabel'
in the way in which Coleridge himself tells us he projected its finish, viz., to adapt it to the taste of the
day; bring it into closer resemblance, we presume, to
the 'Lay of the Last Minstrel.' What truly critical
friend of Coleridge would not have implored him to
desist from such design! 'Christabel' in itself is as
unique and matchless as a torso of Phidian art. Who
wants the torso completed "to suit the taste of the
day"? It is as a fragment that 'Christabel' will be
an eternal study to poets contemplating lyrical narrative. Had it been completed to vie with the 'Last
Minstrel,' Coleridge would have resigned his own
superiority of melody, expression, and form, for a very
hazardous comparison with Scott in the construction of
metrical fable attuned to the popular ear. But, groans
Mr. Joseph Cottle, and many deeper-mouthed than Mr.
Joseph Cottle have "barked back" the groan — "How
much it is to be deplored that one whose views were

so enlarged as those of Mr. Coleridge, and his conceptions so Miltonic, did not, like his great prototype (Milton), concentrate all his energies so as to produce some one august poetical work which should become the glory of his country!"   As in this choragic groan may be heard a chorus of groans irrational, let us hear, from the Man of genius groaned at, his own idea of this one august poetical work on which his energies should have been concentrated, and for which, therefore, we should have lost the all over which those energies were dispersed.   Coleridge himself tells us in a letter to Cottle that which he meant by an august poetical work. He says, "I should not think of devoting less than twenty years to an epic poem; ten years to collect my materials, and warm my mind with universal science.   I would be a tolerable mathematician. I would *thoroughly* understand Mechanics, Hydrostatics, Optics, and Astronomy; Botany, Metallurgy, Fossilism, Chemistry, Geology, Anatomy, Medicine; then the minds of men in all travels, voyages, and histories. So would I spend ten years; the next five in the composition of the poem, and the five last in the correction of it."   Lives there a true poet or a sound-judging critic who could form any sanguine notion of an epic poem thus conceived *de omni scibili?*   Robert Hall said of Dr. Kippis, "He put so many books on the top of his head that he crushed out his brains."   Would the brain of mortal poet bear for ten years the weight of so many sciences, and not feel the poetry crushed out of it?   Where is the chance that a man should end as a Milton who starts as a Newton?   That a large flame requires a large fuel we need no philosopher to tell us. A poet who would grasp the largest form of poetry

(viz. the Dramatic or the Epic) should have the largest.
amount of knowledge; granted. But the largest form
of poetry excludes, except as auxiliary ornament, the
aids of positive science. The reason is perfectly clear.
Poetry is an art, and as an art it deals with types
unalterable and imperishable; it deals with human
nature in its cardinal passions and everlasting aspirations. But science differs from art in being essentially
progressive — alterable from year to year. In hydrostatics, botany, metallurgy, medicine, all our knowledge is so capricious and transitory that an encyclo-
pædia treating on such subjects is out of date if it be
ten years old. There are no revised editions of pictures and statues and works of fiction when the mind
that created them has passed from earth. The fuel required for the flame of poetry is unquestionably knowledge. — knowledge of the human heart — knowledge of passion and sorrow and joy — of aspiration
and abasement — of vice and virtue — of good and
evil. In Coleridge's programme of study for an epic
poem all this knowledge is left out. And if we now
look critically at such examples as he has left us of his
practical power to construct artistic fable in the whole-
ness and unity of completed form, we must acknowledge it was precisely that power which he wanted,
and in which no study of truth through physical
science, "of men's minds through travels, voyages, and
histories," and no mastery of musical language and
felicitous expression, could have supplied his inherent
defect. For we have his tragedies finished *ad unguem*
according to his notions of tragedy; and while these
elaborated performances, whatever their detached beauties, which we would rather reverentially magnify

than churlishly depreciate, suffice to show that Coleridge wanted the indispensable elements of dramatic construction, they no less convincingly show that he would have failed still more in the achievement of epic. That which he lacks is not light, but fire. He has no prolonged sustainment of passion; he can delight the imagination, he cannot enthral the heart. Had he absorbed into the laboratory of his brain all the lore contained on the shelves of the British Museum and the lost library of Alexandria, it could never have been reproduced in the form of such Dramas as, no matter on what principle of art they be constructed — whether on those conceived by Shakspeare, or on those accepted by Corneille, — still hold unlettered audiences under the master-spell of pity or of terror — nor in such creations of epic fable as represent in every human community the heroic archetypes of our common race.

We see, then, no cause for regret that Coleridge did not devote twenty years of his life to manufacture "one august poetical work" out of such raw materials as the positive sciences and books of history, voyages, and travels. Neither do we grieve with less poetical mourners over the embryos of philosophies unborn, that Coleridge did not concentrate the rays of an intellect so widely diffused upon some new History of the Human Mind, or gather into a completed system all his lore in English divinity, and all his speculative deductions from German metaphysics.

For works necessitating a long-continued patience, habits of methodical arrangement, a clear disentanglement of the complicated skein of contradictory opinions in various sects and schools — with a constant and

calm perception of the sage's own theory, and a lucid
and forcible mode of rendering that theory intelligible
to others — we have no reason to suppose that Coleridge had the requisite gifts. He wanted, perhaps, less
the primary than the secondary qualifications which
we find in the Philosopher who can put his whole mind
into a single system, and put his whole system into a
single book.

We must be contented to take even men of genius
as they are, and recognise the fact that, if they had
possessed the qualities they lack, it would have been
to destroy or to neutralize the qualities they possess.
It is enough for us that, with all his asserted indolence, Coleridge has left behind him so goodly an
array of volumes, rich with such diversified spoils —
enough that we retain in so many reminiscences of his
conversation, in so large a remnant of his familiar
correspondence, the adequate record of a Mind that
"has enriched the blood of the world," vital in its influence through age-long generations, alike upon sage
and poet, — kindling new conceptions of beauty, prompt-
ing new guesses into truth.

Goethe has been likened to a cupola lighted from
below. Coleridge may rather be compared to a pharos,
in which the light is placed on the summit, leaving
the shadow of the tower which it crowns stretched at
length on the ground immediately below. But afar,
where the ships move through ocean, the shadow is
invisible, the tower itself disappears, nothing is seen
but the light.

Reluctantly we close the pleasant retrospect of
'Charles Lamb and some of his Companions,' to which,
first invited by Serjeant Talfourd, we have been re-

attracted by the kindred genius of Mr. Procter. In
his recent biography of Lamb, the Poet of 'Marcian
Colonna' has revived the sense of our own obligations
to himself —

"For heavenly tunes piped through an alien flute;"*

while in his simple and touching narrative he has added
much of endearing interest to our knowledge of the exquisite writer whom he loves to honour.

In listening as it were to the uttered thoughts of a
spirit so gently attuned as that of "Elia," so humane,
yet so elevating, the mind —

"tired
Of controversy where no end appears," —

feels that sense of repose, which, to quote the words of
"Elia" himself, steals over him

"whom the Sabbath bells salute,
Sudden; his heart awakes, his ears drink in
The cheering music; his relenting soul
Yearns after all the joys of social life,
And softens with the love of human kind."

* Lamb's verses to the Author of Poems published under
the name of Barry Cornwall.

GRAY'S WORKS.

[First published in 'THE LONDON AND WESTMINSTER REVIEW,' July, 1857.]

GRAY'S WORKS.

[*The Works of Thomas Gray.* Edited by the Rev. John Mitford. 4 vols. Pickering. London, 1837.]

ALTHOUGH Poetry be an art, it is not always, nor is it even often, that the Poet is aware of the steps by which he has passed to eminence. As springs, that supply the fountain, work under ground, so, latent and concealed are the deep and unfailing streams that gather into those reservoirs, which give delight and freshness to the world: yet, not the less for their silence and darkness have the streams flowed through countless veins and strata of the earth, in order that the waters of the fountain might sparkle in the face of day. From the hour of birth to the hour when genius breaks suddenly into fame, the education of the unconscious artist continues on its noiseless progress. The scenes that surrounded his childhood — the first incident that led the eye to observe, the reason to calculate, the heart to feel, the imagination to link together opposite associations, and from familiar materials to combine new forms — all these make an elementary tuition, more essential to the training of the poet than the conscious study of critical principles and æsthetical laws. There is, however, another species of poetical artists in whom we are better enabled to trace the process by

which they have worked out their genius — men who,
though not really more correct or artistical than those
in whom intellect seems to spring from the very wan-
tonness and luxuriance of the soil on which it grows,
are more palpably indebted to labour and to rules for
the accomplishment of their objects — men in whom
method and design are obvious and pervading, and in
whose fabrics, however wonderful and original, we can
detect the care that proportioned every column, the
cement that connected every stone. In the last century
arose two poets, though at a considerable interval from
each other, in whom these opposite principles of poetical
art were strongly contrasted, — Burns and Gray. We
have more knowledge respecting the formation of the
poetical character in Burns than we have respecting
most men of powers equally great; we know by what
influences he himself considered that his mind was
coloured and his imagination warmed, and we find
that it was from the simplest and most familiar sources
that he drew at once inspiration and art. We can
picture to ourselves the grave thoughtful boy thrown
into shade by his livelier brother, listening to the old
nurse's stories of "cantraips, giants, enchanted towers,
dragons, and other trumpery," in which the minstrel
himself recognised the "cultivation of the latent seeds."
He tells us that it was "the life of Sir William Wallace," which "poured the tide of Scottish prejudice into
his veins;" — The boyish pilgrimage on the fine
Sabbath-day to the Leglin wood — the partner in the
harvest that, at the age of sixteen, brought forth at
once the feelings long gathering within, and woke
poetry and love simultaneously — the convivial meetings with smugglers on the coast of Kirkoswald — all

these were the academical degrees through which Burns passed to the master-rank. His enthusiasm, his passions, his contemplative mind, his active physical organization, all contributed to the healthful animation which forms the charm of his works, and which, like the vital principle itself, not only gives to the material forms warmth and glow, but endows them also with symmetry, order, the poise and mechanism of power and motion, and all that makes poetry the art of nature, as "nature is the art of God." We know, indeed, nothing more of the secrets by which enthusiasm begot skill, by which tales of Sir William Wallace passed, in the eternal metempsychosis of the Creative Mind into the ode of "Scots wha hae wi' Wallace bled;" — by which passion, indignation, and regret could convert their bitterness into feelings so true expressed in melodies so artful as those embodied in his Poem to his Illegitimate Child, and in the manly pathos of his Lament. We know how the susceptibilities were awakened, but we cannot tell how they grew into poetry — we know, when the seed was sown, that the soil and the sun were favourable, but we cannot say by what changes in the hidden laboratory the seed broke into the blade and the blade ripened into the harvest. Why enthusiasm should make one man a missionary, another man a soldier, and a third a poet, must ever remain a mystery, which neither Helvetius nor Spurzheim can explain. Burns, though conscious of the influences which formed him into a poet, was unable to tell how he trained his genius into art, yet *an artist* he indisputably was, and it is astonishing how marvellously correct, both in details and as wholes, most of his writings are. He is

11 *

one of the most correct poets that the world has known.
In his smallest pieces the conception is thoroughly carried out; in his easiest lines there is never a word too
much nor too little; his simplicity has in it the best
characteristics of Grecian art.   He is a poet for critics,
and those songs which seem to gush so spontaneously
from the fervid heart of the writer would furnish the
severest lecturer with his happiest illustrations of classical concinnity and completeness.   That Burns was a
great genius every one knows, but the world has been
too apt to consider him, as the world once held Shake-
speare, to be somewhat rude and careless, and his
energy is more conceded than his skill. Yet, if a judicious reader were to take the trouble of comparing
some of the most familiar of his stanzas with the most
elaborate lines of the polished Pope, or the fastidious
Gray, it would be found that the merit of superior correctness would, in nine cases out of ten, be awarded
to Burns. Gray is, indeed, one of the most inaccurate,
precisely because one of the most artificial of poets.
Of this the melodious opening of his greatest and most
careful poem affords an example: —

"The curfew *tolls* the knell of parting day,
    The lowing herds wind slowly o'er the lea;
The ploughman *homeward plods his weary way,*
    And leaves the world to *darkness and to me.*
Now fades the glimmering landscape," &c.

That we may not appear hypercritical for the sake
of our own argument, we will borrow, with some abridg-
ment, the shrewd and sound observations that we find
in the edition we now review. (Appendix cxi.)   The

curfew tolls — 1st. The word *toll* is not the appropriate
verb — the curfew-bell was not a slow bell tolling for
the dead; 2ndly. Long before the curfew tolled the
ploughman *had* wended his way homeward; 3rdly. The
day was not *parting*, when the curfew tolled it had
long since *parted;* 4thly. If the world were left to
darkness in one line, how happens it, first, that in the
very next line — "the *glimmering* landscape fades?"
and, secondly, that we are almost immediately afterwards told that the moping owl is complaining to the
moon? These are not mere verbal criticisms; they are
proofs that the writer is incorrect in his whole picture;
because he does not portray what he is seeing, or has
seen; he is heaping together incongruous images about
evening, collected from books, and compiled in a study.
The incorrectness is equally perceptible in the whole
as in the details. In many other lines of this Elegy
(the beauties of which are, nevertheless, as indisputable
as they are striking), similar inaccuracies abound, more
or less venial 'in proportion as they are faults only in
the expression, such as the barbarism —

"Busy housewife *ply* her evening *care;*"

or the tautology of —

"For them no more the *blazing* hearth shall *burn;*"

or as they are faults in the truth of the image and the
thought, such as those we have touched upon in the
opening stanza. And this, the characteristic fault of
the fastidious Gray, had its origin in his seeking The
Correct in a wrong source, — not drawing it from

practical and actual *observation*, but from verbal rules, and often from graceful imitations of ancient poets. It was but rarely that Gray followed Sir Philip Sidney's advice, to "look in his heart and write."

But in Burns, inferior as was his education, imperfect his knowledge of the square and measure of the architects of verse, the wording is accurate, the picture complete, because, faithful to nature and to truth, he is uttering simply what he has observed, or expressing passionately what he has felt; — and criticism dies without a sign upon his descriptions of nature, or his revelations of sentiment.

In fact, as moral error consists partly in viewing only a portion of the truth, partly in want of faith as to the rest of the truth that it cannot discover, so incorrectness, which is the moral error of the poet, arises from a meagre experience, or from a lukewarm imagination. Hence that poet is, in the proper and scientific sense of the word, the most *correct* who combines the greatest acuteness of actual observation with the most vivifying power of creative enthusiasm.

Yet Gray was a great poet, though his faults lie precisely in the quarter whence his merits have been vulgarly drawn. He was not an accurate writer, and, in the larger and purer sense of the epithet, he was not a classical one; he was not classical, for he had neither the faith, the simplicity, nor the independent originality which constitute the characteristics of the poets of Greece. Learned he was, but the classical poets were not learned. Pindar's rapture never lived in the lyre of Gray, for Gray never knew what the rapture of poesy is. Painfully and minutely laborious, diffident of his own powers, weighing words in a balance,

borrowing a thought here, and a phrase there, Gray
wrote English as he wrote Latin.   It was a dead language to him, in which he sought to acquire an elegant
proficiency by using only the epithets and the phrases
rendered orthodox by the best models. But he was no
vulgar plagiarist — his very deficiency of invention
became productive of a beauty peculiarly his own, and
created a kind of poetry of association; so that in reading Gray we are ever haunted with a delightful and
vague reminiscence of the objects of a former admiration or love, as early things and thoughts that are recalled to us by some exquisite air of music, and in
some place most congenial to dreamlike recollections of
grace and beauty.

"If we glance over the Ode to Spring," the Rosy-
bosomed Hours bring us back to Homer and Milton,
"to paint the purple year" is a literal translation from
the Pervig. Vener. v. 13 *(purpurantem pingit annum)* —
the thought itself on which the ode turns Gray allows
to have been borrowed from Green. But in these con-
tributions, levied from all lands, the excellence of
Gray is felicitously displayed. That excellence was an
admirable delicacy of taste; the ear of his mind was
exquisitely attuned; all the notes he borrows he con-
nects into perfect concord with each other; — and
thought and rhyme are equally harmonious. His poems
are like cabinets of curious and costly gems — the
gems have been polished often by hands long mouldered
into dust, and have glittered in the coronals of many
a foreign muse, but it is for the first time that they
have been so artfully disposed in one collection, — so
well selected, so skilfully displayed. But still it will
be observed, that this dependence on the treasures of

others, this recourse to memory and to research, invariably drew the poet's attention from Nature herself.
Thus, in the Ode to Spring, it is *not* spring that Gray
describes. Let us examine: —

> " Where'er the oak's thick branches stretch
>   A broader, browner shade;
>   *   *   *   *
>   Still is the toiling hand of Care,
>   The panting herds repose;
>   Yet hark! how thro' the peopled air
>   The busy murmur glows!" —

— "the insect youth" that "float amid the liquid
noon," or "show their gaily-gilded trim, quick glanc-
ing to the sun;" these thoughts and lines depict, in
our climate at least, the summer and not the spring.
If Gray had thrown aside his commonplace books,
taken a stroll through the fields in April or May, and
allowed the fields to dictate to him, we should have
lost perhaps a thousand beauties of expression, but
we should have had a poem more consistent with the
truth.

But though in things external Gray is not an accurate painter, because, either not a close observer of
nature herself, or, what is more likely, not a faithful
translator of what he had observed, — yet in those
veins of sentiment and thought that streak with such
beauty the composition of his poems, he is usually
original and truthful. The *reflections* in his celebrated
Elegy — the sweet and tender pathos of the sentiment
that pervades the Ode to Eton College — are drawn
from deep and sincere springs. It is one characteristic

indeed of Gray, that he embodies thoughts the most simple in a style the most artificial.

As life itself is a constant school to all of us, so it is to his mode and habits of life that we must look for the distinguishing peculiarities of the author of the Elegy in a Country Churchyard. An accomplished, secluded, half-unsocial scholar — living for the most part in the learned cloisters of a college — slowly and indolently acquiring vast stores of graceful learning — his taste was naturally more cultivated than his imagination or his passions. It requires something of the bustle and stir of active existence to make a man lean firmly on his own powers, and to call into vivid reality the faculties that observe, imagine, and invent. But Gray, surrounded by men yet more idle than himself — remote from the emulation and excitement of the Republic of Letters — rather filled up his solitary leisure with conceptions of what might be done, than resolutions of what to do: —

"Ten thousand great ideas filled his mind,
But with the clouds they fled and left no trace behind."

Always drawing in new stores, his mind became over-laden with its own wealth, and over-refined and painfully fastidious, from the models which were perpetually before him. Too much honey clogged his wings. Thus made indolent and inert — and the materials and powers within him not being kept vigorous and active by any stimulus from the fierce objects of real life, — when he sate down to compose it was rather to arrange into a new and brilliant shape the expressions, the phrases, the curious felicities of words which he had

noted in his memory, than from the yearning of more
active poets to vent an oppressive emotion, or fix into
immortal being ideal aspirations and haunting visions.
It is singular to observe how frequently the conventual
life of colleges produces the same effect upon the mind.
It is the air of the Castle of Indolence that enervates
even the activity of thought: —

> "A listless climate made, where, sooth to say,
>   No living wight could work, no cared even for play."

In complete and total solitude, if not continued too
long, we are often so driven upon ourselves, that out
of leisure we beget excitement; and our own thoughts
so oppress us,, that we must throw them off by a constant exertion. In total solitude we grow egotists, and
egotism ever longs for a confessional. But this is not
the case with the half-solitude of the college and the
monastery. There, we have just enough of society to
make us indolent, just enough of solitude to make us
dreamers. Those around us have grown reconciled to
the routine of habit — the ablest and the most erudite
are satisfied with the reputation of their monotonous
circle — ambition is but a languid desire — there is
little opportunity to rise — there is no fear to fall.
Poverty does not sharpen the faculties — the hope of
wealth does not excite the passions. Young men who,
as undergraduates, gave the most brilliant promise —
consumed nights in toil — and renounced health, pleasure, all the gold of youth itself — in the desire of a
scholarship or a medal, become fellows and residents
— and emulation seems prostrate and exhausted. They
made a mighty effort in order to be still for ever. The

influence of such a society is wonderfully contagious —
and especially with a man like Gray, whom books
amused rather than excited, and whose fastidiousness
made him more fearful of failure than sanguine of
success. This considered, it is almost surprising that
Gray designed, and even that he did, so much, out of the
beaten track of his existence. And perhaps the slight
stimulus and energy that remained with him, and occasionally stirred his genius into painful action, were
the result of circumstances peculiar to himself in the
earlier part of his life. Maintained at the University
by the exertions of his mother, that very thought may
have inspired the son with the proud wish to repay
her sacrifices by distinction. His travels with Horace
Walpole — perhaps his companionship with that sharp
and acute observer — may have served to ripen such
seeds of energy as all the tares of after-sloth could not
utterly choke. If, on his return to England, he had
fulfilled his original purpose of selecting the legal profession, the forced stimulus of metropolitan life — its
daily and hourly demands upon emulation — the fever
it keeps up, fiercest in the most sensitive frames, might
have necessarily urged the shy proud man into the full
exercise of those powers which, even in their partial
exercise, were destined to attain to one of the most
eminent among the ranks of poetry; for, in proportion
to the pride and the reserve of a man of genius, does
he require a call, a demand, a stretch upon his faculties.
But the fates otherwise decreed. Gray went to Cambridge; and six years of his prime were devoted to
reading Greek!

Gray's odes, like those of Collins, were not popular
at first. An edition of a thousand copies seems to

have disappeared but slowly. His Elegy, as is well
known, spoke at once to the heart of the multitude,
and, at its very birth, it received the stamp of immortality. The reason perhaps of the different reception
accorded to these different species of poetry, is to be
found in a distinction carefully to be noted. Works
that address the common and household feelings —
the emotions — the heart — are brought to a speedy
and universal test. If not popular at first (supposing
that they come fairly before the public), the chances
are, that popular they will never be; like orations to
a multitude, their merit consists in their adaptation to
an audience that, in its main essentials, is always the
same. Hence novels that either excel in pathos or in
domestic interest spring at once into fame; and novels
once famous rarely die. We do not say as much for
romances, which are often but fantastic exaggerations
of a caprice in the public mind. 'Clelia' was as
popular at one time as the everlasting 'Clarissa' at
another. But works that address the taste, the reason,
or the mere fancy (that pale reflection of the imagination), are necessarily slow in their progress; because for
these works judges are more rare, and every man cannot test their merits — they depend upon the few —
they are made or unmade by critics — they do not fill
the atmosphere with a familiar though sudden light,
but are as torches handed from place to place by the
Initiated, until the illumination becomes general.

The ode of modern times, compared with its great
Greek original, must ever want something of its proper
vitality. There was but one age in which the grander
species of lyrical poetry flourished in its full vigour:
the age that preceded the Drama. It was then itself

a kind of drama, inseparably connected with music; not read, but represented before a mighty audience, on solemn occasions, dedicated to themes of national interest and exciting universal enthusiasm. The poetry of the ode had, therefore, essential accompaniments in music, and in a half-developed form of histrionic exhibition. It ceased in Greece as it became merged in the choral songs of the drama which it had served to create. Still, the ode of modern poetry will always be more true to its generical character in proportion as it retains its earliest connection with the lyre, and gives musical expression to such sentiments as are the most readily awakened in a mixed and popular audience. Hence a national hymn is perhaps the nearest approach to the ancient ode; and the 'Scots wha hae wi' Wallace bled,' the 'Mariners of England,' the 'Marseillaise Hymn,' — even 'God save the King,' and 'Henri Quatre,' — have in them more of the true spirit of the classic lyrists than the scholastic poems of Ogilvie, the formal choruses of Mason, or even the elaborate compositions of Gray. But whatever may be disputable as to the precise degree of merit due to Gray's odes, regarded merely in the lyrical character they assume, — as poems of exquisite harmony, splendid diction, and picturesque imagery, they must rank among the most fascinating productions in the language. *Picturesque*, indeed, is the proper epithet to apply to the genius of Gray. His poetry opens, in every winding of its involved sweetness, to such images and prospects as should serve to kindle the sister art. More than any writer of his age, he made words the paintings of things. Like Young, he seeks the attainment of this

object by personifications carried to a faulty excess; —
personifications that present but confused notions, and
are productive but of false glitter; thus, he cannot
speak of hope, but it is "Gay Hope by Fancy fed."
Not only Health is personified as of "rosy hue," but
Cheer also is raised to a rank in mythology, and "of
Vigour born." These unnecessary elevations of commonplace words tend to destroy the effect of the more
worthy and noble personifications (immediately following) of the fury Passions and the painful Family of
Death. Where every line raises an abstract thought
into a mythical being, sufficient boldness of relief cannot be given to those ideas of such inborn warmth and
life as, without an effort, become personifications. In
the 'Progress of Poetry' there is scarcely a line that
does not contain an abuse of that poetic licence which
renders the style animated if sparingly exercised; —
frigid if lavishly indulged. We could readily picture
to ourselves the rosy crowned Loves, even antic Sport
and blue-eyed Pleasures, if we were not overtasked by
being also called upon to believe in the actual in-
carnation of the "Shell:" who again is Parent of
"Airs," and whom "the Voice and Dance obey." Thus
are confused together those ideas which naturally represent persons, such as the Loves and Idalia, and
those ideas, such as an instrument of music, to which
no personification ever can be attached. Even the gorgeous and justly celebrated description of Cytherea
herself is greatly injured by this obtrusive impertinence.
We go with the poet while he tells us, —

"Where'er she turns the Graces homage pay;" —

we see the dream of Praxiteles embodied when we are told how,

> "With arms sublime that float upon the air,
> In gliding state she wins her easy way;" —

but the picture is suddenly lost, the vitality of the creation fades away, and we find but a show of words before us, when we are told that]

> "O'er her warm cheek and rising bosom move
> The bloom of young Desire, and purple light of Love."

Here Desire and Love being also personified, merely to express the goddess's complexion, the unity of the main personification of the Goddess herself is destroyed. What we took for the true Florimel changes into the false one, and the glow and motion of life melt into the shape of snow. We have the less reluctantly taken on ourselves the ungracious task of noting these faults in a great poet, because their very glitter blinds the young whom it dazzles, and conduces to imitations at variance with all pure taste and genuine feeling. Although we maintain that Gray's odes are not conceived in the true spirit of the national lyric, and although, even as poems, they are not without great faults, yet we cannot agree with the editor of the volumes before us, and with some other critics, that Gray would have found a more felicitous range for his genius in didactic poetry. In his fragment on Education and Government, he seems to us to lose all those distinctions which impart to his odes, however borrowed in details, an original stamp and impress when

viewed as wholes. In this fragment his style languishes
under the influence of Pope. The thoughts are battered
out into thin tautologies. Such as

> "those kindly cares
> That health and vigour to the soul impart,
> Spread the young thought, and warm the opening heart."

The incorrectness of his phraseology and metaphors becomes also more evident in the close confines of the
heroic metre: for instance, —

> "What wonder, in the sultry climes that spread
> Where Nile, redundant o'er his summer bed,
> From his broad bosom life and verdure flings,
> And broods o'er Egypt with his watery wings,
> If, with adventurous oar and ready sail,
> The dusky people drive before the gale?"

Here the people are *sailing* through something that we
were told, in the two lines immediately preceding, was
brooding over the land with "watery wings;" the Nile
as a person, and the Nile as a river, being both before
us in the same sentence and in utterly opposite senses.
These faults do not appear to us redeemed by any
great vigour of thought or largeness of conception in
the subject and opening of the poem itself. And we
very much doubt whether, with all his learning, Gray
had sufficient grasp of mind, or sufficient confidence in
his own originality and depth, for a great philosophical
poem.

The character of Gray's poetry, to a certain extent,
pervades his correspondence. It is true, as we shall
again notice before we conclude this article, that his

style in prose was essentially different from his style in verse; yet in both there is the same fastidious mind — the same curious and varied learning, accompanied by that happy and elegant neatness of humour in which his lighter poems excel. We think that his correspondence is also stamped by the main defect of his poetry — it wants *heartiness.* It would be unfair to say of a man to whom national gratitude is due, and whose secret nature we can do no more than conjecture, that he lacked warmth of heart; yet that warmth is not visible where we would look for it most. To the letters of his early friend, West, which are often so beautifully touching — letters full of the inexpressive yearnings — the aching desires — the morbid yet gentle infirmities of the poetical temperament — his replies seem dry and unsympathizing. Even when poor West, condemned to a death too early for himself, and perhaps for the world, writes of the cough "that will go on, shaking and tearing me for half an hour together;" and when, in that melancholy play with disease, which has so much pathos in its humour, the young poet sends him those painful Latin verses on his malady, beginning with

"Ante omnes morbos importunissima tussis," &c., —

Gray's jesting answer, "You are the first who ever made a muse of a cough," jars strangely upon the moral taste. When Gray writes to Wharton that his aunt had had a stroke of the palsy, he dismisses the complaint in a line or two, and hurries on to gossip about Lady Swinburne — Grapes — Evelyn on Forest Trees — Oats, Barley,' and Beans. In another letter to Mason (alluding to the will of the deceased, who

left him joint executor with another of his aunts) he
wittily says, "He has been dividing nothing with an
old woman." Nay, when the mother whom he seems
really to have loved better than anything else in the
world, and to whom he was so deeply indebted, ex-
pires, he says shortly and drily to Wharton, "My poor
mother, after a long and painful struggle for life, expired on Sunday morning; when I have seen her
buried I shall come to London, and it will be a particular satisfaction to me to find you there. If you can
procure me a tolerable lodging near you," &c.

Whatever affections Gray possessed, they do not
seem to gush forth vividly and freely. And we suspect that it was this moral torpor or frigidity which
chilled the current of his poetical fancy, and makes us
feel, even in his most elaborate and fervid splendours
of diction, a certain want of the fire of human passion,
and the impatient eloquence of genuine emotion. There
is indeed always something wanting to inspiration —
something stinted in genius — wherever we cannot
discover an acute susceptibility to the affections. Yet,
so curiously constituted are we human beings, that it
was from, perhaps, this deficiency, that Gray derived
many of the excellences of his character — his calm
of temper, so free from the irritability and jealousies of
the literary commonwealth — his philosophical spirit
of independence (the offspring of his indifference to the
common but passionate objects for which men barter
away their freedom of will) — the stately, yet not hypo-
critical, decorum of morals to which the lively world-
liness of Walpole was unable to mould itself. In the
even balance of all his emotions Gray preserved himself from every vice; — virtuous generally, inasmuch

as he carried no one virtue into a passion. Ambition
never allured, Pleasure never intoxicated, Love never
engrossed him. His inspiration, as we before said,
was a highly cultivated taste operating on a most harmonious ear. It must, however, be observed, while
we are on the subject of his taste, that, though his
judgment upon ancient literature was most felicitous,
refined, and just, he failed lamentably in a right appreciation of his contemporaries: While he expresses an
admiration that does for once carry him into enthusiasm for the hollow rant of Ossian, he speaks with the
utmost contempt of the *talent* of the 'Nouvelle Heloise.'
Of Collins, his rival, he says, "that he deserved to
last some years, but will not." Of 'Joseph Andrews,'
he observes, "that the incidents are ill-laid and without invention, but the characters have a great deal of
nature." And "Parson Adams is *perfectly well!*" He
evidently rates that wonderful fiction very little above
the run of novels, and hurries away with complacent
preference to Marivaux and Crebillon. He thinks David
Hume "continued all his days an infant, but had unhappily been taught to read and write." He considers
Voltaire only showed genius in his dramas. This
want of the "prophetic eye" as to contemporaries is the
more remarkable, as Gray appears particularly free from
jealousy. After all, Dr. Johnson has been hardly
treated for his criticism on our author, for the Doctor
never spoke so disparagingly of Gray as Gray himself
spoke of the most illustrious books and men of his
own time. It was as if the vast quantity of ancient
furniture which the Poet had collected together, and
skilfully arranged in his memory, prevented the intrusion of anything new from being received with wel-

come. He had formed his mind as his friend Walpole formed his castle of Twickenham, only for the museum of a particular class of antiques and curiosities. Although there is no such thing, perhaps, as too much *knowledge*, there certainly is such a thing as too much *reading*, especially when the reading is not made a part of a system, or conducive to some definitive object. It is like crowding the memory with problems from which no new corollary is to be deduced. Gray read till it became a mechanical habit with him indolently to take in learning — which, from the want of vigorous habits of writing, was never fairly digested into knowledge. — With all his accomplishments in classical lore, in history, heraldry, antiquities, architecture, botany, &c., there was no subject which he seems to have known thoroughly, or from which he strikes new results. He acquired rather than studied. He contemplated rather than thought.

Gray's *style* in prose, as exhibited in his correspondence, is confessedly delightful. Though somewhat quaint, it is an easy quaintness. He was infinitely more natural in prose than verse. Horace Walpole lets us into the secret of this. "Gray," says that piercing reader of such characters as came within the scope of his actual observation, "*never wrote anything easily but things of humour;*" — and humour, his natural gift, is the characteristic of his correspondence. If not the best letter-writer in the language, he is the best letter-writer of all the professed *scholars*. Addison himself does not more happily combine humour with elegance; nor can even Walpole throw a more intellectual grace over familiar trifles.

Besides whatever other causes might contribute to

Gray's artificial construction in poetry, one is to be found, perhaps, in the fashion of the time. As each age of eminent writers usually proves its emancipation from the prescriptive shackles of the last, by a total contrast of manner and style, so the concise and easy fluency of Addison, Swift, and Steele, and the spontaneous and unsought nobleness, the *senatorius decor*, of Bolingbroke's diction were, in the early part of the reign of George III., forsaken by authors of great influence and renown, for a phraseology and mode of expression eminently artificial. Words were built up into palaces, no matter how commonplace the thought that was to inhabit them. Johnson, Gibbon, Junius, even Burke (though less systematically), seem to have avoided, as a rock, the periods and expressions into which the English language would naturally fall in conversation. Criticism as well as authorship, in that day, occupied itself with exclusive care to these *verborum minutiæ*. Whatever critical review then existent we look into, we find two words given to the thought of the author and fifty to his style. It was a matter of grave dispute, not only by Gray and his correspondents, but by the commonest Scaligers of a periodical, whether antiquated words are to be admitted into modern poems — whether such and such epithets have been used by the best authors — whether the rhymes of "obscure" and "poor" be not a serious objection to a whole poem — with a hundred other frivolities — the topknots and patches of the muse. Criticism itself was never (scarcely even in our own day) so unconscious of its own great principles. Gray, whose prose writings were almost wholly confined to epistles, could not have exercised in that province,

from which not even critics could pretend to banish the
only appropriate charm of the Familiar, the new ideas
of art that flourished amongst the eloquent and learned.
He, therefore, poured the contemporaneous spirit of
prose into verse, which was the sole form of composition he took up as an art. In this, to a certain degree,
Young, Akenside, and Thomson were his rivals. But
Gray, from labour and research, surpassed them all in
artificial pomp and rhetorical melodies.

As is more often the case than the world supposes,
in Gray the man and the poet appear in perfect harmony with each other — the whole being was graceful,
fastidious, painstaking, and artificial. We see the poet
in the fair stiff character of the handwriting, in the
neatness of dress, precise "even to a degree of finical-
ness and effeminacy," in the grave formality of mien and
manner; and even, if we might venture on a poor joke,
there is something characteristic of the author in his
aversion to *fire*. We can readily believe that, when
at his ease, his natural vein of humour broke forth,
and that he was a charming companion, too widely accomplished to be a pedant; as readily can we understand that, with the high-born and uncongenial Walpole, the proud scholar was the "worst company in the
world" — "so circumspect in his language, that it
seemed unnatural though it was only pure English!"
The commonest traits recorded of his habits are characteristic: even to the flowers arranged in his windows
and about his room, and the extraordinary exactness
and order of "his books, papers, and all his chattels."
He is said, somewhere, never to have been on horseback in his life. We can believe it. There was something too rudely vigorous in that hearty exercise to

suit with our notions of the "formal, plump person," the
delicate features, and the "too much dignity" of the man.

The influence of Gray's poetry has not passed
away, though it be not very visibly traced. It is true
that Runic Odes and Elegies on Ruins no longer fill
our magazines; but the spirit survives the form in
which it breathed. Gray was the first to pay elaborate
attention to the glitter of epithets and the ornate and
overburthened richness of diction. We may detect his
influence wherever we now find these characteristics.
We look round in vain for inheritors of the simple
graces of Goldsmith, but Gray lives again in that wide
host of bards who seem to think of the Muse as peasants think of the Queen, that she cannot walk in the
garden without a crown and sceptre — "with gems on
all her fingers and rings on all her toes!"

Perhaps in that reaction of taste reserved for some
succeeding generation it will be discovered how much
the glare of diction — the profuse pomp of each individual line — mar the effect and unity of a poem;
how much they tend to break up the whole work into
glittering fragments, and how much the strength and
simplicity of passion are enfeebled by an excess of
vocabular decoration.

Gray lamented, at the close of his life, that he
had done so little in literature. He had done enough
to secure immortality, and, so far as vanity and pride
could administer consolations to indolence, he had therefore no cause for regret. But, coupling the expression
of that complaint with the association of the time when
it was uttered, and when his feet were on the threshold of

"The warm precincts of the cheerful day,"

we incline to hope that he thought rather of his species
than himself — rather of stores of instruction and delight lost for ever to the world, than of additional
laurels to an imperishable name. That he had done
so little, as we before said, we do not wonder, viewing
his mode of life, his diffidence of his powers, and,
above all, the lukewarm character of those passions
which are at once the nerves and pulses of the soul.
In more busy and exciting life, in which the energies
might have been strained, the affections kept in exercise, and solitary genius and human interests have been
brought into closer connexion, Gray might have been
not what shallow moralists would consider a more
virtuous or a more blameless man, but one who would
have left far larger legacies to mankind. We might
not have gazed with cold approval on the same calm
regularity of life; we might have recognised more errors, but we might have received more benefits. When
we avoid the temptations of active life and a stirring
career, no error may be detected in us, yet we are less
really virtuous than men in whom many errors are
visible, but by whom a greater number of temptations
have been resisted, and in whom virtues have produced
wider and more social results. He who is deeply impressed either with the holiness of a cause, or the
value of the truths he preaches to mankind, is not of
that sober but unsound philosophy which keeps him
free from the disputes and contests of his kind. Those
from whom the world derives most are usually men of
strong passions and large social sympathies — the passions and the sympathies lead them into many errors,
and call out all, whether of good or evil, that the
genial warmth of their human nature can conceive;

but we must take the evil with the good, nor quarrel with the winds that make the life and freshness of the intellect, though they sometimes produce a storm. It is not only the philosopher of whom it may be justly said, that, had he not erred, he would have done less (*si non errasset fecerat ille minus*) — the same must be often said of patriots, reformers, poets. Where we have most to be grateful for, there we have often most to forgive. This consideration may induce us to forgive the error, not for the sake of the error, but for the sake of the counterbalancing virtue.

Still, while the world fastens with delighted avidity upon the occasional infirmities or excesses of men whose crests shone in every field, whose barks ploughed every sea, in which a glory could be won or a truth discovered for their species, — while it condemns them for the very heat and force of the nature which kindled and produced so much, — we must not wonder at the comparative indolence of genius grown an egotist — of literature preferring the cloister to the crowd; — we must not wonder that the prudent should shrink from earning the racks of an inquisition as a consequence of discoveries in truth, and hug themselves in the security of that applause which awaits an intellect that, suppressing passion, is contented to obtain renown with the fewest possible indiscretions and the smallest possible service to mankind.

SIR THOMAS BROWNE.

[First published in 'THE EDINBURGH REVIEW,' October, 1836.]

SIR THOMAS BROWNE.

Sir Thomas Browne's Works, *including his Life and Correspondence.* Edited by SIMON WILKIN, F.L.S. 4 vols. 8vo. London, 1836.

THE name of Sir Thomas Browne is one of considerable importance in the history of English literature. His writings made a strong impression on his own time, and they still command, among all who turn for inspiration and delight to our earlier authors, a vivid admiration. Johnson has been his biographer; Coleridge and Hazlitt his critics; but we are yet without any dispassionate estimate of his works, or any clear analysis of the texture and character of his mind. The hard sense of Johnson was not calculated to enter into the visionary and ecstatic enthusiasm of the Knight of Norwich; nor did his critical canons furnish him with an adequate rule whereby to test a philosophy that had nothing of the severity of logic, or a style which did not derive its singular beauties from the methodical correctness of its arrangement, or the regular cadence of its periods. Johnson never once appears to be alive to the *poetry* of Browne, whether as exhibited in his diction or his thoughts. He never examines, much less accounts for, the startling phenomena of an intellect that reconciled so many extremes

— in some things so devout, in others so sceptical.
The sturdy rejector of vulgar errors was yet the credulous believer in witchcraft; and the philosopher, who
"had of the earth such a minute and exact geographical
knowledge, as if he had been by Divine Providence
ordained surveyor-general of the whole terrestrial orb," *
could pause amidst his gravest chapters to notice the
old story in Ælian about Æschylus and the eagle, as
an argument against the system of Copernicus.** Johnson acknowledges Browne to have been a very eminent
man; but it is principally to his erudition that the
homage is rendered. Of his style the author of Rasselas
says, "It strikes but does not please . . .   His tropes
are harsh, and his combinations uncouth." The Doctor
allows that he has "great excellences," as well as
"great faults." But what these excellences are, is very
unsatisfactorily explained by antitheses applied principally to mere diction; or by praises like the following: — "His innovations are sometimes pleasing, and
his temerities happy."   And when the Doctor very
sensibly observes that "it is on his own writings that
Browne is to depend for the esteem of posterity," we
are scarcely prepared for this saving sentence — "of

* 'Some Minutes for the Life of Sir Thomas Browne.' By
John Whitefoot, M.A., reprinted in Johnson's Life.

** "It is no small disparagement unto baldness, if it be true
what is related by Ælian concerning Æschylus, whose bald
pate was mistaken for a rock, and so was brained by a tor-
toise which an eagle let fall on it. Some men, critically disposed, would from hence confute the opinion of Copernicus,
never conceiving how the motion of the earth below should
not wave him from a knock perpendicularly directed from a
body in the air above." — Browne's Works, vol. m. p. 365.

which he will not easily be deprived while *learning*
shall have any reverence among men." Learning
Browne, certainly had — learning vast and varied.
But his learning forms a very small part of his claims
to the attention of posterity; and, had he only that
merit to depend upon, we suspect that Mr. Wilkin
would not have employed nearly twelve years of his
life on the present edition of Browne's works, nor
ourselves have willingly devoted twelve pages to his
memory. A reader even superficially acquainted with
Sir Thomas Browne, will be amused to perceive the
uneasy pains with which the grave lexicographer en-
deavours to tame down the wild and eccentric subject
upon which he has fallen, to his own level of probable
motives and ordinary conduct. He is convinced that
the first surreptitious edition of the *Religio Medici* "was
conveyed to the press by a distant hand," so that the
circulation of a false copy might be an excuse for
publishing the true; and then gently moralizes upon a
fraud which he himself invents, as "inimical to the
confidence which makes the happiness of society."
Undoubtedly, the stratagem supposed by Johnson has
been practised by some authors; but one more egre-
giously foreign to the majestic self-esteem of Browne, or
more contradicted by all internal evidence, could not
well have occurred to the ingenuity of conjecture.
When, in the spirit of his gorgeous and Platonic mys-
ticism, Browne asserts that "his life has been a miracle
of thirty years, which to relate were not history, but
a piece of poetry," Johnson can only observe, that "a
man may visit France and Italy, reside at Montpellier
and Padua, and at last take his degree at Leyden,
without anything miraculous." He fairly confesses that

he believes there is no hope of guessing rightly at the
signification of this arrogant boast; and then proceeds
himself to guess that it is but the conclusion at which
every human being, if he had leisure and disposition
to recollect his thoughts and actions, might arrive.

If Johnson, from want of sympathy with the Abstract
and the Visionary, gives no satisfactory analysis of
Browne as an author and a man, Coleridge and Hazlitt,
unfitted for the task by a fault precisely the reverse,
do not appear to us to supply the deficiency. Hazlitt
himself has disposed of the remarks of his eloquent
contemporary with concise and summary justice. But
when he favours us with his own definitions, it is not
Browne criticised, but Browne imitated. Deep calleth
unto deep. The Obscure of the author is elucidated
by the Unintelligible of the commentator. What can
we possibly learn of Browne by being told that "the
antipodes are next-door neighbours to him, and dooms-
day is not far off;" "that nature is too little for the
grasp of his style — that it is as if his books had
dropped from the clouds, or Friar Bacon's head could
speak."* If the "romantic prettinesses" of Coleridge
had not thrown much light upon the subject, certainly
no better success has attended the cloudy metaphors
and colossal conceits of Hazlitt.

We had hoped that an edition professing to contain
so complete a collection of the works of so singular an
author — an edition which, as already mentioned, occupied the labours of the editor for nearly twelve years
— would have supplied the want of which we com-
plain; — filled up an important gap in historical criti-

* Hazlitt's 'Lectures on Dramatic Literature,' p. 293.

cism; — and presented the general reader with a clear
and elaborate view of the merits and peculiarities of
one, nor the least, of those gigantic writers, who conducted the progress of language and of mind through
that memorable interval which, commencing with the
imperial pomp of Bacon, closed with the stern simplicity of Locke. This task has not, however, been
included in the designs of the editor. He has attached,
indeed, to the biography by Johnson a supplementary
memoir, which exhibits great research and care, and
furnishes us with some novel information. But what
we principally desired is still. wanting. We confess we
do not very greatly care whether the Christian name
of Browne's father-in-law was Sir Ralph or Sir Thomas;
nor are we highly interested in the information afforded
to the worthy editor by "Augustus Brigstocke, Esq.,
of Blaenpant, county Cardigan," — that "Anne, sixth
daughter of Sir Edward Browne (eldest son of Sir
Thomas) had no children." These, and other matters
of genealogical knowledge, furnished , to us by the industry of the editor, we think might have been ad-
vantageously exchanged for an enlightened criticism of
the author's works, and a searching and candid appreciation of his intellectual character; assisted by such
evidence as may be collected from his own correspondence, and testimony of his contemporaries. But to
this negative complaint, not of what he has done, but
what he has omitted, we confine our animadversions
on Mr. Wilkin's execution of his pleasing duty. He
has enriched this edition not only with some of Browne's
miscellaneous essays hitherto unpublished, but with a
mass of interesting and valuable correspondence; and
in this he has provided many materials for the task,

which too modestly he has declined himself to accomplish.

Thomas Browne, descended from an ancient family in Cheshire, was born in 1605, educated at Winchester and Oxford, took his degree of master of arts, practised physic in Oxfordshire, travelled into Ireland, thence into France, Italy, and Holland, obtained his doctor's degree at Leyden, and settled as a physician at Shipden Hall, near Halifax. So far there is nothing peculiar in what we know of his history. His record is not in restless actions, but in adventurous and roving thoughts. He wrote a book, and his true history began. This work, entitled *Religio Medici* (the Religion of a Physician), lay for several years unknown to the public. The writer professed to consider it but an exercise to himself, "contrived in his private study," and not intended for publication. There is no reason to dispute the assertion. But it was shown to friends — it was transcribed by admirers — and in the seventh or eighth year its composition, an anonymous and very incorrect edition of it found its way into the press. It attracted, at its first appearance, the attention of the subtlest minds. Sir Kenelm Digby reviewed it for the satisfaction of my Lord Dorset. The author acknowledged and revised it — edition followed edition — annotators enriched, scholars translated it. Some found the author an Atheist, others a Papist. Alexander Ross sought to crush it with a hostile reply; Levin Nicol von Moltke, to bury it with notes; Guy Patin speaks of the impression it made in Paris — confesses the book has *des gentilles choses*, but doubts its orthodoxy, and half regrets the man is alive, "because he may grow worse, not better:" Buddeus reviled all phy-

sicians, in wrath at the impiety of the English doctor;
while, with greater justice, Conringius fervently wished
every theologian were as pious. Thomas Browne, the
obscure practitioner, rose at once to a level with the
most famous wits and the most erudite dreamers of the
time. In the interval between the composition and
the formal publication of this remarkable work, the
young physician had married the daughter of a Norfolk
gentleman, and settled at Norwich. Four years after
its publication appeared the *Pseudodoxia Epidemica*, or
'Inquiries into Vulgar and Common Errors,' a work of
brilliant learning and consummate ingenuity. Browne's
name was now established. Scholars pressed on him
their correspondence upon subjects the most various;
criticisms and encomiums were showered upon his head;
and, at last, as a climax or a bathos to his career, he
was knighted at Oxford by Charles the Second.

The most remarkable of Browne's subsequent works
are — 'The Garden of Cyrus, or the *Quincuncial
Lozenge*, or Net-work Plantations of the Ancients,
Artificially, Naturally, Mystically considered;' and
'*Hydriotaphia;* Urn Burial, or a Discourse on the Se-
pulchral Urns found in Norfolk.' In his miscellaneous
tracts, as throughout his whole correspondence, may
be found proofs of his grasping and inquisitive mind,
his multiform and copious knowledge; but on the four
works enumerated, viz. — The *Religio Medici*, the 'Inquiries into Vulgar and Common Errors,' the 'Garden
of Cyrus,' and the 'Urn Burial,' — rests his fame as
a writer of extraordinary powers of thought and language. It is the general characteristics of these writings that we propose briefly to examine.

It seems to us that a principal error of those who

13*

have bewildered themselves and their readers in endeavouring to describe and dissect the genius of Browne
— who have been so much at a loss to account for its
singularities and contradictions, and who have only
attempted to seize its subtle spirit in meshes of antithesis and hyperbole — arises from this cause: they
have regarded the man apart from his age — they
have set him up as a moral curiosity, who thought ·
"that the proper object of speculation was by darken-
ing knowledge to breed speculation," and who "loved
to converse chiefly with the spectral apparitions of
things;" — they have thought (and what is worse,
written) of a man living in the seventeenth century as
if he were living in our own day — as if he *voluntarily*
adopted the strange errors, and, from constitutional
temperament, combined the motley paradoxes they
find in him — as if he insisted upon rounding every
study with a dream, and losing every fancy in a labyrinth. The result of this view is, that they have represented a very enlightened and studious man as a
rare and incomprehensible anomaly that never existed
out of Laputa, and had no archetype except in that
illustrious philosopher who passed his time extracting
sunbeams from cucumbers.

But the moment we begin to look around us — to
contemplate the literary character of the time — to
compare the psychological nature of the man with that
of his contemporaries, the mystery dies away; the
marvellous fades into sober colours; and Sir Thomas
Browne, like most other men of genius, is but an
author of great imagination and original habits of
thought and study, reflecting back upon us the fantastic light that he received from the influences that

gathered and played around him. In the earlier stages of the literature of a nation, the demarcations between prose and poetry are comparatively faint and confused. The prodigal superstitions, the credulous errors, from which men emerge into the dawn of truth, still linger around the footsteps of the hardiest adventurers. They enter the domains of reason guided by the imagination, and carry not only the language but the temperament of poetry into the severest provinces of prose. Whoever looks into our own early literature will find a strong illustration of this general truth. When, fresh from the giant impulse of the Reformation, the intellect of England broke forth under Elizabeth, a variety of causes combined to quicken and exalt the imagination. The defiance of Rome — the discovery of America — the effects of the press — the almost simultaneous burst of the Greek, the Roman, the Italian poetry upon the wonder and emulation of men, born precisely at an age when thought was most broadly and deeply agitated by political circumstances — were not events that tended to divide the poet from the philosopher. On the contrary, no channel of research, however guarded and fenced about, could resist the rush of the great deeps so universally broken up. Poetry flowed into every course, and sparkled upon every wave, in which men could launch what Bacon has so nobly called the "ships of time." The Greek and Italian authors exercised to the utmost the strength of the language to find adequate translation for their unfamiliar beauties — a profusion of new words and new combinations was the result of the new ideas — the nervous and concise Saxon style became gorgeous with foreign riches, while its periods grew long and stately

to the swell of a borrowed music, and, oppressed with
their own triumphs, marched, laden and encumbered,
amidst the spoils of nations. Whoever turns from
Chaucer and his earlier successors to the literature of
Elizabeth and James, will see how completely the
revolution, produced in great measure by translations,
had changed the genius of the language from the
simple to the splendid. The wonderful translation of
the Bible familiarized the ear to, and coloured the
language with, the expressions of the East. The Reformation was our Pisistratus — the translation of the
Bible was our Homer. A new inspiration and a new
audience were produced; for the most popular book in
England was the most glorious poetry in the world.

To the sacred volume, which, in a form at once
popular yet sublime, was brought home to every man's
breast, succeeded the marvels of classical invention.
The gigantic images of Homer — the royal majesty
of Virgil — were contrasted, or wildly amalgamated,
with the chivalrous grotesque of Ariosto, the adventures of Tancred, the enchanted gardens of Armida.
Even in history — the boasted province of fact, the
fictitious embellishment was the first imparted to the
popular mind of England; and the romances of Plutarch
were cherished and admired long before our ancestors
appreciated the grave profundity of Thucydides — the
tragic epigram of Tacitus.

These importations were hailed with the delight of
novel impressions. Of acquisitions so important a
scholar could not but parade his knowledge; quotations,
and allusions, and authorities crowded his pages and
guided his conclusions. He did not only quote the
authors, he believed in them. He supported an axiom

out of Plutarch or Ælian. If he could have written a treatise upon the doctrine that two and two make four, he would have been enchanted to find a passage in Ovid's Metamorphoses to authorize the proposition. What coloured his thoughts animated his style. Living amidst poetry, its soil clung to his steps whenever he walked abroad. His disquisitions required little more than the mere form of verse in order to become poems. To say nothing of the 'Arcadia' of Sir Philip Sidney, the exceeding popularity of which attests the taste of those scholastic coteries that then constituted "THE PUBLIC," we have only to open the 'Advancement of Learning,' to see how the Attic bees clustered above the cradle of the new philosophy. Poetry pervaded the thoughts, it inspired the similes, it hymned in the majestic sentences of "the wisest of mankind." A very masculine sense — a very observant and inductive mind, in Bacon, prevented the imagination getting the better of the reason; and to those natural gifts must be added the soberizing effect of an early entrance into life — the dry pursuits of law and politics — and a vast practical knowledge of mankind. But the sense of Bacon was not exempt from the prejudices, any more than his style was devoid of the poetry, of the time. He who wrote the *Novum Organum* did not disbelieve in witchcraft. In fact, as some kings have transmitted to posterity, in their single person, the image and representative of all that is glorious in an age, so James I., not as a monarch but a student, embodied all of his own time — except the glory; he had the learning and the pedantry, though not the genius, of the age; he had an unlimited credulity, and an insatiable appetite for the mar-

vellous; he had the notion that in apophthegms, and
aphorisms, and historical fables, and poetical maxims
lay the craft of government and the philosophy of experience; he quoted all the Latin he could remember;
and he believed unhesitatingly in ghosts and witches.
All these were not the exclusive peculiarities of James I.;
they were the characteristics of the great bulk of
English scholars in his time. It was reserved for a
vicious and degenerate period to correct the literary
faults of a virtuous and a great one. There are two
cures to the errors that belong to superstition; one is
the influence of an experimental philosophy, the other
is that of a gay and polite scepticism. Perhaps the
wit and ease, the profligacy and *insouciance* of the
court of Charles II. did as much as causes more solemn
and acknowledged, to counteract the old Gothic superstition; and the light hand of court poets and court
freethinkers brushed away from the page of philosopher
and poet the clinging devotion of the old beliefs, and
the gorgeous pedantry of the old expressions. The
short and clear succinctness of the French diction began
to break up the colossal sentences of the earlier English.
The petulant and lively spirit of French disquisition
began to undermine the bastions and outworks with
which men had fenced round the citadels of their
faith. Time, in its usual progress, and the mighty
events of the Civil War, had raised up new generations
of thoughtful and anxious men; who, by combining
research with practical ends, took philosophy out of
the fairy meads in which, with dreams peopling every
tree, she had so long wandered. To a small and
scholastic, well-born and accomplished tribunal of
readers, succeeded a large, and miscellaneous, and

sturdy public. A popular style, and popular subjects, were necessary to ensure popular favour; gradually our literature lost its euphuism, and went back to something of its Saxon origin. It was not for gallant and graceful nobles, intoxicated with the Italian Helicon, and "enamelling with pied flowers their thoughts of gold,"* neither was it for clerkly and enthusiastic students, making their memory the museum for all antiquities, that Locke wove his plain and unembellished periods. It was in the wide circle of a stern and a practical public that he found space to wield the iron flail that demolished those stately and glittering errors, which, in a preceding generation, were the idols of the wise. But, while a growing people became the audience of the philosopher, who shall say how far a licentious court, with which nothing was too sacred for a jest, prepared the way for his opinions? The Rochesters were the pioneers of the Lockes.

But it was before this second revolution began — it was while, indeed, the fashion of composition, at once pedantic and poetical, which characterised the reign of James, was daily growing more pedantic and more poetical under that of his unfortunate son, till it found its euthanasia amidst the Latin flowers with which Milton crowned and buried it, that Sir Thomas Browne received his intellectual education and lavished its fruits. Though he lived on amidst the wits and freethinkers of the time of Charles II., "he wore the cloke and bootes" of the old style. He probably read little of the works of his younger contemporaries; for in his correspondence he scarcely notices the cur-

* Sir Philip Sidney's 'Arcadia'.

rent literature of his day.   Even Hudibras — the
opinions, the learning, the humour of which must have
been delightful to his taste — appears only to draw
from him an erudite comment upon the antiquity of
burlesque poems.*   He seems more at home with
Hipponactes than with Samuel Butler.   He continued
to the last to live apart and aloof, among his ancient
authors, and his quaint but sublime thoughts; a
scholar by habit, a philosopher by boast, and a poet
by nature.

Viewing Browne, then, in this light, associated
with such of his contemporaries as were similarly
educated, placed, and influenced, the more startling
contradictions in his intellectual character are easily
solved.   It is true that, with a luminous understanding and a cautious and, in some respects, sceptical
mind, he believed in witchcraft.   But so did others,
with even broader views and acuter comprehension.
Bacon, but little his senior in time, and far less inclined by temper to revere ancient belief erroneously
propped on scriptural authorities, was no wiser upon
this point.   The marvellous so largely entered into
the temperament of every scholar, that, if checked in
one channel, it was sure to cast its humours through
another.   Sir Kenelm Digby, who gravely argues
against astrology, believed in the wonderful effects
of sympathetic powders — is respectfully doubtful of
chiromancy — but persuaded that "at the approach
of the murderer, the slain body suddenly bleeds again."
If, when asked by "My Lord Chief Baron" whether
the fits of an old woman were from disease or the

* See 'Works,' vol. iv. p. 253.

Devil, Sir Thomas Browne answered, that "they were heightened by the Devil co-operating with the malice of the witches," we are not to find his excuse in Dr. Aiken's slovenly dogma, that in his mind "fancy and feeling were predominant over judgment," nor to adopt all the fantastic apologies of pseudo-metaphysical admirers. His excuse was in the trial itself — in a Lord Chief Baron (who, much more a man of the world than the studious physician, should have been a much deeper philosopher in such a case) putting the question, and summing the evidence — in a jury of twelve men finding a verdict of guilty. There was nothing in Browne's genius or in his studies — we do not say that should have rendered him wiser than Bacon — but wiser than twelve Englishmen, with a Lord Chief Baron to boot, upon a matter of witchcraft, then almost a matter of religion. Nay, his very learning only plunged him deeper into error; since it supplied his memory with all past instances of witchcraft, sacred and profane, and even assured him "there had been a great discovery of witches lately in Denmark!" Still less can we wonder at the Knight's leaning towards astrology; or (with Newton, equally cautious as bold, in our recollection) at an amusing curiosity about the philosopher's stone. The truth of the saying of Luther, that "the human mind is like a drunken peasant on horseback — set it up on one side and it falls on the other," — is startlingly visible, if applied to the giants of the past when examined by the merest pigmies of the present. The great men who have lived before us have lighted us from their knowledge to a survey of their follies. While we breathe and move, while we imagine and invent, we ourselves are laying up new stores for the ridicule of posterity.

Like his contemporaries, Browne's thoughts were strongly steeped in a passion for the marvellous and recondite; like his contemporaries, he was a reverent and enthusiastic scholar; and with his contemporaries he shared also the redundant periods — the florid diction — the exuberant poetry, which were thought to give classic beauty and importance to prose. How much in these latter attributes he resembles the greatest of his coævals may be seen on comparison with Jeremy Taylor and Milton.

When all that belongs to poetry, except the rhythm, glowed from the sober pulpit, or found its melodious way into the ungenial and angry elements of political dispute, or theological dissertation, there is no reason why critics should be so amazed to behold it bright and living in the pages of enthusiastic reverie or ideal contemplation. This poetical spirit pervaded the reasoning, as well as the expressions, of the writers of that time. When Jeremy Taylor wishes to prove the insensible progress of "a man's life and reason," he does not set about it by a syllogism, but a picture. He is not contented with a simple illustration — he raises up an elaborate landscape. "As when the sun approaches towards the gates of the morning, he first opens a little eye of heaven, and sends away the spirits of darkness, and gives light to a cock, and calls up the lark to matins, and, by and by, gilds the fringes of a cloud, and peeps over the eastern hills, thrusting out his golden horns like those which decked the brow of Moses, when he was forced to wear a veil, because himself had seen the face of God, and still, while a man tells the story, the sun gets up higher, till he shows a fair face and a full light, and then he shines one whole day, under a cloud often, and sometimes weeping great and little showers; even so is a man's reason and his life!"

It is in the same poetical spirit of *painting* thoughts, that Browne often convoys to us his meaning. Thus, at the close of his 'Garden of Cyrus,' wishing to denote that it is late, he tells us "that the Hyades (the Quincunx of Heaven) run low — that we are unwilling to spin out our awaking thoughts into the phantasms of sleep — that to keep our eyes open longer were but to act our antipodes — that the huntsmen are up in America, and they are already past their first sleep in Persia." On this Coleridge exclaims, "Was there ever such a reason given before for going to bed at midnight? to wit, that if we did not, we should be acting the part of our antipodes!" Begging pardon of "the old man eloquent," we should say that Browne did not conjure up these images for the cold purpose of "giving a reason." He was not arguing upon the matter — he was delighting himself, as he sought to delight the reader, by such vivid and rich associations and shapes as the idea of sleep and midnight could evoke. He was not writing as a logician — but a poet; and, so far from being alone and peculiar in this mode of expression, reasons (if so they are to be called) equally far-fetched and exuberant, as applied to some simple proposition, may be found in abundance, not only in the purple eloquence of Jeremy Taylor, but the complacent dissertations of Sir Kenelm Digby, and even in the interminable prosings of Alexander Ross. Literature was still in that stage when

things were presented to the eye, not in the brevity of
words, but in the life of pictures. The arts of composition resembled even less the Egyptian hieroglyph
than the Mexican painting.

In Browne, the scholar and the sage could never
subdue the poet. He felt this himself. He was often
conscious that, as the poet, he said many things which
he could not gravely defend as a philosopher. Thus,
in the advertisement prefixed to the '*Religio Medici*,'
he warns the reader, that "there are many things delivered rhetorically — many expressions therein merely
tropical; and therefore, also, there are many things to
be taken in a soft and flexible sense, and not to be
called unto the rigid test of reason." We believe that
this warning, prefixed to the *Religio Medici*, is applicable, though in a less degree, to all the works of
the author; and that hence many of his critics have
confounded the fantastic embellishment, the wild conjecture, or the quaint and sweet perversity of a sportive
genius, with the assertions of grave and positive belief.
Thus, our author did not conceive that he was advancing the most sensible and practical, but the most
pleasing and solemn argument in favour of gardens,
when he observes, "that Paradise succeeds the grave
— that the verdant state of things is the symbol of
the resurrection — and that to flourish in the state of
glory we must first be sown in corruption." Neither,
probably, when commenting on marriage and the sexual
ties, did he mean us to conceive it to be his deliberate
wish that "men might procreate like trees:" he merely,
in a quaint extravagance, expressed the usual desire
of philosophy to escape the tumults of the passions;
or conveyed the trite and ancient morality, that pos-

session sates, and that the coarser gratifications are unworthy follies.

Perhaps this twofold way of examining things is
more common amongst writers than we are aware;
especially with men like Browne, who rather write
to throw off an exuberance of sentiment and thought,
than for the stern design of effecting some particular
and defined object. Of a mild and kindly temperament, fond of his books and his curiosities, and spin-
ning his subtle and aërial thoughts from materials
which the crowded world casts out of its bustling way
into nooks and corners — moderate as a politician,
averse to all disputes in theology, inclined in both to
leave things in their beaten course, beneath the shelter
of unexamining veneration — there did not exist for
Sir Thomas Browne those great and exciting interests
which gird up the loins of a man's mind, and make
him in earnest in all that he undertakes.   Even
in philosophy, he rather philosophized, than can be
called a philosopher. If he was curious, observant,
and laborious, it was in those solemn trifles and minute
prodigies which amuse the leisure and enrich the
memory, but do not educate the mind to great practical
results.   He did not keenly exert his reason, unless
he was seduced to it by one of the brilliant visions
which delighted his fancy. Thus, perhaps, his most
argumentative work, the one in which he most de-
liberately proceeds through the links of effect and
cause, is that in which he attempts to prove the universal operation of *quincuncial* forms and combinations
throughout the works of nature, and the mystical application and importance of the number FIVE! —
"Quincunxes," as Coleridge pithily says, "in heaven

above, quincunxes in earth below, quincunxes in the
mind of men, quincunxes in tones, in optic nerves, in
roots of trees, in leaves, in everything."

We cannot subscribe to the grave opinion of the
editor, as to the importance of this theory, nor attach
any very reverential faith to "Mr. Macleay's persever-
ing and successful advocacy of a quinary arrangement."
But if Sir Thomas Browne required an apology for
devoting his learning and his genius to such a subject,
the apology is before us when we see that, in the
nineteenth century, his wildest conceits have their admirers and followers: as Browne himself well and
gracefully expresses it — "as though there were a
metempsychosis, and the soul of one man passed into
another, opinions do find, after certain revolutions,
men and minds like those that first begat them." In
fact, Browne neither adopted this subject of the quincunx purely as a brilliant whim, nor yet as a wholly
serious and important discovery in philosophy. The
thought charmed his imagination — it afforded scope
for his curious and scattered learning — for his golden
and fantastic thoughts. It was of a nature that united
both his leading attributes, a taste for the learned and
a passion for the marvellous. He saw that he could
please himself by a work congenial to his thoughts and
studies; and, not less, that he could please the public
by a very remarkable composition. And how much he
considered all the farfetched illustrations and anecdotical
learning in which he indulged, in the light of episodical
ornament, rather than of sober argument; digressions
intended to keep alive the reader's interest, and beautify
his work; in short, how much he regarded such ex-
traneous matter as *an art of composition*, may be seen

in his correspondence. Thus, for instance, in giving his son some hints in the meditated publication of a 'Journey into Upper Hungary to the Mines,' he specially reminds him to add the story of the man that put a snake's head into his mouth in the bath, and of the hussar who bathed in a frost at midnight. He tells him "that he need not be so particular as to give the full account of separating the metals in this narration, but bids him *remember to put in the green jasparcoloured tomb at Larissa, in the barber's shop.*" In short, the advice of the great master is that of a man accustomed to think less of the plain practical nature of any selected theme, than of all the embellishments of anecdote and allusion which may be wrought in "purple patches" upon the stuff. That Browne himself believed in the operation of his darling quincunx, may perhaps be possible; just as he believed in apparitions and sorcerers, but perhaps with the same unexamining and poetical faith; for it is difficult to know when that writer is gravely and honestly in earnest, who tells us that "he has one common and authentic philosophy he learned in the schools, whereby he discourses and satisfies the reason of other men; another, more reserved and drawn from experience, whereby he contents his own."* Whether, in the discourse on the quincunx, the disciple of Pythagoras meant to satisfy the reason of other men, or by experience to content his own, it is difficult to determine. Perhaps he thought little about it; and did not mean to found a philosophy, but to write a book.**

* 'Religio Medici,' vol. n. p. 105:
** A chapter in the more serious work of the 'Pseudodoxia

But if it be disputable whether, in the higher or stricter sense of the word, Browne was a philosopher, no one has ever written sentences more beautifully philosophical. He was worthy to be a disciple of the sage who said, "man was born to contemplate." His pages are filled with a lofty and ideal morality, and his maxims are bright with luminous, if unconnected truths. In some respects he was, among the prose-writers of that day, what Wordsworth is among the poets of this — dedicating even the familiar to the beautiful, and not disdaining "to suck divinity from the flowers of nature." He cannot allow ugliness in a toad or bear — and "even that vulgar and tavern music, which makes one man merry, another mad, strikes in him a deep fit of devotion, and a profound contemplation of the FIRST COMPOSER. There is in it a hieroglyphical and shadowed lesson of the whole world and creatures of God — such a melody to the ear as the whole world, well understood, would afford the understanding." It is from such hints and suggestions of thought that Browne, like Wordsworth, plumes his wings and raises himself beyond 'the visible

Epidemica,' makes it, however, highly probable that Browne put little faith in his own ingenious deductions in the Garden of Cyrus, namely, chapter XII., book IV., "of the great climacteric year, that is, sixty-three." In this chapter he contends with great vigour against the very doctrine of the efficacy of numbers that he advocated in defence of the quincunx: and observes that "not only one set of numbers, but all or most of the digits, have been mystically applauded," and says, that, though "God made all things in number, weight, and measure, yet nothing by them, or through the efficacy of either," &c.

diurnal sphere.' A temperament somewhat common
to both was in both fed by similar political tenets, and
theological veneration; apart from the anxious and exciting cares of men who struggle actively with or
against the multitude. The *Religio Medici* is one of
the most beautiful prose poems in the language; its
power of diction, its subtlety and largeness of thought,
its exquisite conceits and images, have no parallel out
of the writers of that brilliant age, when Poetry and
Prose had not yet divided their domain, and the Ly-
ceum of Philosophy was watered by the Ilissus of the
Nine.

It is difficult to conceive a deep and a just thought
more eloquently expressed than in the following words:
"Nature is not at variance with art nor art with nature
— they being both the servants of His providence.
Art is the perfection of nature. Were the world now
as it was the sixth day, there were yet a chaos.
Nature hath made one world and art another. In belief all things are artificial, *for nature is the art of
God.*"

We cannot refuse to our readers, well known as it
is to many, that noble piece of egotism, in which all
believers in our spiritual immortality may share: —

"For my life it is a miracle of thirty years, which to relate were not a history, but a piece of poetry, and would
sound to common ears like a fable.* For the world I count

* This boast, which Dr. Johnson could not explain, and
even the superrefining Sir Kenelm Digby took literally,
evidently refers not to external and bodily adventures, but to
the progress and operations of the soul. Nor, while in this

14*

it not an inn but a hospital, and a place not to live but to die
in. The world that I regard is myself, it is the microcosm
of my own frame, that I can cast my eye on — for the other
I use it but like my globe, and turn it round sometimes for
my recreation. . . . The earth is a point not only in respect
of the heavens above us, but of that heavenly and celestial
part within us. That mass of flesh that circumscribes me,
limits not my mind. That surface that tells the heavens it
hath an end, cannot persuade me I have any. . . . Whilst I
study to find how I am a microcosm or little world, I find
myself something more than the great. There is surely a
piece of divinity in us — something that was before the
heavens, and owes no homage unto the sun. Nature tells me
I am the image of God as well as scripture. He that understands not thus much, hath not his introduction or first lesson,
and hath yet to begin the alphabet of man."

Coleridge and others have spoken of the egotism
of Browne; but Browne was not an egotist, though
he wrote one work which, not composed for publication, but as a closet confession of his own opinions,

passage the author alludes to such moral and spiritual mys-
teries as have been wrought within himself, does he mean to
imply that his life has been more miraculous than that of another; since in a former passage ('Rel. Med.,' vol. II. p. 21) he
utters the same sentiment, but applies it generally. "*We
carry*," he says, "with *us* the wonders we seek without *us;*
there is all Africa and her prodigies in *us*," &c. It is not
because, as Dr. Johnson imagines, Browne thought himself
distinguished from all the rest of his species, but because he
thought himself *like* them, that he calls his life a miracle.
Thus, in the very passage built upon the assertion that his
life is a miracle, he says that "*he who understands not thus
much has yet to begin the alphabet of man.*"

was necessarily egotistical. It is rather remarkable, on the contrary, that, despite the great success of the *Religio Medici*, and the delicious temptation to go on in the same strain which a man incurs when he has once made the world a confidant, and finds it listen to all he says of himself, it concluded, as it began, his self-dissections. His tale once told, Browne seems to have felt, like Goethe, after the composition of his Werther — as if he had unburdened his mind of anxious secrets; the confession was made and the absolution given. He wrote the book while young, unsettled, and unmarried. Youth is generally an egotist. Most young gentlemen and young ladies, if they write at all, write greatly about themselves. A settled life, household cares and affections, scatter their thoughts insensibly over a wider surface; and sentiment becomes less intense and more diffused.

The *Pseudodoxia Epidemica*, or 'Inquiries into Vulgar and Common Errors,' was Browne's second, and, from its extent and elaborate learning, perhaps his most important work. It is, indeed, in this performance, that we lose sight, in great measure, of the ideal and extravagant poet, and find ourselves with the sober and laborious scholar. The style has little, if any, of the eccentric flights, or stately music, of the knight's other works. It is, indeed, dry, quaint, and pedantic, as was the peculiarity of the day; but has not the ornament and digression which form, elsewhere, the peculiarities of the writer. It is evident that, as he himself says in his preface, he addresses his pen unto the "knowing and leading part of learning." The work properly consists of two main divisions; the one devoted to the correction of such errors (mostly in

chemistry or natural history) as he encountered in his
professional pursuits; the other to the examination of
miscellaneous matters which came before him in his
capacity of a curious and indefatigable student. In
the first, it is noticeable how much his profession served
to sober and restrain the wild and speculative temper
he displays in all else. That profession made, indeed,
the great link between himself and the common world
— it tied him down to the practical: the moment he
gets rid of it he is in the seventh heaven. In his remarks as a chemist and naturalist we cannot but observe a habit of cautious and zealous experiment. Many
of the then popular fallacies he refutes with plain common sense, or by the testimony of actual experience;
and his observations and inductions contain the outline
and suggestion of some of the important discoveries of
modern science. The fatal and unexploded errors of
the alchymists, indeed, occasionally vitiate his most
ingenious arguments; and these he sufficiently venerated, not, in some instances, to submit their dogmas
to that test of experiment which he enforced towards
authorities not a whit less equivocal. In natural
history, also, his passion for the marvellous breaks out
at times. He stoutly rejects the basilisk and the griffin;
but he believes it not impossible that elephants may
have spoken rationally; and says, with earnest pleasantry, "that to those who would attempt to teach
animals the art of speech, the dogs and cats that
usually speak unto witches may afford some encourage-
ment."*

* We ourselves have witnessed an example of the curious
and credulous exaggeration which has construed certain ar-

The nature of the more miscellaneous essays may be conjectured from the following titles: —

In Book IV. (on many popular and received tenets concerning man), "That Jews stink,' — 'On Pigmies.'

In Book V. (of many things questionable as they are commonly described in pictures), 'Of the Picture of Dolphins,' — 'Of the Picture of Haman Hanged,' &c.

In the Seventh Book (of popular and received tenets, chiefly historical, and some deduced from the Holy Scriptures), — 'Of Methuselah,' — 'That a Man hath one Rib less than a Woman,' — 'Of the Wish of Philoxenus to have the Neck of a Crane', &c. With these, however, are interspersed many of more gravely philosophical and antiquarian importance; such as 'The River Nilus;' the 'Origin of Gypsies;' 'Of the Blackness of Negroes,' &c.

Nor are we to suppose that, in many of those subjects which now seem to us so obsolete and frivolous, Sir Thomas Browne was engaged in attacking errors without life and defence. Scarce the absurdest

ticulations in animals into rational speech. Some time since, in travelling through Italy, we heard, in grave earnest, from several Italians, of the prodigy of a Pomeranian dog that had been taught to speak most intelligibly by Sir William Gell. Afterwards, in visiting that accomplished and lamented gentleman at Naples, we requested to hear an animal possessed of so unusual a gift. And, as the friends of the urbane scholar can bear witness, the dog undoubtedly could utter a howl, which, assisted by 'the hand of the master in closing the jaw at certain inflections, might be intelligibly construed into the words, "Damn grandmamma!" Such a dog with such an anathema in his vocabulary, would have hanged any witch in England three centuries ago.

delusion he demolished but had its stubborn champion;
and every inch of the bridge, from Fable to Truth,
was fought with all the knight-errantry of men who
see in Ignorance the beloved country in which they
were born, and for which they are contented to die.
No invaders ever found patriots so desperate, as a man
who attacks a prejudice finds the peaceful possessors
of its realm.   Error lives in the hearts of its subjects;
it is the most venerated and beloved of monarchs.
Thus Sir Thomas Browne could not even assert, in opposition to the ancients, that garlic did not hinder the
attraction of the loadstone, but what an antagonist
started up to declare that the ancients could not be
mistaken; and, therefore, they must have had "a *stronger
kind* of garlic than is with us!"   Another critic (whose
lucubrations are, however, confined to manuscript *), in
opposition to Browne's scepticism as to the existence of
griffins, clenches the question by asserting that he has
himself seen a griffin's — *claw.*   Yet both these commentators were men, not of the ignorant multitude, but
of the learned few.   Alexander Ross (the first referred
to) is in many of his notions even more enlightened
than Browne.   The *Pseudodoxia* is the book of 'Popular
Fallacies' of the sixteenth century; not so valuable,
perhaps, from the subjects it embraces, as the spirit in
which it is conceived — a spirit of bold, but not irreverent scepticism, built upon experimental induction.
    In the 'Garden of Cyrus' and the treatise on 'Urn
Burial' we again see the dreaming and poetical mind
that breathes its beauty through the *Religio Medici.*
Of the main object of the 'Garden of Cyrus' we have

---

* Sir Hamon l'Estrange, quoted vol. ii. p. 173.

already spoken. Of the ingenuity and learning with
which the idea is followed out through innumerable
forms, it is impossible to convey an adequate conception.
The genius of the author never proceeds to conclusions
in a straight line of argument; it undulates and serpen-
tines through a landscape of fertile images, wherever it
can find a sunbeam, or repose upon flowers. With
what grace and eloquence this remarkable writer has
in the following passage* availed himself of an old
Aristotelian sentence the reader will judge: —

"Light that makes things seen makes some things invisible. Were it not for darkness, and the shadow of the
earth, the noblest part of creation had remained unseen, and
the stars in heaven as invisible as on the fourth day, when
they were created above the horizon with the sun, or there
was not an eye to behold them. The greatest mystery of
religion is expressed by adumbration, and in the noblest part
of Jewish types we find the cherubim shadowing the mercy-
seat. Life itself is but the shadow of death, and souls departed but the shadows of the living. All things fall under
this name. The sun itself is but the dark Simulachrum, and
light but the shadow of God." **

Both in the 'Garden of Cyrus' and the 'Urn
Burial' the author has resort to the ancient scholastic
art of exalting as much as possible the nature of his
theme by the grandeur of the exordium. In the first,

* 'Garden of Cyrus,' vol. III. p. 436.
** It was said by Aristotle that "light is the shadow of
God." And the passage in the text is but a series of the
most poetical illustrations of that sublime aphorism.

mindful of his own profession, he observes upon its
antiquity and sacred origin, "that physic may plead
high from that medical act of God in casting so deep
a sleep upon our first parent; and chirurgery find its
whole art in that one passage concerning the rib of
Adam." Yet, preferring, as in duty bound, the dignity
of the theme to that of the author, he proceeds to remark that even medicine can have "no rivalry with
garden contrivance and herbary; for if Paradise were
planted the third day of the creation, as wiser divinity
concludeth, the nativity thereof was too early for horos-
copy. Gardens were before gardeners, and but some
hours before the earth." In like manner our author
commences the 'Urn Burial' by making the world itself a grave. "That great antiquity, America, lay
buried for thousands of years, and a large part of the
earth is still in the urn unto us." It is injustice to the
spirit of such passages to consider them merely as
pieces of far-fetched and humorous quaintness — their
extravagance is that of a wild but noble poetry. They
are absurdities only to those who consider the author
as the logician — they are fanciful, yet appropriate
flights, if we regard him as the poet.

Like the 'Garden of Cyrus,' the subject of the
'Urn Burial' afforded to Browne a theme especially
congenial to his motley erudition and creative imagination. But as in the latter he had no whim to enforce,
no system to pursue, so his genius is far less restrained
and perverted; and for noble thoughts, and in lofty
diction, the 'Hydriotaphia' greatly excels the 'Garden
of Cyrus.' The author reviews the customs of burial
from all time and in all nations. He brings before us
a panorama of graves. But this is done in the spirit

of a poet conversing with antiquity. He is happy to
take an illustration from the shades of Homer. The
beryl ring on the finger of the mistress of Propertius,
when she appeared to him as a ghost, assures us that
"the dead buried with them the things wherein they
delighted." No touching sentiment that can be ex-
tracted from the dry pedantries of learning escapes
him. The sole point in the biography of Domitian
that can please us is introduced with the careless delicacy that belongs to a master hand. "The ashes of
Domitian were mingled with those of Julia." — "Unsatisfied affections conceived some satisfaction to be
neighbours in the grave, to lie urn by urn, and touch
but in their manes." No criticism ever so wholly misrepresented a work as that of Coleridge upon this
beautiful treatise. He tells us that it is "earthy;" "that
graves and sepulchres are redolent in every line." "You
have now," he says, "dark mould, now a thigh-bone,
now a skull, then a bit of mouldered coffin, &c., or
the echo of a November psalm wafted on a November
wind, and the gayest thing you shall meet with shall
be a silver nail or gilt Anno Domini from a perished
coffin-top." In the first place, as Mr. Hazlitt justly
observes, "with such things you do not meet at all in
the text;" and, secondly, which Mr. Hazlitt omits to
observe, so far from the subject being treated in a
gloomy spirit, its darker parts are relieved by a prodigal fancy, and exalted by all that belongs to a
Christian's imperishable hopes. He who recalls the
light and cheerful customs of classic sepulture — the
perfumed ashes, the urn "laden with flowers and ribbons" — will scarcely conceive that a less gloomy
character belongs to the Gothic terrors and dreary as-

pect of a modern charnel. But Browne views not the
contrast in this light — he sees the Christian burial
through the rites that typify resurrection — he thinks
that "Christians have handsomely glossed the deformity
of death by civil rites which take off brutal termina-
tions." Nor, if his subject necessarily lead him to
dwell upon the vanities of human life, does he ever
fail to soften that bitter truth by some sweet or elevated
recurrence to the life beyond. It is in this sense that
he thus concludes his remarks upon "pyramids, arches,
obelisks, those irregularities of vainglory and wild
enormities of ancient magnanimity."

"To subsist in lasting monuments, to live in their productions, to exist in their names and predicament of chimæras,
were large satisfaction unto old expectations, and made one
part of their Elysiums. But all this is nothing in the metaphysics of true belief. To live indeed is to be again ourselves, which being not only a hope, but an evidence in noble
believers, 'tis all one to lie in St. Innocent's churchyard as in
the sands of Egypt. Ready to be anything in the ecstacy of
being ever, and as content with six feet as the moles of
Adrianus."

Of his tolerant and thoughtful spirit, whether as
applied to the physical infirmities of some trembling
martyr, or to the fame of a long-calumniated, because
long-uncomprehended heathen, we select the two following examples:—

"The contempt of death from corporal animosity pro-
moteth not our felicity. They may sit in the orchestra and

noblest seats of heaven who have held up *shaking hands in the fire*, and *humanly* contended for glory."

"Epicurus lies deep in Dante's hell, wherein we meet with tombs enclosing souls which denied their immortalities. But whether the virtuous heathen who lived better than he spake, or, erring in the principles of himself, yet lived above philosophers of more specious maxims, lie so deep as he is placed, at least so low as not to rise against Christians, who, believing or knowing that truth, have lastingly denied it in their practice and conversation, were a query too sad to insist on."

Of the more weighty and solemn peculiarities of his style the following passage will furnish an adequate and sufficient specimen: —

"Who knows whether the best of men be known, or whether there be not more remarkable persons forgot than any that stand remembered in the known account of time? Without the favour of the everlasting register the first man had been as unknown as the last, and Methuselah's long life had been his only chronicle. Oblivion is not to be hired. The greatest part must be content to be as though they had not been, to be found in the register of God, not in the record of man. Twenty-seven names make up the first story before the flood; and the recorded names ever since contain not one living century. The number of the dead long exceedeth all that shall live. The night of time far surpasseth the day, and who knows when was the equinox? Every hour adds unto that current arithmetic which scarce stands one moment. And since death must be the Lucina of life, and even Pagans could doubt whether thus to live were to die — since our longest sun sets at right descensions, and makes but winter arches, and therefore it cannot be long before we lie down in darkness and have our light in ashes — since the brother of death daily haunts us with dying mementoes, and time, that grows old in itself, bids us hope no long duration — diuturnity is a dream and folly of expectation. Darkness and light divide the course of time, and oblivion shares with memory a great part even of our living beings — we slightly remember our felicities, and the smartest strokes of affliction leave but short smart upon us. Sense endureth no extremities, and sorrows destroy us or themselves. To weep into stones are fables. Afflictions induce callosities — miseries are slippery, 'or fall like snow upon us, which notwithstanding is no unhappy stupidity. To be ignorant of evils to come, and forgetful of evils past, is a merciful provision in nature, whereby we digest the mixture of our few and evil days, and our delivered senses not relapsing into cutting remembrances, our sorrows are not kept raw by the edge of repetitions. A great part of antiquity contented their hopes of subsistency with a transmigration of their souls — a good way to continue their memories, while, having the advantage of plural successions, they could not but act something remarkable in such variety of beings, and, enjoying the fame of their passed selves, make accumulation of glory unto their last durations. Others, rather than be lost in the uncomfortable night of nothing, were content to recede into the common being, and make one particle of the public soul of all things, which was no more than to return into their unknown and divine original again. Egyptian ingenuity was more unsatisfied, contriving their bodies in sweet consistencies to attend the return of their souls. But all was vanity, feeding the wind, and folly. The Egyptian mummies, which Cambyses or time hath spared avarice now consumeth. Mummy is become merchandise. Mizraim cures wounds, and Pharaoh is sold for balsams." *

* Upon this profanation of applying mummies "to base medical uses," the author has a similar idea, less solemnly expressed, in his treatise on mummies, first published in the present edition. "Shall Egypt," he says, "lend out her antients

. . . . "There is nothing strictly immortal but immortality. Whatever hath no beginning may be confident of no end, which is the peculiar of that necessary essence that cannot destroy itself, and the highest strain of omnipotency to be so powerfully constituted as not to suffer even from the power of itself — all others have a dependent being, and within the reach of destruction. But the sufficiency of Christian immortality frustrates all earthly glory, and the quality of either state after death makes a folly of posthumous memory. God, who can only destroy our souls, and hath assured our resurrection, either of our bodies or names hath directly promised no duration. Wherein there is so much of chance that the boldest expectants have found unhappy frustration, and to hold long subsistence seems but a scape in oblivion. But man is a noble animal, splendid in ashes, and pompous in the grave, solemnizing nativities and deaths with equal lustre, nor omitting ceremonies of bravery in the infamy* of his nature."

No one can read this beautiful passage without being deeply impressed with the wrong done to the author by those who consider him only valuable for his learning or amusing from his quaintness.

The above works are, as we have said, the best of Sir Thomas Browne's productions. To these, however, are added in the present collection 'The Christian Morals,' to an edition of which Dr. Johnson prefixed

unto chirurgeons and apothecaries, and Cheops and Psammetichus be weighed unto us for drugs — shall we eat of Chamnes and Amasis in electuaries and pills?" &c.

* Dr. Southey in his 'Colloquies' proposes to read "infimy" for infamy. The emendation is ingenious but wrong; infamy is the proper antithesis to "bravery" in the old signification of the latter word.

his biography of Browne — a work containing most of
the worst faults of the author's style, with far less frequent and elevated evidence of its beauties, but still
pregnant with occasional sentences of noble morality,
expressed with exquisite felicity of diction. Perhaps,
too, in proportion as we miss the sublime flights and
vein of charmed and unearthly contemplation of the
Religio Medici, we gain in homely sagacity and practical sense. The nature of the subject — the office of
a moral teacher to others — necessarily imposed much
restraint upon the fancies the writer might indulge,
when, as in the *Religio Medici*, conversing as it were
with himself. We pass over the more trifling of the
miscellaneous works hitherto published, which contain
little very valuable, except as evidence of the lively
and indefatigable scholarship of the man, and the singular questions to which he delighted to apply it; —
fishes, birds, and insects, cymbals and *Eopalic* verses,
languages and garlands, artificial hills and burrows,
the situations of Sodom, Admah, and Zeboim — such
are among the subjects which form the pastime of his
leisure. Nor should we wholly omit mention of a very
curious catalogue, in which he has drawn up, for the
despair of biblomaniacs unborn, a series of what, alas!
he too justly calls "rare and *generally* unknown books"
— such as 'A Poem of Ovid writ in the Getic Language,' 'A Submarine Herbal, describing the several
vegetables at the bottom of the sea,' and 'The Oneiro-
critica of King Mithridates!'

Of these and other miscellanies contained in the
valuable edition of Mr. Wilkin, we content ourselves
with saying that they tend to increase our admiration
of the piety or research, the perseverance or ingenuity

of a man, whose very eccentricities sharpen our interest
in his character and pursuits. And this interest is yet
more excited by the very curious family correspondence
which Mr. Wilkin has judiciously introduced into the
present edition. It is delightful to see this recondite
scholar — this contemplative and refining dreamer —
in the centre of his happy nor unworthy household.
The correspondence of his elder son Edward (himself
afterwards a distinguished physician) is singularly
amusing. Edward appears to have inherited much of
his father's passion for his profession. He had also,
unconsciously perhaps to himself, much of the paternal
eccentricity in pursuits and studies. But though possessed of fair abilities, with untiring perseverance and
zeal, he had nothing of the knight's brilliant fancy
and subtle intellect. In his whole journal (inserted in
the correspondence) not a spark of poetry is to be
found. He travelled much, and through lands then
little visited by our countrymen, but even adventure
cannot extract much more from Mr. Edward Browne
than the names of places and persons. He never
stumbles on a vivid image or an original remark. He
is quaint and solemn, but lifeless; like the ghost of
one of his father's most pedantic periods. In fact he
strongly reminds us of Moses in Goldsmith's charming
tale; and indeed the worthy knight has, through the
correspondence, a little resemblance to the Vicar, while
Dame Dorothy, his lady, has all the generic features
of the notable Mrs. Primrose. But we must allow the
embryo doctor to speak to his own occupations through
the medium of his own journal kept in his youth.

"January 1663-4. — On the 2nd he cut up a bull's heart
and took out the bone, &c.

"On the 3rd he heard Mr. Johnson preach at Christ Church, and Mr. Tenison at St. Luke's Chappell, and took notice that the sun rose in an eliptical or oval figure."

On the 5th he dined with Mr. Howard, "where wee dranke out of pure golde, and had the music all the while," and on the 7th he opened a dog. He spent the 9th chiefly in observing the knee-joint of a calf, and receiving a visit from Monsieur Buttet, "which plays most admirably on the flagelet, bag-pipe, and sea-trumpet." January the 14th was signalized by the discovery "that a monkey hath fourteen ribs on each side." The said monkey did not escape so easily, if indeed it be identical with the animal of which, on the 23rd, we find a noticeable entry. "Boyled the right forefoot of a monkey!"

The student was not, however, so devoted to his more scientific amusements as to forget recreations less sublime. "On January 28th, after spending the morning in seeing oxen killed, he partook of a dancing at Mr. Houghton's till almost four o'clock in the following morning," — a proof that our sober ancestors were not on all occasions exempt from our own vice of unseasonable hours. So again, if on February 10th Mr. Edward dissected a badger, he relaxed his mind on the 13th by drawing valentines at Mr. Howard's. Independent of the grave oddity of this journal, it is interesting from its description of the hospitable gaieties at the house of a country gentleman of the first rank — Mr. Howard, afterwards, by creation, Lord Howard of Castle Rising, and Earl of Norwich, and, by the death of his brother, sixth Duke of Norfolk. It is pleasant, as the editor remarks, to perceive the friendly and equal terms on which this munificent and accomplished gentleman mingled with the inhabitants of the town.

"He kept his Xmas this year (1663-4) at Norwich so magnificently as the 'like hath scarce been seen. They had dancing every night, and gave entertainment to all that would come. He built up a room on purpose to dance in, very large, and hung with the bravest hangings I ever saw. His candlesticks, snuffers, tongs, fire-shovels, and andirons were silver. A banquet was given every night after dancing, and three coaches were employed to fetch ladies every afternoon — the greatest of which would holde fourteen persons" (so omnibuses are no modern invention!) "and cost 500*l.* without the harnesse, which cost six score more."

The young man afterwards went abroad, and consumed a longer time in travelling than his father approved; but, having sown his wild oats, returned to England, settled in London, and appears, while yet young, to have realized an income from his practice of about 1000*l.* a-year. He attained high professional honours, became Censor of the College of Physicians, and seems to have been a fashionable doctor to people of quality. It was Dr. Edward Browne who attended the penitent death-bed of that most brilliant of English profligates, the Earl of Rochester.

The knight's second son, Thomas, is a more interesting character than Edward. Sent abroad at the early age of fourteen, a disposition frank, bold, and manly, enabled him to make his own way without committing any errors to induce his father to repent so confiding a trust in the steadiness of a boy. He en-

15*

tered the navy in 1664, took part in the Dutch war,
and highly distinguished himself, throughout a short
but promising and proud career, for ability and courage.
His letters display far more spirit and life than those
of his elder brother. He is evidently enamoured of
his profession, and speaks of it with the zeal and gusto
of a gallant spirit to which danger is pleasurable excitement.

"I thanke you" (he says in one of his letters to his father)
"for your directions for my cares agaynst the noyce of the
gunnes, but I have found that I could endure it: nor is it so
intolerable as most conceave, especially when men are earnest
and intent upon their business, and unto whom muskets
sound but like pop-gunnes: *it is impossible to express unto another how a smart sea-fight elevates the spirits of a man, and
makes him despise all dangers.*" *

All the wild enthusiasm which the father devoted
to peaceful pursuits — all the grave earnestness with
which Edward plodded on from "boyling the foot of a
monkey" to lecturing at Surgeons' Hall — this young
seaman felt for his noble and active calling. In him
met many of the qualities that form our ideal of the
English sailor, not only the joyous daring, but the
gentle and generous nature. When the seamen are dis-
tressed for want of pay, he says —

"While I have a penny I cannot but relieve them of whose
fidelitie and valor I can give so good testimonie." "I am
much satisfied" (he adds in the same letter) "that I have got

* Vol. i. p. 129.

my boy Will Blanchot's pension settled for his life, having
had his thigh broake by a splinter in the last fight butt one.
. . . . It will be hard to meet with a boy so boald and useful
in a fight, though I have another that doeth well. I shall
take all the care to bind him out, and I hope it is already
done by those I have employed about it. His father was
chief gunner of our shippe at Bergen, where hee was slayne,
and his sonne left to the wide world, till *I tooke him into my
care.*"

Well might his father say of him, with honest and
delighted pride, "God hath given you a stout but a
generous and merciful heart withall, and in all your
life you could never behold any person in miserie but
with compassion and reliefe, which hath been notable
in you from a childe." But our young hero was not
of the Smollett school of sailors — children and dunces
the moment they touch land. The hereditary love of
knowledge was strong in his breast. He reads Lucan
"while riding in Plimmouth Sound;" and characteristic-
ally enough admires the "noble straynes" of that
energetic and warlike poet. The knight, while repeat-
ing the praises he hears of his son's skilful seamanship,
cannot omit expressing his delight to find that he is
"not only Marti but Mercurio." He congratulates him
on the success with which he has "read divers bookes
at sea, especially Homer and Juvenal, with Lubine's
notes." This accomplished and excellent young man
unhappily did not live to fulfil the sanguine expectations generally formed of him. After his return to
England, Mr. Wilkin reasonably laments that all trace
of his existence is lost. "A solitary allusion in a letter
written many years after, adverts to him in terms
which prove that he had been long dead;" but how

and where he died, the editor has not been able to
ascertain.*

The favourite daughter of our author, Mrs. Lyttleton,
adds a new feature of interest to this charming family.
A single sentence in one of Sir Thomas Browne's
letters to her affords a beautiful sketch of her feminine
and pious character. "Thou didst use" (he says) "to
pass away much of thy time alone and by thyself in
sober ways and good actions, so that noe place, how
solitary soe ever, can be strange to thee, nor indeed
solitary, since God, whom thou servest, is everywhere
with thee."

Of Dame Dorothy, his wife, we are assured, by
the knight's contemporary and eulogist, Whitefoot, that
she "was of such symmetrical proportion to her worthy
husband, both in the graces of her body and mind,
that they seemed to come together by a kind of natural
magnetism." Of this marvellous sympathy, however,
Dame Dorothy's correspondence affords no satisfactory
evidence.   She appears to have resembled the general-
ity of provincial ladies in that day — to have been
skilful in potting game, and making a "pretty kind of
safe wine;" while the laconic brevity of her letters de-
notes a modest consciousness of the weary difficulty
with which the good lady threaded the labyrinth of
grammar and orthography. She was evidently a thrifty
and careful housekeeper.   She enforces plainly upon
her sons those cautions of frugality and economy which

* Works, vol. i. p. 116.   In the 'Supplementary Memoir,'
p. 75 (note 4), Mr. Wilkin hazards, indeed, a conjecture that
his death was in September, 1667; but no satisfactory reason
is given for the surmise.

the gentler and more delicate father only tenderly
hints; and she seems to have been equally careful of
the piety and the breeches of her favourite grandson
"Tomey." But the worthy pair lived happily together.
Probably the plain shrewdness of Dame Dorothy was
a proper adjunct to the aspiring intellect of her husband. And perhaps that man, however gifted, has
reason to be contented with his nuptial lot who can
find in his helpmate 'the staff of common sense, and
the pillow of sincere affection.'

The family, with its peculiarities and contrasts,
forms a cheerful and pleasant picture. With some
little licence of chronology, we may imagine it such
as it might have been when it smiled its welcome upon
the graceful and accomplished Evelyn, on his visit to
the knight, then in the height of his fame. We can
see the quaint old house, and garden, "being a paradise and cabinet of rarities, and that of the best collec-
tions, especially medals, books, plants, and natural
things."* We can transport ourselves to the principal
chamber, pleasingly littered, not perhaps to the taste
of Dame Dorothy, with the last received and examined
"rarities;" — plants collected abroad by the knight's
sailor son — or a relic of the ostrich which excited so
earnest curiosity in his more scientific heir — or the
Druid urns which called forth the immortal thoughts of
the *Hydriotaphia*. Sole token of the ostentation of the
loyal scholar, we gaze on that high chimney-piece,**

---

* Evelyn's Account. See 'Supplementary Memoir,' vol.
I. p. 94.

** "In the drawing-room of the house in which he lived,
there is over the mantelpiece, and occupying the entire space

wrought with the arms of the gay king from whose
sword the knight of Norwich had received his chivalric
honours. Nay, we can fancy we see the grave Edward, ever eager for knowledge, holding the button of
the courteous and courtly Evelyn, while the fair Elizabeth, "who passed away much of her time alone," is
gliding noiselessly along the threshold. The frank
sailor (for we must have him still alive) is drawing for
the favoured "Tomey" the picture of "The monstrous
Tartar." Dame Dorothy is meditating upon the "shews
of the supper;" with now and then a regretful sigh
that "the gold upon her daughter's manto gown att a
little distance goes but for buf-colored silke."* And
the knight himself, touched with a green old age, is
before us as we picture him from the lively delineations
of those who knew him. There he is, pointing to some
new "botanicall," middle sized, and plainly garbed,
just returned from his garden, with "the cloke and
boots which he ever wore;" grave and sober of aspect,
slowly aroused to conversation, cheerful and animated
when his powers are called forth, and, in the sensitiveness of the quick poetical temperament, *blushing* with
the emotion that his own ideas, whether couched in
wit or eloquence, create in him.**

The time has long past when the creed of the
author of *Religio Medici* was a matter of dispute. He

---

to the ceiling, a most elaborate and richly ornamented carving of the royal arms of Charles II."—*Sup. Mem.*, vol. i. p. 92.

  * Vol. i. p. 249.
  ** See Whitefoot's description, vol. i. p. 44. "His modesty
was visible in a natural habitual blush, which was increased
upon the least occasion."

was not only a very orthodox Christian, but a very orthodox churchman. He clung to an establishment with the resolute vigour of a man who feels that, if he were to wander away an inch from the magical circle, a thousand imps of imagination would hurry him off into pathless wastes, or down an unfathomable void: "Where the scripture is silent" (he says with considerable unction) "the church is a text; where that speaks, it is but a comment." Perhaps, indeed, there is no period in English history in which religion exercised so powerful and direct an influence over men's minds, as the space from Elizabeth to Charles the Second. The universal concession of the Bible, and the removal of that daily control upon conjecture which belongs to the priesthood of Rome, brought divinity home to every man's hearth and heart: he was free to study and to interpret every doctrine and every text. A revolution of faith was united with a great era in liberty of opinion. Men were at once fanatics and sceptics — fanatics in their own sect, sceptics of all authority that differed from it. Hence numberless varieties of belief, combined with stern and rigid enthusiasm. All revolutions are faithful to the spirit of their origin; the Reformation was the triumph of opinion against authority. It sowed seeds which necessarily sprung up into great good and great evil. On the one side, earnest piety, inquisitive knowledge, heroic devotion to truth; on the other, all the chimeras of superstitious heresy, all the extravagance of political speculation. Bacon and Hampden were in much the offspring of the Reformation; but so also were Syndercomb and Prynne. Philosophers and patriots, fifth-monarchy-men, saints and levellers, all were the distant progeny of the first great

impulse which released the spirit of mankind from the
thraldom of hereditary prescription. The whole reign
of Charles the First belongs to the history of religion.
Living in that reign, affected by its influences, the
contemplative and eager mind of Sir Thomas Browne
plunged itself betimes into the mystical abysses of
theology. Perhaps his sagacity was soon deterred from
attempts to find a boundary for the infinite; perhaps
his tolerant and benevolent temper was soon revolted
from speculations which in his day induced the wildest
follies and the harshest bigotry. He therefore settled,
while yet young, into the large philosophy of passive
belief. "Since" (he says) "I was understanding to
know that we know nothing, my reason has been
pliable to the will of faith." But still, more or less,
his sense was darkened by the vast shadow which he
refused to penetrate, and under which the age reposed.
Hence most of the prejudices that detract from his
knowledge — his belief in witches, his disbelief in
Copernicus. He imagined the one was proved, the
other condemned, by the scriptures; and to his mind
they both belonged to that part of inquiry which
he thought it no sin vaguely to dream about, but an
offence and a folly too curiously to examine. It is
thus, we have before intimated, that most of the contradictions in his intellectual frame are to be accounted
for. They were those of the age rather than of the
man. As from the same general causes came the religious spirit and poetical treatment of his subjects, so
also in the universal language of the time we see the
reason for its occasional singularity and quaintness.
Every one, then, was quaint; — the Roundhead, the
Cavalier, the Poet, the Scholar. Each man sought a

style and diction of his own; and the general eccentricity gave a generic likeness to the individual examples. This also arose from circumstances apparent to every student of our literary history. Upon a nation not accustomed to the light, an immense blaze of fancy and intellect had been suddenly shed. Taste was not formed — critics were not known — through so mighty and so tempting a wilderness guides were not received. The common taste of the common multitude is the best critic; but the common multitude was disdained by all. Each man of genius studied, thought, and composed for himself or for the few; and strove to distinguish his toils from those of his rivals, by a consummate elaboration of painful oddities. Writers were anxious to frame a sort of anaglyph for themselves, incomprehensible to the vulgar; and Browne himself exultingly remarks, that, "if elegancy proceedeth, we shall in a few years be fain to learn Latin to understand English." The vulgar could not cope with the scholars; but in the popular fanaticism they found a language for themselves; and the ignorant Puritan rejoiced in a vocabulary as little English and as little intelligible as the dainty affectations of the most conceited academician.

Thus far, in some of his higher attributes, and some of his weaker qualities as a writer, Sir Thomas Browne was the creation of his times. But his calm toleration of spirit, "condemning no man for his opinions," his candid and modest discussion of facts and principles, were the result of his own remarkable sweetness of disposition, and the retired, though not inactive, habits of his life.

Of the force and majesty of his style in its better

portions sufficient evidence has been presented to the
reader. He enriched, rather than corrupted our language,
by an inundation of Latinisms, necessary, perhaps, to
,science, and, if judiciously managed, ornamental in
poetry. The next step was that taken by Milton, who,
not contented with Latin expressions, sought to form
the whole language anew upon a Latin construction.
Here, as in all fashions of literature, when the last
step of the change is made, a new fashion is sure to
be the successor. An *architectural style*, once elaborated,
remains to be admired or condemned, according to the
taste or associations of the beholder — a landmark of
the everlasting progress of language — but the writers
of the next generation are the last to imitate or adopt
it; for them, like the houses of our grandfathers, it is
old-fashioned, not antique.   Time rolls on, and the
obsolete diction, like the old-fashioned house, contracts
a venerable and majestic sanctity in our eyes.   Dr.
Johnson censures the exploded diction of Browne and
of Milton; the diction of Dr. Johnson is more exploded
than theirs.   In almost every age, when *a people* have
become *readers*, there are two schools of composition;
— the one closely resembling the language commonly
spoken; the other constructed upon the principle, that
what is written should be something nobler or lovelier
than what is spoken; that fine writing ought not so
much literally to resemble, as spiritually to idealize,
good talking; — that the art of composition, like every
other art, when carried to its highest degree, is not the
representation, but, as Browne expresses it, "the *perfection* of nature;" — and that, as music to sound, so
is composition to language.   A great writer of either
school reaches the same shore, and must pass over the

same stream; but the one is contented with the ferry, the other builds up a bridge — one goes along the stream, the other *above* it. Of these two schools of composition, the Eloquent and the Familiar, the last, often lightly esteemed in its time, and rather commanding a wide than a reverent audience, passes, with little change and little diminution of popularity, from generation to generation. But the first stands aloof — the edifice of its age — copied not for ordinary uses, however well formed by scholars in exact and harmonious symmetry. Royal, but unprolific, it is a monarch without a dynasty. It commands, is obeyed, adored — dies, and leaves no heir. Gibbon and Junius are imitated but by schoolboys and correspondents to provincial newspapers; but the homely Locke, the natural Defoe, the familiar Swift, the robust if boorish manliness of Cobbett, leave their successors; and find (perhaps unconsciously) their imitators, so long as the language lasts. This is no detraction from the immortality of greater and more imaginative minds. It is the characteristic of their immortality, that, though they inspire, they are not copied: mediately or immediately the spirit of Milton has had its influence on almost every great poet that has succeeded him — but poetasters alone have mimicked the machinery of his verse. He who has really caught the mantle of the prophet, is the last man to imitate his walk. As with poets, so with those prose-writers who have built up a splendid and unfamiliar style; — after the first rage of contemporaneous imitation, no one of sound taste or original talent dreams of imitating them. They are not, however, the less certain of duration. Their spirits live apart in the sumptuous palaces they have erected: Men, it is true, do not fashion after palaces their streets and thoroughfares; but Windsor Castle is not less likely to last, because Windsor Castle was not the model for Regent Street.

There was one other characteristic of our author, which we must touch upon ere we conclude; because it perhaps makes the true reason why, with all his genius and learning, his wonderful subtlety of thought and power of diction, he never accomplished so much as he might have done, and will never, perhaps, command a very numerous and popular audience. Meek and amiable as he was upon single topics and towards single opponents, he borrowed from the Roman poets what he could not have done either from Greek philosophy or Holy Writ — a fierce and unenlightened disdain of what he calls "that great enemy of reason, virtue, and religion — the MULTITUDE."

It is true that he was too refined and too just to include in this censure, as the vulgar reasoners of later times have done, only the subordinate masses. He acknowledges also "a rabble amongst the gentry." But the error is the same, when it implies a contempt for the opinions, interests, and pursuits of the great bulk of mankind, however divided and classed. It is not without truth that Aristotle likens the Multitude to a complex animal, with many feet, with many hands, with many faculties, with many virtues, each member contributing a something more or less valuable to the perfection of the whole body. And as a picture, collecting only excellences and avoiding deformities, will be found more beautiful than any single original in nature with whom it can be compared, so the excellences of that complex entity the Public may sometimes sur-

pass those of the most accomplished prince or of the
most virtuous council. It is true, as Aristotle allows,
that so great a compliment to the Multitude cannot
admit of universal or even of general application. On
the contrary, in every age some men tower above the
masses of mankind, often their guides, sometimes their
martyrs. We do not mean that good and great minds
are to bend to popular caprice, or worship the popular
idols. It is their duty to advocate and enforce such
truths as they believe essential, yet unacknowledged.
But it is equally their duty to do so, not from disdain,
but from affection for the public; — heartily sym-
pathizing with their interests, while endeavouring, with
equal courage and temperance, to correct their errors.
Such is the position and such the character of the most
venerable and beneficent reformers of their land and
time. But, with all the follies of the mass, we doubt
whether a history of the wise *few*, or a history of the
despised *many*, would contain the greater number of
ludicrous blunders and melancholy excesses. How
long ago, and how justly, was it said, that "no sick
man ever dreamt such crudities as waking philosophy
has embodied in its systems"! The philosophy of an
age is often, indeed, but the condensed essence of its
follies. And Browne himself, while registering his
vehement and lofty contempt of "that great monstrosity,
the multitude," takes from the multitude his sole excuse
for his own belief in witchcraft, chiromancy, or the
anti-Copernican system of the solar motion.

It was a consistent result of this unwise and passionate disdain of the Public that Browne wasted so
much of his genius upon scholastic frivolities. He

had no sympathy with the great business of men. In
that awful year, when Charles I. went in person to
seize five members of the Commons' House — when
the streets resounded with shouts of "Privilege of Parliament," and the king's coach was assailed by the
prophetic cry "To your tents, O Israel!" — in that
year, in fact, when the civil war first broke out, and
when most men of literary power were drawn by the
excitement of the crisis into patriotic controversy on
either side — appeared the calm and meditative reveries of the *Religio Medici*. The war raged on. It
was a struggle between all the elements of government. England was torn by convulsion, and red with
blood. But Browne was tranquilly preparing his *Pseudodoxia Epidemica;* as if errors about basilisks and
griffins were the paramount and fatal epidemic of the
time; and it was published in due order in that year
(1646), when the cause which the author advocated,
so far as he could advocate anything political, lay at
its last gasp. The king dies on the scaffold. The
Protectorate succeeds. Men are again fighting on paper
the solemn cause already decided by the field. Drawn
from visions more sublime, forsaking studies more intricate and vast than those of the poetical Sage of
Norwich, diverging from a career bounded by the most
splendid goal, foremost in the ranks shines the flaming
sword of Milton; Sir Thomas Browne is lost in the
quincunx of the ancient gardens; and the year 1658
beheld the death of Oliver Cromwell, and the publication of the *Hydriotaphia*.

We do not blame, while we account for, the seeming unconsciousness of Browne to the stormy events

around him: if he despised the multitude, he was naturally lukewarm to the struggles of either party between which the multitude was divided; and, no doubt, he would have brought Archimedes and Lucretius to establish the sublimity and grandeur of a philosophy so little disturbed by the roar and strife that raged below. But this temperament is not congenial to practical efforts of mind. Divorced from the ends and interests of the million, the genius of one man, howsoever great, is apt to run riot amongst trifles. Therefore it is that, throughout all the seven books of an inquiry into 'Popular Errors,' by a man of singular acuteness enlightened by singular learning, no searching comment attends a single error directly injurious to the political or social happiness of mankind. Therefore it is that the inquirer himself, while professing to expose the blunders of the people, disdainfully boasts, that *for* the people, "whom books do not redress," his work is not intended. Therefore it is that, throughout all our author's gravest and loftiest idealism, there is something of the whimsical frivolity of a man who lives alone, with no occupation so attractive as that of sporting with his own fancies, and caressing his own conceits. Therefore it is that, while Sir Thomas Browne will always command the admiration of poets, and the respect of scholars, he will find, we fear, the justice of retaliation in the indifference of the ordinary public. Amongst writers who have won to themselves listeners in all time and from all men, the social principle is invariably strong. They come home to our thoughts and passions, our waking objects and ideal dreams, by the eloquence of a sympathy with ourselves. They have struggled for us, or they have felt with us. Their immortality rests less upon our tastes than our affections; and it is precisely because the multitude has *not* been, for them, a monster, that their genius appeals to a universal test and an everlasting tribunal.

PITT AND FOX.

[*First published in* 'THE QUARTERLY REVIEW,' *Sept. 1855.*]

16*

PITT AND FOX.

[*Memorials and Correspondence of Charles James Fox.* Edited by LORD JOHN RUSSELL. Vols. I. and II. London, 1853.]

THE time has perhaps arrived when Englishmen may regard, not without predilections, but freed from such passions as forbid a calm survey of the grounds on which those predilections have been formed, the characters of men who commanded the confidence or excited the dread of our contending grandsires. Political interests are invested in new combinations of party, — from the eternal problems of civilization new corollaries are drawn, since Fox identified his name with the cause of popular freedom, and Pitt' was hailed as the representative of social order.

Statesmen are valued while living, less according to the degree of their intellect than to its félicitous application to the public exigencies, or the prevalent opinions. Time, like law, admits no excuse for the man who misunderstands it. Hence, in our estimate of contemporaries, we pass with abrupt versatility from one extreme to the other: "*Mors ultima linea rerum est*" — death must determine the vanishing point in the picture before we can estimate the relative size of each object expressed on the canvas.

In examining the Memorials and Correspondence of Mr. Fox, recently edited by the most distinguished of his surviving disciples, our eye often turns from the prominent hero to linger where an opening in the group that surrounds him vouchsafes a glimpse of his lofty antagonist; and strange does it seem to us that so much in the character and career of Mr. Pitt has been left to the mercy of commentators,* who could not fail to misinterpret the one from the hostility they professed to the other. In securing from future ages an impartial judgment, Mr. Fox has this striking advantage, that, perhaps less than any of our great public men, do his actions need the investigation of latent causes, or his idiosyncrasies require much skill in analysis or extensive acquaintance with mankind. It was his notable attribute to lay himself open on all sides, whether to applause or to reproach. And thus, while, on the one hand, his familiar letters render yet more transparent his amiable and winning qualities, and the graces of his cultivated and affluent genius, so, on the other, they compel our attention the more to his signal defects as the leader of a party, or the councillor of a nation. But though in detail criticism may suggest remarks not without novelty or instruction, the salient attributes of the man, regarded as a whole, will remain the same: and the additional light thrown upon the portrait does not provoke the question whether or not it be placed at its proper height upon the wall. Far less clear to the discernment of the last age was the character of Pitt; and even in our day, men, wonder-

* We need scarcely say that Lord Stanhope's admirable 'Life of Pitt' was not published when this article was written.

ing that genius should have been so long fortunate,
have but little examined the properties and causes
which made the fortune a necessary consequence of the
genius. In the demeanour of Mr. Pitt, a certain stately
reserve baffled the ordinary eye; in his political action
there was a guiding tendency towards practical results,
which is liable to misconstruction by the ordinary intelligence. It was his fate to incur, from his earliest
manhood, those grave responsibilities which separate
the minister charged with the destinies of a nation from
the theorist in legislation, who, free to contend for
what he deems good in the abstract, is not bound to
consider how and when to effect it. Hence, so little
was known of Mr. Pitt out of his own chosen circle,
in private, that Mr. Fox speaks of him "as no scholar."
And few indeed among the supporters of the majestic
minister, who cheered his awful irony or imperial declamation, could have believed that he had ever been
the gayest of gay companions met to sup in the
hostelry of Eastcheap, and vie with each other in apt
quotations from Shakspeare. On the other hand, in his
public character — so little have his true opinions
been subjected to candid investigation, that he has
been represented as an apostate from popular freedom
and a champion of absolute rule; while Lord Holland
would kindly mitigate his guilt as one or the other by
the charitable assurance that Pitt had very few fixed
principles at all. He has been accused of making war
for the cause of the Bourbons; the Bourbons accused
him of ignoring their cause altogether. He has been
charged with prolonging the war to prop his selfish
ambition almost at every hazard; while, fresh from the
Malmesbury Correspondence, Lord Brougham invites

us to notice how "sincerely desirous he was of making
peace with the French Directory almost at any price."
According to Macaulay, Pitt was a wretched financier;
while Lord John Russell laments that no junction between Fox and Pitt allowed the nation to see "the one
adorning and advising his country in foreign affairs,
the other applying to the management of our finances the
economical principles of Smith and the wise frugality
of Sully." It may well be worth while to re-examine
a character thus carelessly rated, thus ill comprehended,
and to ascertain what really were those qualities which,
in a time unparalleled for the grandeur of its public
men, raised Mr. Pitt to a power pre-eminent over all.
And, although there is no great general analogy between the circumstances that now surround us or the
dangers that threaten, and the stormier attributes of
the time in which Mr. Pitt achieved his fame, still, in
the prosecution of a war* in which great blunders have
been committed and lofty reputations have fallen into
obloquy and odium, suggestions not without their value
may arise from the 'contemplation of a character which
inspired the public confidence in proportion to the degree of the public peril.

William Pitt, the second son of Lord Chatham, was
born on the 28th of May, 1759. Like his great rival
Mr. Fox, and unlike great men in general, his childhood was remarkable for precocity of intellect. Of
his two brothers, one was destined to the army, the
other to the navy. William was selected for the career
of the bar and the senate. From the age of six to fourteen, educated at home under the eye of Lord Chatham,

* The Crimean war.

all his faculties were trained towards development in
public life. During those eight years the popularity
of the elder Pitt had rapidly declined. The Great Com-
moner had passed to the House of Lords. He had
formed that motley and feeble cabinet, made familiar
to posterity by the exquisite satire of Burke, to which
he had contributed nothing save his name, in the defence of which, to borrow Chesterfield's brief definition,
"he was only Earl of Chatham and no longer Mr. Pitt,"
and from which he altogether retired in 1768. Infirmity and disease grew upon him. He was much confined to his room. He had leisure to form the mind
and inspire the ambition of his favourite son.

It was not only in scholastic studies that the grand
old man encouraged the boy's natural eagerness to excel; it was not enough even in childhood to read and
to remember. Lord Chatham early instilled those two
habits of mind which call from the inert materials of
learning the active uses of purpose, the reproductive
vitality of original deductions, — the habits to observe
and to reflect. He led the young student to talk openly and boldly upon every subject, and to collate his
first impressions with a statesman's practical experience.
The exceeding tenderness which the great Earl, so imperious in public life, exhibited to his son, appears in
the letters Lord Chatham addressed to William at the
early age of fourteen. They have almost a mother's
familiar kindliness and yearning affection, with just
enough of the father's unconscious greatness to sustain
masculine ambition, and animate the sense of duty, not
by dry admonitions but by hopeful praise: "Your race
of manly virtue (he writes to this boy of fourteen) is
now begun, and may the favour of Heaven smile upon

the noble career! How happy, my loved boy, is it that
your mamma and I can tell ourselves there is at Cambridge *one* without a beard, and all the elements so
mixed in him, that Nature might stand up and say
'This is a man!'"

Such words, and from such a parent, might not
only stimulate all the energies of a generous son, but
they serve, perhaps, to account for that remarkable conviction in his own powers, that firm quality of self-
esteem so necessary in public life, which from first to
last was the distinctive peculiarity of William Pitt.
Nor was it only by this wise familiarity of conversation
and intercourse that Lord Chatham mechanically educated his son towards the adoption of his own career.
He accustomed the boy to recite aloud, and, no doubt,
took occasion to inculcate those arts of oratory so difficult to acquire in later life — the distinctness of elocu-
tion, the modulated change of voice, the bye-play of
look and of gesture, in which Lord Chatham himself
was the most accomplished master of modern times. It
was, perhaps, the conviction that the arts of oratory
are closely akin to those of the stage that led Lord
Chatham to encourage William before he went to the
University, not only to write a play in verse, but to
take a part in its performance. Yet more useful, perhaps, than the performance of the play was its composition in verse. Rarely, indeed, has it happened that
an eminent orator has obtained distinction as a poet;
but rarely also has it happened that an eminent orator
has not indulged in verse-making. No other study
leads to the same choiceness of selection in words, or
enforces the same necessity to condense thought into a
compact compass. Bolingbroke, Chatham, Burke, Fox,

Sheridan, Pitt, Canning — all made verses at one time of their lives, though Sheridan and Canning alone, of that immortal seven, have left us cause to regret that they did not cultivate in verse any uses not rigidly confined to the embellishment of prose. Nor did Lord Chatham neglect to exercise an influence over the direction of William's graver studies. The Earl prudently, indeed, left to professional teachers the legitimate routine in the classic authors, but he made it his particular desire that Thucydides, the eternal manual of statesmen, should be the first Greek book which his son read after coming to college; "the only other wish," says Bishop Tomline (William's college preceptor), "ever expressed by his Lordship relative to Mr. Pitt's studies, was, that I would read Polybius with him." But to William himself Lord Chatham's literary recommendations were less restricted, and they directed him to the study not only of the historical and political master-pieces of England, but also of the logical arrangement and decorous eloquence which characterise the literature of the national Church. The sermons of Barrow especially seemed to Lord Chatham "admirably calculated to furnish the *copia verborum*." *

* Barrow's amplitude of style is not unfrequently discernible in Pitt. But Barrow's more poetical attributes — his bursts of passionate fervour — his glowing use of personification — his felicity in adapting high thoughts to sonorous expressions, appear more congenial to Chatham's style of eloquence than that of his son. There are parts in Barrow which we could well fancy Chatham to have spoken. For instance, the sublime passage beginning, "Charity is a right noble and worthy thing," &c.

In 1773, when little more than fourteen, William went to Pembroke Hall, in the University of Cambridge. It was, perhaps, an advantage to his moral habits, and to his undivided attention to study, that he was so much younger than his contemporaries. A boy of fourteen could scarcely participate in the pleasures that allure young men from eighteen to twenty. Even then, however, his tutor tells us "that his manners were formed and his behaviour manly." His conversational powers were already considerable, and his range of study was singularly wide and comprehensive. Even then, too, his habits indicated the bias of the future orator. The barber who attended him, on approaching the oak door, frequently overheard him declaiming to himself within; and at a yet earlier age he had been accustomed to listen to the debates in the House of Commons, and repeat to his father the general purport of the arguments on either side. A severe illness attacked him soon after his entrance at the University, and much interfered with his residence during the first three years, but does not seem to have greatly interrupted his educational progress. There were these remarkable characteristics both in the quality of his learning and the mind that was applied to it. Although not fond of composition in the dead languages, nor ever attaining to that perfection in the elegant pastime of adapting modern thoughts to ancient tongues, which is the favourite Academical test of scholarship, he yet devoted especial and minute care to detect the differences of style in the classic authors; and we are told by his tutor that "his diligent application to Greek literature had rendered his knowledge of that language so correct and extensive that, if a play of Menander or

Æschylus, or an ode of Pindar, had been suddenly found, he would have understood it as soon as any professed scholar."

Lord Wellesley confirms this authority by his own, which carries with it more weight. That indisputable scholar, whose classical compositions may bear no disparaging comparison with Milton's and Gray's, says of Pitt, in maturer life, "He was perfectly accomplished in classical literature, both Latin and Greek." . . . "With astonishing facility he applied the whole spirit of ancient learning to his daily use." Lord Grenville has often declared that "Mr. Pitt was the best Greek scholar he ever conversed with." Yet he had not habituated himself in boyhood to construe classical authors in the ordinary way, viz. literally, and word by word, "but read several sentences in the original, and then gave the translation of them, interpreting with almost intuitive quickness the most difficult author;" a peculiarity which evinces the tendency to generalise and express details by the comprehension of the whole, rather than arrive more slowly at the whole through the detached examination of details. Thus his observation was searching and careful; but it was more directed to essentials than minutiæ. He took great pleasure in philological disquisitions and the true niceties of language; little pleasure in the lesser exercise of acuteness that would amend a trivial error in a doubtful text; — great pleasure in studying the peculiar means by which poets obtain effect in expression; little pleasure in analysing the laws of the metre they employed. His mind, in short, was critical only so far as criticism was necessary to the object in view; and in the tastes of his studious boyhood he evinced that preference for the

Practical, that strong seizure of some definite purpose, in which is to be found the main secret of his after greatness, and of some of the defects and failings with which that greatness was inseparably blended. He acquired what would now be called but an elementary knowledge of mathematics and natural philosophy. His tutor, indeed, thinks that he would have made a wonderful progress in pure mathematics, had his inclination to that abstruse science been indulged. This we venture to doubt. No test of the capacities requisite for mastery in the more recondite regions of abstract philosophy is established by a readiness in the solution of elementary problems. There are few logical minds which the clear deductions of Euclid do not strengthen and delight. But for achievements in science, as the minute investigator, the subtle discoverer, we apprehend that qualities are required the very opposite of those which in William Pitt shunned all results that were not broad and palpable — employed genius to heighten and adorn the robust substance of common sense, and by adherence to reasonings the most familiar, or appeal to passions the most elementary — convinced the plain understanding of a popular assembly, and commanded the heart of a free nation, which a similar policy on certain measures adopted by a minister who had philosophized more, and felt less, would have driven into terrible revolt.

William Pitt went just so far into mathematics and natural science as fitted him the better for active life, and went no farther. He said himself, and truly, "that he found their uses later, not merely from the actual knowledge conveyed, but rather from the habit of close attention and patient investigation." So also in metaphysics. He seems to have contented himself with a thorough knowledge of Locke's 'Essay on the Human Understanding,' of which he formed a complete and correct analysis. "He indicated no inclination to carry his metaphysical studies farther." In other words, it was the nature of his mind to adopt such studies as could collaterally serve the vocation of an accomplished statesman; to halt from those studies where they deviated into directions in which they would naturally demand the whole man; and out of all researches to select by preference those which would furnish the largest outlines of valuable ideas to the use of an intellect rather simple than refining; rather positive than subtle; rather grasping at Truth where she emerged into the open space than stealing through the labyrinth to surprise her in her cell. We must be pardoned for these references to certain points in the earlier education and tendencies of this famous man, which may seem too familiar to reiterate; since our readers may thus arrive at perceptions into the nature of his general intellect which do not seem to have been suggested to his biographers.

Thus trained and prepared William Pitt entered into life — too soon his own master. He had attained the age of nineteen when his father died. In 1780 he was called to the Bar, and went the Western Circuit. In the same year he lost his eldest sister, Lady Mahon, and his brother James, of whom he says, in a letter to his former tutor, "he had everything that was most desirable and promising — everything that I could love and admire; and I feel the favourite hope of my mind extinguished by this untimely blow. Let me, however (he adds), assure you that I am too tried in affliction

not to be able to support myself under it." Whether
from the desire to distract his thoughts from such
causes for grief, or from the native buoyancy of spirit
which belongs to genius in youth, it was in the winter
of that year that we find him supping nightly at
Goosetree's club, more amusing than professed wits,
entering with energy into the different amusements of
gay companions, and displaying intense earnestness in
games of chance. Of these last, however, "he perceived," says Wilberforce, "the increasing fascination,
and soon after suddenly abandoned them for ever."
Indeed, in the January of 1781, William Pitt, having
unsuccessfully contested the University of Cambridge
at the general election in the previous autumn, was
returned to Parliament for the borough of Appleby,
by the interest of Sir James Lowther, but at the re-
quest of the Duke of Rutland. From that date the
ordeal of such temptations as beset the idleness of
youth was past.

It is scarcely possible to conceive a more gloomy
combination of discredit and disaster — of dangers
from without and within — than that which threatened
Great Britain, when the son of Lord Chatham first
entered the august assembly in which his father had
left many to divide his mantle, no one to claim his sceptre.

Abroad, the condition of our affairs was such as the
boldest statesman might have contemplated with dis-
may. In America, a war that had become odious to
the feelings, and humbling to the spirit of the English
people, was slowly burning down into barren ashes;
temporary successes inspired no exultation at home; a
secret sentiment of their ultimate futility made the
people echo the assertion of Fox, that Clinton's cap-

ture of Charlestown and Cornwallis's victory at Camden "were matters less to rejoice at than deplore." Two years before, France had acknowledged the independence of the American Colonies, and was now our declared foe. Her resources were then unknown; they were represented by our leading orators, and popularly believed, to be far beyond the power of British commerce and wealth to encounter. Turgot's wise warnings had been disregarded. Necker had enveloped the general finances of France in profound mystery, and the boldness of his loans concealed the exhaustion of his means. Here even the sagacity of Burke was deceived: misplaced indeed was the splendid panegyric he pronounced on the hollow expedients of the Genevese financier: "Principle," exclaimed the orator *nescius futuri* — "principle, method, regularity, economy, frugality, justice to individuals, and care of the people, are the resources with which France makes war upon Great Britain."* Holland was already on the side of the Americans, and preparing to join France in the acknowledgment of their independence. Spain had arrayed against us fleets that excited more dread than her earlier Armada. In 1779 the island had been scared by a Proclamation charging all officers, civil

---

* Burke lived to exclaim upon reading Necker's History of his own Administration, "Ah, if the practice of the author had corresponded to his theory!" Wise was the reply that Burke received from Necker's apologist, and the distinction it implies should be remembered in our estimate of every genuine statesman: "The theory depended on the author alone, the practice on all that was around, with, or against him."

and military, in case of an invasion, to cause all horses, oxen, cattle, and provisions to be driven from the sea-coast to places of security; and had an enemy, in truth, set foot upon our shores, we possessed not, according to the assurance of the Secretary at War, a single General in whom the army could confide. "I don't know," said Lord North with his usual exquisite drollery, "whether our Generals will frighten the enemy, but I know that they frighten me." Meanwhile Gibraltar was besieged by forces greater than had ever before honoured a solitary stronghold. Russia, Denmark, and Sweden had entered into common treaties, constituting an armed neutrality, and maintaining a principle that forbade to belligerent powers the right of searching the vessels of neutral states and involved the pregnant seeds of that actual hostility with England which Russia, at least, almost openly desired. We had not on the Continent a single ally. Nor did we stand only against the great potentates of Europe; we stood against its public opinion, while we continued to sink in its respect for our power. In the contest with America we had neither the support of popular sympathy nor the dignity of military success.

Not only our armies had been defeated, but our maritime power had been humbled. Hostile fleets had paraded their flags before Plymouth: a miserable buccaneer, Paul Jones, had harried our Northern shores in a single frigate — insulted the Scottish coast with a descent — plundered an Earl's house with impunity — spiked the guns of Whitehaven fort — burned two vessels, and carried off 200 prisoners. Admirals were condemning the Admiralty, and dividing Parliament against each other. The Court was supposed to take

part against its absent naval commander; and the ac-
quittal of Keppel by the court-martial, to which Burke
had attended him "to witness his agony of glory," had
been followed by public illuminations — not more designed to honour the hero than to mortify his Sovereign. Naval successes indeed there were to chequer
these ominous prospects, but the naval service itself
was demoralized; Keppel, coldly re-appointed, refused
to serve, other officers of distinction threw up their
commissions, and a general mutiny in the great fleet
assembled at Torbay was with difficulty appeased.

At home, trade was everywhere depressed; the public
spirit, disheartened against the national enemies, trans-
ferred its wrath to the national rulers; monarchical
institutions shook beneath the violence of party and
the general discontent. Language that went to a length
which an ultra-radical now-a-days would call revolu-
tionary, was held, not by the populace and their de-
magogues alone, it was thundered from the lips of
peers — it lightened from the eloquence of sages.
Burke's famous motion for Economical Reform had
produced effects on the public mind far beyond what
his sagacity foresaw, or his philosophy could approve.
Economy, as is usual in times of distress, became connected with some constitutional change which should
go to the root of the evils alleged. Public meetings
inflamed the provinces; and so great a multitude had
assembled at Westminster, that troops were drawn out
and stationed in the immediate vicinity. In the midst
of this excitement a motion, to the effect that the influence of the Crown had increased, was increasing, and
ought to be diminished, was supported by the Speaker
of the House of Commons, adopted with an immaterial

17*

amendment by the Government itself, and carried, thus
amended, by a majority of eighteen.   Very shortly
afterwards, the Duke of Richmond introduced into the
House of Lords a motion for annual parliaments, and
a suffrage little less than universal; and as if to prove
how unfit were the commonalty for the power to which
it was thus proposed to exalt them — how faint would
be the hope of enlightening the councils of the state,
by transferring legislation to the wisdom of numbers —
at that very period a madman was at the head of the
mob, and the "No Popery" riot of Lord George Gordon
was raging through the streets.   Members of the House
of Commons were compelled by the *sans-culottes*, whom
a Duke would have elevated into voters, to put on
blue cockades, and shout out "No Popery" — the
rabble were thundering at the doors of the House of
Commons — in the lobby a lunatic was haranguing
crowds, half fanatics, half thieves — when the very
motion for annual Parliaments in the Lords was interrupted by the roar of the multitude — and a motion,
whether or not the peers should sally out in a body
to rescue their fellows, was decided in the negative, for
fear the mace that should symbolize their dignity should
be stolen by the pious assemblage it would assuredly
not have awed.

Such were the circumstances under which Parliament (prorogued July 8th) had been suddenly dis-
solved on the 1st of September, 1780, and that new
Parliament assembled, in which Providence had selected the agent for the preservation of the English
throne.

At this time Lord North's administration, still out-
wardly strong, was inwardly undermined.   Lord North

himself had long been impatiently anxious to retire, and only retained the seals at the urgent entreaties of the King. The main body of the Opposition comprised two parties, which, but for personal jealousies, would have easily amalgamated their political opinions — viz., first, the scattered remnants of Lord Chatham's more exclusive following, of whom Lord Shelburne was the chief representative in the Lords; Dunning and Col. Barré the most influential organs in the Commons. Secondly, the Whigs, properly so called; formidable alike from their number and their union, the mass of property which they represented, and the parliamentary eloquence with which their opinions were enforced. Never did the Whigs, since the palmiest days of Walpole, stand so well with the people as towards the close of Lord North's administration. It was not only that they comprised the greatest houses and the loftiest names in that more powerful section of our Aristocracy, by the aid of which William III. had achieved his throne, and the House of Brunswick secured its ascendency; but during their penance in opposition, the questions they had advocated had restored them to the popular favour, which the Newcastle administration had lost. They had outlived the national prejudice excited against them by their early resistance to the American war. The public were as hostile to the continuance, as they had been favourable to the commencement, of that luckless struggle. Burke's great orations — in which the zeal of the partisan took the imposing accents of patriotism guided by philosophy — had produced a powerful effect upon the more calm and reflective minds which lend authority to 'popular opinion; and if the private errors of Mr. Fox himself scared the timid and

shocked the decorous — errors palliated by youth,
sanctioned by fashion, redeemed by social qualities at
once loveable and brilliant, and leaving no stain upon
the masculine virtues of sincerity, courage, and sense
of honour — little impaired the effect of his genius
upon an audience chiefly composed of men of the
world, or upon the ordinary mass of the public, in an
age that had made an idol of Wilkes. And that great
orator, from the height of the position to which he had
stormed his way, could have seen little save the coronets
of nobles, who smiled upon his progress, between himself and the loftiest place below the throne.*

Nature bestowed on Mr. Fox the qualities which
are certain to command distinction in popular assemblies. He possessed in the highest degree the temperament of the orator, which, equal to the poet's in
the intensity of feeling, is diametrically opposed to the
poet's in the direction to which its instincts impel it.
For the tendency of the last is to render into the ideal
all which observation can collect from the practical,
and the tendency of the first is to gather from the ideal

---

* At this time Fox *practically* led the opposition in the
House of Commons, though he does not appear to have been
formally recognised as the Whig leader in that House, to the
deposition of Burke, until as a Cabinet Minister he naturally
took precedence over his elder friend. At the death of Lord
Rockingham, Burke, who had hitherto been regarded as the
special representative in the House of Commons of that
nobleman's opinions, had, by acquiescence in an office of
inferior dignity, resigned the power, even if he retained the
ambition, to contest Fox's supremacy as the successor of
Lord Rockingham, and the chief of the Whig party in both
Houses.

all which can serve and adorn the practical. Hence logical argument is the death of poetry and the living principle of oratory. In the union of natural passion with scholastic reasoning Mr. Fox excelled all who have dignified the English senate. He required no formal preparation beyond that which a mental review of the materials of a question in debate suggested to a mind rich in a copious variety of knowledge, and so charged with intellectual heat that it needed but collision to flash instantaneously into light. Yet an intellect so active and a fancy so teeming as Mr. Fox's must have been constantly at work in the moments most apparently idle. Mr. Fox might have spent the night in a gaming-house, hurried off to Newmarket at daybreak, returned just in time to open a debate in the House of Commons — but who shall say that during those hours he had found no intervals in which his reason was arranging a course of argument, and his memory suggesting the appropriate witticism or the felicitous allusion? He was not only endowed with the orator's temperament, he was consummate in the orator's art; and whether in oratory, poetry, painting, or sculpture, no artist attains to that excellence in which effort concealed steals the charm of intuition, unless his art be constantly before him — unless all which is observed in ordinary life, as well as all which is studied in severer moments, contributes to the special faculties which the art itself has called into an energy so habitually pervading the whole intellectual constitution, that the mind is scarcely conscious of the work which it undergoes. But perhaps of every art that of the parliamentary orator is the one in which the least obvious sources supply the most popular effects. Even the gossip of commonplace minds furnishes a barometer of public prejudice to counteract or of public opinion to respect. The talk of the clubs suggests the topics which will best tell with a party; while every man who narrates an anecdote or quotes a poem may suggest a grace to the discourse, an intonation to the voice, an effect to the delivery. Those, indeed, notably err, who, judging only by the desultory social habits and dissipated tastes of Mr. Fox, conclude that his faculties attained their strength without the necessary toil of resolute exertion. The propensity to labour at excellence, even in his amusements, distinguished him throughout life. "At every little diversion or employment" (says his nephew Lord Holland), "chess, cards, carving at dinner, would he exercise his faculties with wonderful assiduity and attention till he had attained the degree of perfection he aimed at. It was this peculiarity which led him many years afterwards, when asked how he contrived, being so corpulent, to pick up the out-balls at tennis so well, to answer playfully, 'Because I am a very painstaking man.'" Perhaps it was this earnestness to excel, even in trifles, that conduced to his errors, and frittered away his robust powers of application. When persons accused him of idleness as a legislator, it was because he was fagging hard to be a fine gentleman. The exuberant vitality of his nature, like that of Alcibiades and our own Henry St. John, could not exhaust itself in a single field of ambition. Pleasure was essential to his joyous energies, but he could not take pleasure as a mere relaxation. He took it as an active pursuit, and sought, from that love of approbation which accounts for the frivolities of great men, to wring from the pursuit a distinction. If a

gamester, — to be of gamesters the most reckless; if a
rake, — of rakes the most daring. With Fox, too,
labour was necessary for all achievements. Nature had
not given to his person the beauty which allowed St.
John to please without an effort, nor to his voice the
felicitous music by which Chatham could sway the soul
of an assembly. Therefore to be the prince of beaux
and gallants in the drawing-room, or the speaker at
whose rising members rushed to their seats or crowded
the eager bar, demanded in Fox a degree of study and
toil which were disguised by the outward ease with
which superior strength smiles under its own exertions.
And though, as we have before said, Fox required no
formal preparation to make a speech, he had gone
through elaborate preparation to become a speaker. Not
only from his earliest boyhood had politics engaged his
thoughts; not only before he was of age had he accomplished himself in the learning which best befits the
orator, arms his memory with facts and enriches it with
illustrations; but in the zest with which he entered into
theatrical performances he was already meditating the
effects which art might give to an utterance in itself
unmelodious. And Lord Holland justly observes, "that
the power of expressing passion by the tones of his
voice had, no doubt, been brought to perfection by his
exertions on the stage."* But, more than all, Mr. Fox
sought the excellence which practice alone confers, in
the arena in which his triumphs were to be achieved.
The House of Commons has a kind of oratory so

* Fox produced some of his most thrilling effects by what
actors call "the run upon two voices," viz., suddenly sinking
from his sharp, high key-note into a deep, low whisper.

peculiar to itself that there is no greater misfortune to
eloquent men on entering that assembly than to have
matured the theory of their art (though they may well
have established its groundwork) in any other school.
It was his very success at the bar which injured the
effect of Erskine in the senate.   And had Burke entered Parliament at that earlier age when the mind is
yet keenly alive to the finer influences round it, he
would never have incurred those faults of taste which
so often offended his audience.   The colours of genius
are determined by the ray incident on the first prism,
and the light once decomposed by refraction, no further
refraction can again decompose.   It was thus no sub-
sidiary cause of Mr. Fox's parliamentary success that
his taste formed its style in the House of Commons —
an eloquence indigenous to the soil and not trans-
planted; its beauties and defects grew up together; and,
as the first were those which could be most generally
appreciated, so the last were those which could be most
readily excused.   Entering Parliament before he was
of age, the ardour of his nature soon flung him into
the thick of debate.   For five years he spoke on every
question but one, and he said he regretted he had not
spoken upon that.   But his earlier speeches were not
long, like Burke's; they did not take the form of essays;
they were so close to the matter of debate that the debate
would have seemed incomplete without them.   Thus the
audience grew familiarised to faults which had a certain
charm, not only because they imparted to effects that were
learned at the theatre, but learned too well to appear
theatrical, the air of natural passion and "negligent
grandeur," but because they gave to the merits which
redeemed them the thrilling suddenness of surprise, and

the orator was patiently allowed to splutter and stammer out his way into the heart of his subject, grappling, as it were, with the ideas that embarrassed his choice by the pressure of their throng, till, once selected and marshalled into order, they emerged from the wildness of a tumult into the discipline of an army. Mr. Fox was thus not only an orator, but pre-eminently an orator for the House of Commons. And though he gave to his invectives an angry and distempered enthusiasm which would not now be tolerated, and which even then was a gross defect that detracted from his authority and impaired his position; yet, upon the whole, his speeches were more characterised than those of any of his contemporaries by the tone of a man of the world, who, accustomed betimes to the best society, can be wise without pedantry, pleasant without flippancy, and is not vulgar even when he puts himself into a passion. Thus at the age of thirty-one Charles Fox stood forth before the public — the foremost hero of an united, numerous, and powerful party; he himself, says Horace Walpole, "the idol of the people," adding to his advantages of intellect and position the inestimable blessing of an Herculean constitution, which no labours seemed to weary, no excesses to impair. Never did chief of a party inspire more enthusiasm amongst his followers, never was political sympathy more strengthened by personal affection. What became of that party, under the guidance of that leader? We shall see.

At this time a tall, slender stripling, ten years younger than Mr. Fox, with no social fame, with few personal friends, scarcely known even by sight to his nearest connexions, with manners that rather repelled than allured ordinary acquaintance, at once shy and

stately with the consciousness of merits unrevealed, took
his undistinguished seat below the gangway, and under
the gallery, by the side of a young Whig county member
(George Byng), who survived to witness the passing of
the Reform Bill and attain the venerable distinction of
Father of the House of Commons: —

> "Abstulit clarum cita mors Achillem,
> Longa Tithonum minuit senectus."

Plain in feature, but with clear, grey, watchful eyes
— with high and massive forehead, in which what
phrenologists call the perceptive organs were already
prominently marked — with lips which when in repose
were expressive much of reserve, more of pertinacity
and resolve, but in movement were singularly flexible
to the impulse of the manlier passions, giving a noble
earnestness to declamation and a lofty disdain to sarcasm — this young man sate amongst the Rockingham
Whigs, a sojourner in their camp, not a recruit to their
standard. He had, indeed, offered himself to their
chief, but that provident commander had already mea-
sured for his uniform some man of his own inches, and
did not think it worth while to secure the thews of a
giant at the price of wasting a livery and disappointing
a dwarf.

The incident is curious, and illustrative of reflections from which future leaders of the Whigs might
deduce a profitable moral.

When William Pitt, in 1780, sought first to enter
Parliament as a candidate for the University of Cambridge, he wrote to Lord Rockingham for his interest,
and concluded his letter in words by which honourable

men imply support in return for assistance. "I have only," writes the son of Lord Chatham, "to hope that the ground on which I stand, as well as the principles which I have imbibed, and which shall always actuate my conduct, may be considered by your lordship as some recommendation."

Will it be believed that the Marquis of Rockingham does not answer this letter dated the 19th of July till the 7th of August? and then makes no apology for the delay, but replies with laconic frigidity, "I had the honour to receive your letter some days ago. I am so circumstanced from the knowledge I have of several persons who may be candidates, and who indeed are expected to be so, that it makes it impossible for me in this instance to show the attention to your wishes which your own as well as the great merits of your family entitle you to."*

That Lord Rockingham's interest might be pre-engaged was natural, but he does not state it to be so: he implies *preference* for other candidates, but not *pre-engagement* to them; and that, supposing he was "so circumstanced" as to render it "impossible" to aid his applicant in contesting the University, he should have found amongst the numerous boroughs at the disposal of the Whig leader no seat for a recruit whose very name would have been so important an addition to the Whig strength, and who might have served as a connecting link between the Chathamites and the Rockingham party, argues grave deficiency in

* 'Memoirs of the Marquis of Rockingham, and his Contemporaries,' by George Thomas, Earl of Albemarle, vol. II. p. 423.

political tactics. But when Lord John Russell expresses eloquent regret that at a subsequent period
Mr. Pitt and Mr. Fox did not act together, we submit to him that — in rejecting overtures which, had
they been cordially accepted, would have necessarily
made Mr. Pitt, on his entrance into public life, not
the rival but the follower of Mr. Fox — Lord Rockingham, if never less of a prophet, was never more of
a Whig. The Whigs of that day were the Hebrews
of politics. Regarding themselves as a chosen race,
the privileges of their creed were to be inherited at
birth, not conceded to proselytes. They courted no
converts, even amongst those whom they aspired to
govern. Over Edom they might cast their shoe, and
Moab they might make their washpot; but no Tory
from Edom, and no Radical from Moab, has right to
claim admission into the sacred tribes: in the eyes of
the rulers of Israel, Lord Chatham's son was a — Gentile.

Thus, unpledged to any political chief, but imbibing from his father opinions irreconcilable with Lord
North's administration, on the 26th February, 1781,
Mr. Pitt first rose in Parliament in support of Burke's
renewed bill for Economical Reform in the Civil List.
It is a remarkable proof, which we do not remember
to have seen observed, of Pitt's isolation from all
sections of party, that Lord Shelburne's friends did
not attend this debate, and that he was not therefore
acting more in concert with them than with the
followers of Lord Rockingham. Of this speech Lord
North declared that it was the best first speech he
ever heard. Lord John Russell considers it a signal
instance of Mr. Fox's generosity, that he hurried up
to the young member to compliment and encourage

him in this "sudden display of talents nearly equal
to his own." The praise of generosity is unmerited.
Mr. Fox cannot be called generous, though he may
justly be called wise, in applauding a young man
for an admirable speech on a motion which Mr. Fox
and all his party supported. An old member overheard the praise, and said, "Ay, old as I am, I
expect to hear you both battling in these walls as
I have done your fathers before you." The man of
fashion, disconcerted by the awkward turn of the
compliment, looked foolish; the boy lawyer answered
with equal readiness and felicity of expression, "I
have no doubt, General, you would like to attain the
age of Methuselah." If we examine this first speech
with some critical attention, and compare it with others
known to have received Mr. Pitt's careful revision,
there is good internal evidence, that not only its
substance but its diction is preserved to us with
sufficient accuracy to enable us to judge of the causes
which assigned to it so signal a success. We can
gather from it, first, the fact that the delivery must
have been very striking, for it is precisely one of
those speeches which ill delivered would have failed
in effect, below the merit of the substance — well
delivered would have obtained more applause than the
substance itself deserved. It is always so in the House
of Commons where the language rises above the level
tenor of debate, and the argument avoids apt personalities to grasp at general principles. Take for instance passages like the following: —

"They ought to have consulted the glory of their royal
master, and have seated him in the hearts of his people, by

abating from magnificence what was due to necessity. . . . .
It would be no diminution of true grandeur to yield to the
respectful petitions of the people; the tutelage of that House
might be a hard term, but the guardianship of that House
could not be disgraceful to a constitutional King. . . . .   But
it had been said that the saving was immaterial . . . . it proposed to bring no more than 200,000*l.* into the public coffers;
and that sum was insignificant, in the public account, when
compared with the millions which we spend.   This was
surely the most singular species of reasoning that was ever
attempted in any assembly.   The calamities of the crisis
were too great to be benefited by economy!   Our expenses
were so enormous that it was ridiculous to attend to little
matters of account!   We have spent so many millions that
thousands are beneath our consideration!   We were obliged
to spend so much, that it was foolish to think of saving
any!"

    A practised observer of parliamentary effects will
at once acknowledge — that sentences like the above,
if spoken, especially by a very young man, with
frigidity or feebleness, would fall flat on the ear as
the rhetoric of schoolboy premeditation — while, if
uttered with warmth, assisted by the earnest bye-
play of countenance and gesture, they would be as
sure of loud cheers to-day as they were in 1781.   The
aid of delivery thus taken for granted, the speech
justifies the impression it created; the language is
precisely of that character, which when well spoken
the House of Commons is most inclined to admire —
dignified, yet animated — pointed and careful, yet
sufficiently colloquial — the beauties it avoids are
those by which the House of Commons is least seduced.   So with the matter — it embodies the gener-

ous sentiments, to which all popular assemblies the most willingly respond, in arguments that take the broadest objections of the adversaries, and do not fatigue attention by entrance into small details and subtle reasonings. More perhaps than all other elements for parliamentary success, the speech exhibits the two qualities which, when present, give repute to mediocrity, — when absent, impair the efficiency of genius, viz., readiness and tact.* Waking thus "to find him-

* Wraxall erroneously ascribes to Pitt's *maiden* speech a sarcastic witticism which he spoils in the telling. Lord John Russell gives the words on the authority of Mr. Adams, but does not seem aware of the occasion on which they were delivered, and apparently antedates them. They were not uttered in Pitt's first session in Parliament, but the second, in going into Committee of Supply on the Army Estimates, Dec. 14, 1781. To give due force to the witticism, and to rescue it from the character of presumption which Lord John's authority assigns to it, his Lordship should have stated correctly the substance of the charge which the witticism barbed. Pitt was not accusing the Minister, as Lord John says, "of grave *neglects*," but the Ministers in general of *want of union*. "Is it to be credited," he said, "that a Ministry ignorant of each other's opinions are unanimous? The absurdity is too monstrous to be believed, especially when the assurance is made at a moment when the Ministry are more disunited than ever." Here that veteran placeman, Wellbore Ellis, began whispering to Lord North and to Lord George Germaine, whose personal courage had been so gravely called in question; and Pitt, checking his invective, said, "But I will pause till the unanimity is a little more settled — until" [here comes Mr. Adams' version of the happy taunt] "the Nestor of the Treasury Bench has composed the differences of Agamemnon and Achilles." — See *Hansard's Parliamentary Debates*, vol. xxii. p. 843.

self famous," Pitt did not fall into the error by which
Burke at the onset of his career had cheapened his
eloquence and damaged his position.   Pitt did not
speak "too long and too often."   Only three speeches
of his in his first session are recorded; and when the
session was over, he had done more than prove himself an orator — he was acknowledged as a Power.
The very contrast between his years and his bearing
but increased the respect which accompanied the
popular admiration.   Men regarded as a kind of
sublime prodigy a youth so unbending to follies, and
uniting such ample resources with such calm self-
reliance.   The solitude of his position rendered its
height more apparent.   He continued to hold himself aloof from the recognised chiefs of opposition.
Fox and Shelburne alike might sue for his aid,
neither one nor the other could lay claim to his alle-
giance.   No doubt this reserve was in part the result
of profound calculation.   As yet it was only as a subordinate that he could have joined a party, and he
who once consents to become a subordinate must go
through the hackneyed grades of promotion before
he can rise to be a chief.   Let Genius venture itself
boldly against Routine, and the odds are that it will
win the race by the help of its wings.   But if it seek
its career in Routine itself, it must resign the advantage
of its pinions, and trust to the chance of outwalking
those two fearful competitors — Length of Service and
Family Interest.   It is true that the first is somewhat
slow in its pace, but then it has ten years start on
the road; it is true that the last cannot bear much
fatigue, but then, instead of its own slender legs, it
makes use of my lord's chaise and four!   But if Pitt's

isolation from the Whigs was due in part to his political sagacity, it was due also in part to his personal tastes. To a man of his temper there could have been no allurement in the brilliant society of the Whigs, with all the looseness of its wit, and all the licence of its fashion.

Who can fancy William Pitt at his ease in the social orgies at Brookes's, or amidst the gay coteries of Devonshire House, or exchanging jests with Sheridan, or sauntering into the levées of St. James's Street, in which Fox, "his bristly black person and shagged breast quite open, and rarely purified by any ablutions, wrapped in a foul linen gown, and his bushy hair dishevelled, dictated his politics with Epicurean good humour"? * There — where the principles of a loan and the assaults on a government were relieved by broad jokes on the last scandal, the slang of the turf, and the irreverent spectacle of the boyish heir to the crown imbibing lessons of royal decorum and filial reverence from the men whose ribald talk against his father was echoed back to the court from the gossip of every drawing-room and club; there — what figure

---

* Horace Walpole. To which Lord Holland adds a note: — "This description, though of course a strong caricature, yet certainly has much humour; and I must needs acknowledge, from my boyhood recollections of a morning in St. James's-street, has some truth to recommend it." Probably in 1783 the description had less caricature than when Lord Holland, at a later period of his uncle's life, recognised the partial truth of its outlines. Fox in his earlier youth, when serving under Lord North, had been remarkable for foppery in dress. He adopted slovenly habits in espousing popular opinions.

18*

would have been so inaccordant to the genius of the
place as the stately son of Chatham, with his imperial
tenacity of self-esteem, and his instinctive deference
for the fair proprieties of life? If it be unjust to suppose that Pitt, especially in his youth, was any foe to
mirth, — for the mirth of men of gallantry, men of
fashion, men of polite morals, he was too austere in
his principles, and too decorous in his tastes.   We
fear that we must allow that in such a society William
Pitt would have been quizzed.   As, therefore, his
private temperament and inclinations were not attracted
towards intimacy with the Whigs and their illustrious
leader, so, even where at that time he politically agreed
with Mr. Fox, there was so essential a difference in
the modes with which the two men treated the same
questions, that their intellectual intercourse would have
failed for want of sympathy.   One distinction between
them is pre-eminently noticeable: it continued throughout life, and contains much that made the one supported by the people even in his most rigorous enact-
ments, the other deserted by the people even in his
most popular professions. Mr. Fox identified himself
with principles in the abstract, Mr. Pitt rather with
the nation to which such principles were to be applied.
The one argued and viewed the great problems of
state chiefly as a philanthropist, the other chiefly as a
patriot. This distinction is not merely theoretical —
it affects the practical treatment of mighty questions.
He who thinks with Mr. Pitt embraces for change the
consideration of season, and refers a speculative principle to the modifications of practical circumstance.
And the wisdom of such view of the art of statesmanship is apparent in this, that, where the politician

avows it frankly, consistency is not violated nor a
principle damaged when he is compelled to say,
"There are considerations connected with the actual
time that will not allow me the safe experiment of a
theory to which I am otherwise friendly." But where,
on the contrary, the politician rigidly asserts that the
principle he affects must be carried at all hazards, he
loses character, and injures that principle itself, if,
when he comes into power, he finds that he is no more
able to carry it into law than the predecessor whose
milder doctrine he had attacked as untenable. But
whatever may be thought of the abstract superiority
of either creed, there can be no doubt that, in action,
the man who is more habitually seen to make his first
object the interests of the nation, will obtain the
greater degree of national support; and the man who
works towards his end according to the instruments at
his disposal, will be more likely to achieve some positive result than he who, absorbed in shaping his object
according to his own ideal, insists on a circle with
tools only fit for a square.

It is unnecessary to narrate the events, or refer to
the debates, of the two following sessions, till the
capitulation of Lord Cornwallis's army and the fall of
Minorca led to the resignation of the amiable minister
who had borne with such easy good humour the assaults
of his enemies and the disgrace of his country. Two
public men then stood forth, pre-eminent for the royal
selection of chief minister, — the Marquis of Rockingham and the Earl of Shelburne. The first has been
singularly felicitous, the last as singularly unfortunate,
in those elements of posthumous estimation, which the
comments of contemporaries afford. The Whigs have

been the chief annalists of that time, and they were as friendly to Rockingham as they were hostile to Shelburne. It is not from Lord Holland nor from Mr. Allen that we have a right to expect an accurate judgment of the man with whom Fox so vehemently quarrelled, and by whom, in the stage-plot of cabinets, Fox was so pleasantly outwitted. On the other hand, the grateful praise of Burke has assigned to Lord Rockingham a place among statesmen to which nothing in his talents or career affords any solid pretension. Lord Rockingham, indeed, was a man whose respectability of character must be not less frankly admitted, than the inferiority of his capacities. We have read with attention Lord Albemarle's 'Memoirs' of this wealthy nobleman, and the skill of the editor has rendered the reading very light and amusing, by keeping Lord Rockingham himself almost hid from the eye. The memoirs indeed would be rendered still more amusing if, in a future edition, the marquis could disappear altogether. Bold as the doubt may be, we question whether Lord Rockingham, take him altogether, was not the dullest man whom England ever saw in the rank of first minister. "*Doctrina sed vim promovet insitam*" — perhaps the natural sterility was redeemed by artistic culture? Flattering supposition!

"Horse-racing," says Lord Mahon* of this favourite of fortune, "was his early passion and pursuit. He afterwards became a lord of the bedchamber, and was thought perfectly well fitted for that post. When in 1765 the idea was first entertained of appointing him to a high political office, the King expressed his sur-

* Now Earl Stanhope.

prise, 'for I thought,' said his Majesty, 'I had not two
men in my bedchamber of less parts than Lord Rockingham.'" Nevertheless in 1765 the ex-lord of the
bedchamber was at the head of his Majesty's government — and that government is entitled to respect for
the excellence of its intentions, nor less to our gratitude for the instructive lesson it bequeathed, viz. that
excellent intentions unaccompanied by vigour and
capacity can neither give permanence to governments
nor avail for the guidance of states. Doubtless it is a
merit in a sack to be clean, but a clean sack stands
on end no more than a foul one — if it is empty. As
a party adviser Lord Rockingham is said to have exhibited, in private, plain good sense and sound judgment: these qualities appear little in his correspondence,
less in his actions, least of all in his speeches. In
Parliament his highest efforts in his best days were but
slovenly commonplaces dropped forth with painful hesitation. Latterly he had grown timidly averse to speaking at all, and had settled down to the confirmed state
of a nervous valetudinarian. But whatever Lord Rockingham's defects, he had the great advantage which
mediocrity alone possesses, — none of his party were
jealous of him. He had another advantage in the high
rank and the immense wealth which invest with imposing splendour the virtue of common honesty, and
give to the sobriety that comes from constitutional
languor the loftier character of sagacious moderation.
At all events he was ingenuous and simple. "His
virtues," according to Burke's epitaph, "were his arts."
To sum up — no statesman living was more worshipped
by his party — less beloved by his sovereign — was

regarded by his country with more indifference — or inspired its enemies with less awe.

The Earl of Shelburne (afterwards Marquis of Lansdowne) contrasted the notable tameness of Lord Rockingham, equally by the greatness of his talents and the puzzling complications of his character. Lord Holland tells us in one sentence that "the Earl had no knowledge of the world, but a thorough perception of its dishonesty;" and adds, in the very next, that "his observations on public life were often original and just, and, on individual character, shrewd, sagacious, and happy. I have known," continues Lord Holland, "few men whose maxims more frequently occur to my recollection, or are more applicable to the events of the world, and to the characters of those who rule it." Thus, again, while the same noble critic remarks, that "there was elevation in Lord Shelburne's character," and says, "I have observed traits of real magnanimity in his conduct," he lends his sanction, in the 'Memorials of Mr. Fox,' to the grave imputation against the Earl of systematic duplicity — the vice, above all others, least compatible with "elevation of character and magnanimity of conduct," and implies that the statesman whose youth had been passed in the frank intercourse of camps, and who was allowed by his bitterest detractors conspicuous attributes of courage and decision of character, merited the nicknames of Jesuit* and

---

* Lord Holland, in seeking to justify a charge that he can in no way prove, by bringing a nickname of the day in support of its probability, should have remembered that the same nickname of Jesuit was applied yet more familiarly to Edmund Burke; yet certainly no man was ever less entitled to that appellation in the sense it was intended to convey.

Malagrida. The true secret of judgments so contradictory is to be found in this — Lord Shelburne's was
one of those natures in which both merits and defects
are more visible to the eye from the irregularity of
the surface which draws and reflects the light. Morally
and intellectually, he was eccentric and unequal. His
earlier years had purchased military distinction at the
cost of scholastic instruction. And in his after intercourse with those in whom he saw secret enemies or
doubtful friends, he brought a great deal of the old
soldier's caution; nor where he suspected the ambush
did he disdain the stratagem. Of long-sustained in-
trigue he was incapable; but did he conceive a scheme,
he could guard it with great closeness, and carry it by
a *coup de main*. The politic dissimulation of a Jesuit
he certainly had not; but, on occasion, he exhibited
the wary astuteness of a Spartan. We must concede
the justice with which Burke says of him in a private
letter, that he was "whimsical and suspicious." But
the whims arose from an intellect self-formed, arriving
at its own results in its own way; and though often
changing its directions, unaccustomed to the beaten
track and the professional guide. And if he was suspicious, it must be owned that the charge chiefly came
from men whom he might reasonably think it somewhat
imprudent to trust. Nor was this tendency of mind
unjustified by the peculiar circumstances with which he
was surrounded at various periods of his life. In early
youth he had some cause to guard himself against his
own family: in the noon of his ambition he saw on one
side of him a hostile court, and on the other side a
rival faction, whose aid was necessary to his advancement, and whose jealousies might compass his over-

throw.   But that he had, as Lord Holland asserts, "a mean opinion of his species," is scarcely in keeping with a political theory to which respect for mankind, and confidence in human virtue, make the necessary groundwork.   "Lord Shelburne was the only minister I ever heard of," said Jeremy Bentham, "who did not fear the people."   His political doctrines were indeed of a more philosophical and comprehensive character than those by which the Great Houses invited the aid of democracy to the dominion of oligarchs.   He differed from Mr. Fox and the Whigs of that day in his attachment to the growing science of political economy.   No public man then living better understood the true principles of commerce.   Without sharing the extravagant doctrines of the Duke of Richmond, he was more sincerely in favour of a modified Parliamentary Reform than were the leading partisans of Lord Rockingham. But he had a thorough contempt for all the commonplace jargon bestowed on that subject, and rather held popular liberty essential to vigorous government, than the fascinating substitute for any government at all.

As a Parliamentary speaker, Lord Shelburne showed the same brilliant and eccentric originality which perplexed the judgment of contemporaries in their estimate of the man.   He certainly did not speak like one accustomed to plot and inclined to dissimulate.   Animation was his leading excellence.   Often rash, often arrogant, careless whom he conciliated, whom offended — speaking with impetuous rapidity,* like a man full of

---

* Fox says, in one of his later speeches, that Lord Shelburne spoke, like himself, very rapidly, and it was difficult for the reporters to follow him.

unpremeditated thought — warmed by passionate impulse — exposing himself both to refutation and ridicule, but "repelling such attacks with great spirit and readiness,"* — all authorities concur in the acknowledgment that, in debate, he was generally very effective, and that at times his language itself, though generally unstudied, was felicitously eloquent. Indeed, there are passages in his speeches still preserved to us, which not one of our English orators has surpassed in hardy nobility of thought, and masculine strength of diction. "He was," says Lord Holland, "a great master of irony; and no man ever expressed bitter scorn for his opponents with more art and effect." This is not the rhetoric of a Jesuit: in his vehemence, as in his caution, Lord Shelburne was always the soldier.

Regarded purely as a party leader, Lord Shelburne had some of the highest requisites. "He was munificent and friendly," says Lord Holland, "even to a fault; none of his family or connections were ever involved in any difficulty without finding in him a powerful protector and active friend." "He had discernment in discovering the talents of inferiors" — his person was prepossessing, and his manners, when unrestrained, were sufficiently cordial. On the other hand, as caution was not habitual to him, so he often counteracted its effects by a sudden indiscretion. Though so ready, he often failed in tact, and his energy, though prodigious, was rather fitful than sustained. Often a deep, but too much a solitary thinker, he could not act in sufficient concert with others. And the closeness with which he concealed his plans was partly

* Lord Holland's 'Memoirs of the Whig Party.'

connected with a reluctance to receive advice. With
much kindness he had little sympathy. And as he
lacked the art to conciliate opponents, so he scorned
to recover friends whom an offence on their part, or a
misconception on his own, once estranged from his
side. He was not revengeful, but he was not forgiv-
ing, or rather, if he forgave in his heart, he did not
own it. In these less amiable and attractive attributes,
favourably indeed contrasted by the son, who ultimately
succeeded to his honours, and who yet lives[*] to command the affectionate veneration of all, who, whatever
the differences of party, can appreciate the nature in
which a rare elevation and an exquisite suavity admit
of no enmities, while cementing all friendships — and
which, gracing by accomplished culture a patriotism
not embittered by spleen nor alloyed by ambition,
harmonizes into classic beauty the character of one
with whom Lælius would have eagerly associated, and
whom Cicero would have lovingly described — "*Ad
imitationem sui vocet alios; ut sese splendore animæ et
vitæ suæ, sicut speculum, præbeat civibus.*"[**]

In the eyes of the King, Lord Shelburne possessed
two merits which atoned for speeches that, if not dis-
loyal, were certainly not flattering. First, though
friendly to peace, he desired to effect it on terms that
might least wound the dignity of the crown, and
hesitated therefore to acknowledge unconditionally the
independence of America. And secondly, though driven
to act with Mr. Fox, he disliked him personally little

---

[*] That eminent Statesman, the second Marquis of Lansdowne, was living at the time these pages were written.

[**] Lælius ap. Cic. de Republicâ, lib. II.-XLII.

less than the King did. Accordingly, when George III. found himself compelled to choose between the Earl of Shelburne and the Marquis of Rokingham, the former obtained his preference. There were indeed some previous coquettings with Rockingham through the medium of a go-between, little gifted with the arts of seduction. Lord Chancellor Thurlow was sent to sound the Marquis, but without "authority" — the Marquis refused to treat — he came again — would the Marquis accept the administration and settle the terms afterwards? The Marquis gave a direct negative. The King was in a position that would have been actually impracticable had his obstinacy been such as it is popularly represented, for he had declared in a private letter to Lord North, "in the most solemn manner, that his sentiments of honour would not permit him to send for any of the leaders of Opposition, and personally treat with them." "Every man," adds his Majesty, "must be the sole judge of his own feelings, therefore whatever you or any man can say will have no avail with me." But four days afterwards, a leader of the Opposition was sent for to Buckingham House, and in three days more Lord Shelburne was empowered to form an administration. The Earl went straight to Lord Rockingham and offered him the Treasury and Premiership. "My lord," he said, with a candour little in unison with the duplicity ascribed to his character by Mr. Fox's friends, "you could stand without me, I cannot stand without you." The Marquis was a formalist in point of etiquette — he was disposed to decline, because the King had not sent for himself in person. Mr. Fox and the Duke of Richmond overruled his scruples, and the Marquis suddenly

consented to have greatness thrust upon him. The
King pocketed his honour as the great subject pocketed
his pride, and so, after straining at Lord Shelburne,
his Majesty swallowed Lord Rockingham.   Exactly
ten days from the date of the letter in which George III.
so solemnly repeated his assurance that he could see
'personally no leader of the Opposition — the chief
of the Whigs kissed hands as first minister of the
Crown.

Never, considering the grave disasters of the country,
did an English minister evince a less dignified sense
of responsibility than the Marquis of Rockingham —
never did the mind of professed patriot appear more
narrowed into the petty circle of party jealousies —
never did the diplomacy of a constitutional statesman
commissioned to secure the requisite authority to his
counsels, and yet conciliate the favour of a reluctant
king — so indulge in the spite that must gall his
master, and so admit the elements that must divide
his cabinet. Had Lord Rockingham possessed "the
sound common sense and clear judgment" which his
admirers assign to him, his course was clear. In the
necessary changes in court and state, such a man would
have gracefully consulted the King's personal tastes
and friendships, in appointments not affecting his policy,
in order the more strenuously to insist upon the removal of political antagonists. Lord Rockingham did
precisely the reverse. A harmless inoffensive nobleman
held the office of mastership of the buckhounds. This
nobleman the King loved as a peculiar friend; with
him the royal intellect unbended in happier moments,
and, forgetful of Whigs and Tories, discussed the adventures of the chase. Grimly my Lord Marquis insisted

that the hounds should exchange their master, and the King lose his gossip. George III. stooped to personal entreaty, that this one appointment might be left uncancelled; in vain. He even shed tears — the Marquis remained inflexible — Europe and America were at war with England — and Lord Bateman was a necessary sacrifice to the deities of Peace. On the other hand, if there were a man in the three kingdoms whose exclusion from the Cabinet should have been an imperative condition with the Whig minister-in-chief, it was Lord Chancellor Thurlow. The imperious lawyer had a hearty dislike for the Rockingham party; he was notoriously preopposed to the measures the Marquis was pledged to support. He was not a man to be swamped by the adverse members of a Cabinet, nor to be awed by the rank of a Rockingham or the genius of a Fox. By office he was the Keeper of the King's conscience; in point of fact, the King was rather the keeper of his own. He was sure to report every difference, and exaggerate every error, to the Sovereign, who had accepted the government as a dire necessity, and whom its chief had turned into a personal enemy. Yet the same hand that fortified the stables against a Bateman left the door of the Cabinet unclosed against a Thurlow. But with that smallness of cunning which belongs to smallness of intellect, the Marquis contrived to shift upon Shelburne the responsibility of an appointment which he lacked the courage to resist. In giving a list of those he himself selected for the Cabinet, he left a blank for the office of Chancellor, apparently in compliment to the Earl, whose friendship for Dunning would incline him to offer the seals to that famous lawyer and influential debater. But his true object was, no doubt, to impose upon Shelburne the alternative either of resisting the King and mortally offending Thurlow, or of retaining the Chancellor, and incurring the responsibility of an appointment odious to the Rockingham party. And perhaps Lord Rockingham, dull though he was, could scarcely have been so dull as not to foresee that, of the two evils, Lord Shelburne would choose the last as the least, for the Earl had not the same stern causes to exclude the terrible Chancellor as should have weighed with his colleague. During all the preliminary negotiations, Lord Shelburne had been selected for personal conference with the King, and, as the representative of a party comparatively small to that of the Rockinghamites, the Earl might reasonably consider the royal favour too valuable an element of strength to be thrown away, while Lord Thurlow had been mixed up in the transactions conducted by Shelburne, and his very hostility to one portion of the Cabinet might not be without use to the other.* Lord Shelburne therefore retained Lord Thurlow, and Lord Rockingham assented to the appointment. That, in the blank left to Lord Shelburne to fill up, the Marquis had no desire to advance Dunning, became instantaneously clear, for, when Lord Shelburne propitiated that eminent person to the loss of the Great Seal by elevating him to the peerage, with the Duchy of Lancaster, and a pension of 4000*l.* a year, the Rockingham faction were seized with jealous resentment, and could not rest contented till they had

---

* Thus Horace Walpole observes truly, "that Lord Shelburne having more of the King's favour than Lord Rockingham, the Chancellor would incline the same way."

counterbalanced the Shelburne dispensation of patronage,
by raising to the peerage a partisan of their own, Sir
Fletcher Norton. If Lord Rockingham was sincere in
the expectation that Dunning would be raised to the
Woolsack, the exceeding bitterness with which himself
and the Whigs regarded the compensation afforded by
the pension and peerage, seems strangely misplaced.
On the liberal party generally Dunning's claims were
paramount. It was his motion on the power of the
Crown which had most united the Opposition, and conduced to the downfall of the North Administration.
And not even Fox himself more commanded the ear
of the House, or could less safely have been omitted
from a share in the *spolia opima*. In brief, the more
the history of the formation of the Rockingham government becomes clear, the more the general interests of
the nation, and the nobler sagacity of patriots, appear
to have been forgotten in the miserable jealousies of
rival cliques. The grand object of the Whigs was
avowedly less to consolidate the best government that
could reform abuses and restore peace, than to maintain
the dignity of their coterie against the encroachments
of the Shelburnites. One-half the Cabinet and one-
half the subordinate appointments were rigidly to counterbalance the other half. The Government was thus
composed much on the same principle of symmetry as
that on which Capability Brown constructed his gardens. If one tree was planted to shield from the north
wind, another must be stuck into the ground just opposite, though it only served to shut out the south. If
some eminent man was appointed by Lord Shelburne,
some man, whether eminent or worthless, must be thrust
in by Lord Rockingham. The envies and bickerings

about garters and peerages, and places in the Household, could they have been known to the public, would
have lost for ever, to the ambition of "the Great
Houses," the sympathy of every masculine intellect.
But the most fatal blunder of all was in the places
severally assigned to Lord Shelburne and Mr. Fox.
"'The Foreign Office was, in the improvident regulations of that day, divided between two secretaries of
state: they presided over their respective offices, one
of which embraced the north of Europe, the other the
south and the colonies. The consequences were, that
wherever a diplomatic agency was required for nego-
tiation with joint powers, the same man was furnished
with instructions from, and had to correspond with,
two different principals;"* as each of these principals
employed respectively a separate servant in an affair
which was or ought to have been substantially the
same, it is clear that an arrangement, in which the will
and the dignity of two co-equal officers of State were
perpetually liable to clash with each other, unquestionably required either the most cordial confidence
between the two ministers, or that the negotiations to
be effected should appertain exclusively to one of the
departments. The last was impossible at the formation of the Rockingham Cabinet, in which the primary
measures must needs be negotiations for peace with
France, which was in the one department, and with
America, which was in the other. The first condition
thus became still more requisite, and, in order to meet
it, Lord Shelburne was made Secretary for the south
department, and Mr. Fox for the north, — precisely

* 'Memorials of Fox,' vol. ii.

the two men who, out of the whole junto, most disliked and most suspected each other. Thus to the ceremonial adjustment of conflicting dignities, were alike sacrificed the union of the government and the cause of the nation.

Amongst all the partisans of Lord Rockingham, no one had claim to the veneration and gratitude of the ministers equal to Edmund Burke. His motion on Administrative Reform, and the matchless oration by which it had been prefaced, had given them their popular cry at the recent election, and comprised the pith of their promises to the people. Lord Rockingham's obligations to Burke were beyond all conceivable estimate; they were such as some commonplace Chloe owes to the poet, who converts an original without a feature into an ideal without a flaw. Burke had taken this (doubtless respectable but) very ordinary nobleman up to the celestial heights of his own orient fancy, and re-created into the prototype of a statesman, in times of grave national danger, a mortal whom, if shorn of fortune and titles, no party in a parish, divided on a sewers-rate, would have elected as its champion in the vestry.

It is true that Burke had exhibited, along with the zeal of his ardent temperament, considerable defects in temper and in tact; but those are not defects that necessitate exclusion from Wigh Cabinets, provided the erring man can cover such stains on his dinted armour, not with a veteran's cloak, but a herald's tabard. And whatever those defects might be, the chiefs of the party did not pretend that they sufficed to disqualify Burke for a deliberate adviser. "He had," says Lord John Townshend, "the greatest sway, I might almost say

19*

command, over Lord Rockingham's friends."* They professed in private to respect his counsels; they excluded those counsels from a voice in the Cabinet. Lord John Russell, with the honourable sympathy of a man of letters, allows this slight to one whom posterity regards, if not as the greatest orator of his age, still as the most luminous intellect that ever flashed on the windows of the "Great Houses," to have been "unwise and unjust." But he adds, in apology for his party, that it does not appear at the time that the exclusion of Mr. Burke was resented by himself or by any of his friends. This may be true of Burke's friends — the Whigs, who excluded him — not quite so true of himself.

* 'Fox's Memorials,' vol. II. p. 22.

(*Continuation in* Vol. II.)

END OF VOL. I.

PRINTING OFFICE OF THE PUBLISHER.

www.ingramcontent.com/pod-product-compliance
Lightning Source LLC
Chambersburg PA
CBHW020853020726
47497CB00005B/1380